PHANTOM

Phantom

CARL MICHAELSEN

Boxhead Books

A novel by Carl Michaelsen

Cover by Taylor Piggot

Chapter One
Damascus, Syria

The rotors of the Sikorsky UH-60 Black Hawk thumped rhythmically as the vehicle soared over the battered city of Damascus; the chopper was equipped with sound mufflers to limit the roar of the engine and rotors. Smoke billowed from buildings, infernos raged through the streets, and the distinct sound of AK-47 fire could be heard. However, none of this mattered to Chief Petty Officer Gray Saxon. His only focus was an old warehouse in the far end of the city, right in the middle of enemy-controlled territory.

"You nervous?" Captain Spathe asked, nudging Saxon on the shoulder. Saxon shook his head.

"I don't really get nervous. Just stay on my ass and don't get shot. We'll get her back, don't you worry," Saxon said sternly.

"You DEVGRU guys are a different breed," the captain rolled his eyes. Unlike the rest of the soldiers on the Black Hawk, Gray Saxon was not a Delta Force Operative. Instead, he was a member of SEAL Team

Six's elite Development Group, or DEVGRU—the All-Star team of SEAL Team Six.

"Alright, listen up, guys," Saxon yelled, standing to his full height, just over six feet. "We know that Warrant Officer Cassidy Minor is still alive as of yesterday and in enemy hands. We're gonna drop in on the building, clear it as fast as we can, and bring Officer Minor home. I don't need to remind any of you that we have no backup, no air support, and no QRF. We're all we've got... so stay frosty and let's get this done."

"He's got a real gift with the pep talks," a Delta Operator named Clancy whispered to Spathe. The captain chuckled and shook his head.

"Check your weapons, Master Sergeant."

"90 seconds!" the pilot's voice boomed over the speakers. Saxon placed his helmet over his head and buckled the strap under his chin, then folded his Ground Panoramic Night Vision Goggles over his eyes. Instantly, the darkness outside the Black Hawk was illuminated in a hue of green. He yanked back the charging handle of his MK-18 CQBR carbine, priming the weapon.

The side door to the Black Hawk slowly opened and the squad of operators immediately got to their feet. Luckily for them, there appeared to be no guards on the roof of the warehouse. The pilot expertly lowered the Black Hawk and hovered above the roof.

"Go, go, go!" Spathe yelled. The team rushed out of the Black Hawk and onto the roof, weapons at the ready. As soon as the last operator was off the Black Hawk, the pilot ascended and flew away to a safe distance.

"Team 1, with me," Saxon whispered into his comm.

"Team 2 and 3, on me," Spathe echoed.

The squad broke off into their respective teams, each heading for a door on opposite sides of the roof. Saxon took point, leading the way to the door. He lowered his rifle and tested the handle; it wasn't locked. Saxon waited for his team to stack on the door before he gently pushed it open. A Delta called 'Sugar' was the first man inside.

"Clear," Sugar whispered. "No sign of any activity."

"Move in," Saxon responded.

Moving in absolute silence, the team crept down the rickety staircase and onto the second level of the two-story warehouse. The team's NVGs made it easy to move through the darkness quietly.

"We're clear in the northwest corner," Spathe said through the team's communication system.

"Copy, move on," Saxon responded. Using hand gestures, Saxon ordered two Delta operators to search the offices on either side of the team—both came back having found nothing.

"She must be on the first floor," Sugar said. Saxon nodded in agreement.

"Spathe, we're clear over here. Moving onto the first floor," Saxon whispered, heading back for the staircase. Once again, the team moved down the stairs in silence.

As they hit the ground level, they all heard faint voices. Lights were on in the back offices and there were several guards roaming about the large facility. Saxon held up his fist and the entire team took a knee.

"Spathe, I have eyes on seven... no, eight armed hostiles," Saxon reported. "Gimme your location."

"We're coming down the stairs of the northwest side of the building, over. Let us get into position before you engage," Spathe advised.

At that moment, a blood-curdling scream echoed through the warehouse, sending a chill down Gray Saxon's spine. The scream was from a woman. There was no doubt in Saxon's mind that Cassidy Minor was indeed in the warehouse.

Saxon's mind instantly went to the video as her screaming continued.

Four days earlier, a US Black Hawk helicopter had come under fire and gone down in the outskirts of the city. The very pretty, 27-year-old Warrant Officer Cassidy Minor had been taken captive while the rest of the crew had either died in the crash or been killed off by militants. A day later, Saxon was secretly shown a 'proof of life' video that made him boil with anger; the video was never meant to be shown to anyone in the Special Operations community, for fear of an unauthorized mission to rescue the pilot.

There, on the dirty table, was Cassidy Minor. She'd been stripped of her uniform and was chained to the bed by her wrists and ankles. It didn't take long before two bearded men began violating her. The video was the most repulsive thing Saxon had ever seen in his life. But it was Cassidy's helpless screaming and crying that he heard over and over in his head. Her broken, shattered, and tear-streaked expression at the end of the video permanently ingrained itself into Saxon's consciousness.

When Saxon and Spathe had been discreetly made aware of Cassidy's location, they jumped on the opportunity to rescue her. It didn't matter that they were specifically disobeying direct orders to not launch a rescue mission—Cassidy was one of them, there was no way Saxon would sit idle and let her suffer any longer.

And now, that same scream from the video was ringing in his ears.

Saxon looked back at his team and saw their concerned faces. He flicked the safety off on his rifle.

"Fuck it," he muttered. All of his military logic told him to wait for Spathe to get into position, but his heart was in control now. Saxon turned back to his team. "Go loud!"

Saxon leaped up, steadied his rifle, and pulled the trigger; he fired three suppressed rounds into two bearded militants. They fell over each other, dead before they hit the ground. Immediately, the warehouse erupted into chaos. AK-47 fire blasted all over and 7.62 rounds ricocheted off of almost everything in the warehouse. Saxon somersaulted behind a wooden crate and leaned around the side. He popped off another trio of bullets, wounding another fighter.

"Goddammit!" Spathe yelled over the comms. He turned around to his team. "Move in! Engage, engage!" Spathe cursed under his breath as he took off running toward the sound of gunfire. He had served with Saxon before and he never expected the seasoned operator to be this reckless. The gunfire got louder and louder as more AK-47s joined the fight. Spathe slid on his knees through the doorway and dove behind a crate; he brought his M4A1 up to his shoulder and peered through the ACOG sight. Calmly placing the crosshairs on a militant's head, Spathe pulled the trigger and blew the man's head apart.

Saxon crouched down and weaved around the numerous crates. For a brief moment, he wondered what was inside the crates. A bullet suddenly tore through the air, barely missing his head. He wheeled around and popped off two rounds, dropping the man attempting to flank him. Kneeling beside another crate, Saxon quickly reloaded his CQBR. Spathe's team had provided much-needed support and the number of militants was dwindling. Just as Saxon was about to leap back into the fight, one of the crates caught his eye.

The label on the crate was all too familiar to him: MARS Industries—The world's premier manufacturer for every kind of weapon imaginable.

A grey orb came flying into view, grabbing Saxon's attention. He recognized it instantly.

Grenade.

On pure muscle memory, Saxon threw himself aside just as the grenade exploded next to two crates. The blast shook the warehouse and obliterated two Delta shooters in a blink of an eye.

A second wave of fighters poured out of the office area in the rear of the warehouse and began spraying 7.62 rounds. Another crate erupted in a fiery inferno, gravely injuring another Delta.

Captain Spathe reloaded his M4A1 and tried to work his way over to his dying operator. As he crossed the warehouse, a searing round caught him in the shoulder, spinning him around completely. Another round sliced through his back, burying itself up near his neck. Spathe collapsed to the ground, struggling to breathe.

Saxon's ears were ringing as he crawled onto his knees; his vision was blurry and he felt like he was seconds away from vomiting. He felt around dumbly, breathing a sigh of relief when his hand wrapped around the stock of his rifle. After a few precious seconds, Saxon's vision had cleared enough for him to get back into action.

"Saxon!" Sugar screamed. "We're getting cut up! We need to pull back!"

"Spathe, you copy?" Saxon grumbled into his mic. No answer. Dodging bullets, Saxon moved over to where Sugar and three other soldiers were holed up. "Where's everyone else?" Saxon asked.

"Dead," Sugar shook his head. "They came up behind us, I don't know how we missed them."

"Never mind. Cassidy is here, we need to get her and get the fuck out of here. You guys start falling back, I'm gonna try and find Spathe and Cassidy," Saxon rattled off. He thumbed a fragmentation grenade from his tactical vest and heaved it toward a cluster of fighters; it detonated four seconds later, killing the four militants and blowing their bodies apart.

"Fuck that, we're not turning tail and running," Sugar spat, popping up the fire burst from his own M4A1 rifle. Saxon shook his head. They had lost the element of surprise and the upper hand.

"Then just cover me. I'm gonna find Spathe," Saxon snarled. Sugar and the three Delta operators sprang into action, bombarding the fighters with accurate rounds; they forced a group of fighters back behind cover, giving Saxon the opportunity to dart across the warehouse.

Saxon stumbled over the bodies of two militants and one dead Delta. He moved quickly, desperately trying to find Captain Spathe. He stopped to return fire at a duo of fighters who'd spotted him. The first man dropped but the second was able to get a shot off before Saxon's bullets shredded him. The stray bullet ripped through Saxon's vest and ACU; it pierced his skin and lodged itself in his stomach. He dropped to his knees, gritting his teeth in pain.

"Spathe! Where the fuck are you?" Saxon hissed under his breath. He put his hand over the wound and blood seeped through his fingers.

"Here..." Spathe garbled. Saxon whipped around and saw Spathe laying in a pool of his own blood. He dropped to his knees and tried to assess the damage.

"Fuck. You've been hit a couple of times," Saxon observed.

"I fucking told you to wait for us," Spathe grumbled. Saxon knew he'd fucked up and he knew exactly why he'd been so headstrong.

"I know, Captain. I'm sorry." Saxon went to work trying to stop the bleeding as best he could.

From the back of the warehouse, a militant raised a powerful Russian-made RPG-7 rocket launcher. Sugar's eyes went wide with recognition.

"RPG!" he screamed, loud enough for even Saxon to hear. Saxon heard the whine of the rocket as it flew toward Sugar and the three operators.

The rocket hit a steel ammo crate and exploded on impact, igniting three other crates that were stocked with explosives. Saxon was temporarily blinded from the brilliant flash of the explosion; the eruption blew a massive hole in the roof and set fire to almost everything in the warehouse. Although he had no way to confirm it, Saxon was sure that Sugar and the three remaining operators had been killed.

Saxon was determined to stay by Spathe's side, regardless of the flames licking at his boots. Smoke began filling the warehouse, making it difficult to breathe. Spathe was fading rapidly and there was nothing Saxon could do.

This mission had been his idea, his plan—never in his illustrious military career had Saxon felt so guilty. Not only had he gotten the 11 Delta Force operators killed, but he'd also failed to rescue Cassidy Minor. As the smoke filled his lungs, Saxon heard hurried footfalls getting closer and closer.

Chapter Two

Location Unknown

Chief Petty Officer Gray Saxon swayed in and out of consciousness; he'd been semi-aware of what was happening. After he'd lost consciousness, he must've been moved from the burning warehouse. The next thing he was aware of was being tossed into the back of a beat-up truck. He lost consciousness again as the truck began driving out of the city.

When he finally came to his senses, Saxon was chained to a chair in a dimly lit room. His wrists and ankles were shackled to the legs of the chair. He was still wearing his uniform but his vest and other gear had been stripped off. His stomach wound had been crudely patched up, but it hurt like the devil. As his eyes adjusted to the darkness, Saxon noticed a long table in the corner of the room.

There was a body on the table, under a dirty blanket. He couldn't tell if the person was dead or alive.

"Hey..." Saxon whispered. The person stirred slightly and slowly rolled over.

The bruised and battered Warrant Officer Cassidy Minor peered up from the blanket. She burst into tears at the sight of Gray Saxon.

"Oh my god, Gray!" she cried. She was beyond relieved to see a friendly face.

"Are you ok?" Saxon asked, trying to move the chair closer to her. She sniffed and wiped her eyes, but nodded firmly.

"I think so," she said quietly. "What are you doing here?"

"Looking for you," Saxon said. "Where the fuck are we?"

"I think somewhere near Hobran. They moved me after a group of soldiers attacked the warehouse they were holding me in," Cassidy muttered.

"Yeah, that was me," Saxon grunted. "They wiped everyone else out."

"Fuck! Who was with you?"

"Spathe and his Delta boys."

"Fuck," Cassidy swore again, hanging her head. "I'm shocked the Head Shed signed off on a rescue op."

"They didn't," Saxon chuckled. "Spathe and I didn't care, we heard you were in Damascus and we took off."

"Well, you can kiss your career goodbye, Saxon," Cassidy joked. It relieved Saxon immensely to see that she was still at least in good spirits. After what she'd had to endure, he was absolutely shocked, but relieved nonetheless.

"I'm gonna get you out of here, Cass. I promise," Saxon said, smiling at her. She returned his smile.

Cassidy Minor had always felt a strange attraction to Gray Saxon. He was fearless and a natural-born warrior, but also extremely kind and she had seen he could even be tender. She'd met him almost four years earlier on her first deployment to Afghanistan. He had just joined up with DEVGRU and she flew missions for them regularly. The two had become close over the long deployments, chatting regularly about the stresses of married life, the NFL, and swapping stories from their high school days.

Aside from their tastes in movies and sports, Gray and Cassidy had one major thing in common—they had both married their high school sweethearts before their 21st birthdays. The revelation of this was something they shared a hearty laugh over during a night of drinking on base. Truth be told, neither one of their marriages was going particularly well.

Cassidy's husband, Mark, was a mechanic back home in Arizona and was growing tired of her deployments. The constant time away from each other had strained the relationship immensely; the long distance was extremely difficult for Mark. She'd confessed her annoyance with this to Gray less than a week ago when the two were relaxing on base together, watching Gray's favorite movie, *Sin City*. The sexual tension between the two of them reached a breaking point that night—they relished in the opportunity to be together finally. She'd imagined what it would be like to be with Gray for ages and was beyond relieved to find out that he was even better than she thought he'd be. Both of them had needed the release and they reaped the benefits.

The very next morning, after a night of ravenous and rough sex, Cassidy was abducted after her Black Hawk helicopter crashed inside Damascus. The other pilot and small crew had been killed off by militants, but the savages took Cassidy. Time seemed to stop as she was forced to endure hours upon hours of torture, rape, and interrogation. She had no idea how long she'd been in the hands of the enemy or how long it had been since she'd last slept. Time had lost all relativity for her.

"Gray?" Cassidy whispered. Saxon looked up at her with his tired, dark eyes.

"What's up, Cass?" he asked quietly.

"Thank you. Thank you for coming for me," she said, on the verge of tears again. She had never been one to cry a lot, but the last week's events had brought her to a breaking point.

"You don't have to thank me," Saxon said sincerely. "I'd do it again in a heartbeat."

"You are one of a kind, Gray Saxon," Cassidy chuckled. "So, you got any plans for after?" she asked, wanting to change the subject.

"Well, assuming I'm going to get court-martialed for trying to rescue you, I'd say take an early retirement. Maybe buy a farm somewhere out West. I don't know, I haven't given it much thought," Saxon said honestly.

"I bet Jayne will be happy to hear that," Cassidy smiled, referring to his wife. Saxon lowered his head and scoffed to himself.

"Jayne and I are getting a divorce," he chuckled. "She called me a week ago and told me."

"Are you serious?" Cassidy gasped. "Why didn't you tell me? Or anyone for that matter?"

"The less people know about me, the better," Saxon shrugged. "Jayne told me before I left on my last deployment that she wouldn't be there waiting for me when I got home. I've put her through enough, I don't want her to feel like she wasted her life."

"That's very noble of you," Cassidy said, smiling sadly. "Mark and I aren't too far away from that, unfortunately. He's probably feeling very similar to Jayne."

"Cost of the job, I guess," Saxon admitted. "It's hard to find people who can accept the way we live."

"Mark and I were just too damn young," Cassidy laughed. "We were kids and we just grew apart. It happens, what more can you do?"

"It's a lonely path," Saxon whispered. He looked up at the beautiful and fearless Warrant Officer in front of him. "But it doesn't have to be."

"No, it doesn't have to," Cassidy smiled warmly, picking up on Saxon's subtle hint. "When we get out of here, how about the first round on me?"

"Your money's no good, Minor," Saxon laughed loudly. Cassidy and Saxon shared a laugh, despite their awful surroundings. They both had the impeccable ability to find the funny in horrible situations—something that made Saxon all the more attractive to Cassidy.

The door to the room swung open violently and half a dozen men walked in, followed closely by their stench. Each man was carrying a dirty AK-47, sported a long beard, and wore various turbans over their heads. Saxon and Cassidy ceased laughing immediately, the reality of their situation was about to get much worse. Saxon looked up at the men, his eyes fiery with defiance. The apparent leader of the group knelt down in front of him.

"Hello, Mr. Saxon," the man said in a thick accent. His breath was putrid and disgusting. Saxon pulled away from the man, holding his breath. "My name is Yusuf."

"Great," Saxon muttered under his breath. Yusuf turned and yelled something in Arabic that Saxon didn't understand. He was semi-fluent in the language, but Yusuf seemed to be using a different dialect. One of the militants disappeared into the hallway and came back with a large metal pipe, which was stained in blood. Saxon felt his stomach tighten as the man handed the pipe to Yusuf.

"I'm not a patient man, Mr. Saxon. I demanded 20 million US dollars in exchange for your female pilot. And instead, your government sent you to come and kill us." Yusuf was visibly angry. He gripped the pipe tightly in his right hand.

"They didn't send us," Saxon laughed. He looked up at Yusuf and smiled arrogantly. "My government doesn't give a fuck about lowlifes like you. I did that all on my own. I acted out of orders for the simplest of reasons. I love fucking up your shit."

Yusuf swung the pipe and hit Saxon over the head as hard as he could. Saxon fell onto the floor and blood instantly began pouring from a fresh wound on his head. His vision was back to being blurry and his head felt like it was being pounded by a jackhammer.

"Fuck," he spat.

"Get him up," Yusuf snarled in Arabic. Two men manhandled Saxon back into the chair. Yusuf grabbed him by his hair and looked into his dazed eyes. "You will know suffering, American. The way my people have had to suffer for centuries. You arrogant Americans are a cancer in my country."

"You're gonna have to do better than that," Saxon spoke through gritted teeth. Yusuf smiled evilly and released him. He turned and walked slowly over to Cassidy. She held the blanket close to her and quivered as he got closer.

In one swift motion, Yusuf ripped away the blanket. Cassidy was still wearing her ripped green t-shirt and tattered fatigues. Yusuf motioned for the others to join him. Instantly, Saxon knew what was about to happen. He strained against the chains, desperately trying to get free.

"Leave her alone, you motherfuckers!" Saxon screamed, all the pain in his head disappeared as the adrenaline kicked in. He had to break free now, otherwise, Cassidy was going to be subjected to god knows what.

Yusuf looked back at the struggling Saxon and smiled even more evilly. He reeled back and slapped Cassidy as hard as he could, stunning the pilot and leaving a nasty red mark on the side of her face. One by one, the men began to take turns groping her breasts and running their hands between her legs. Cassidy slammed her eyes shut.

"I swear to Christ, I'll fucking kill every last one of you goat-fuck-ers!" Saxon screamed. His wrists were starting to bleed from pulling so hard against the chains.

One of the men jumped onto the table and pinned Cassidy's wrists above her head. And that was when she started screaming.

Chapter Three
Location Unknown

Neither Saxon nor Cassidy spoke to each other. Saxon wasn't sure if she was awake or not and he certainly wasn't going to do anything to bother her. His wrists were bloodied from trying so desperately to break free from the chains. His entire body was covered in a layer of sweat and his throat was drier than the Syrian desert. But he was in no mood to feel sorry for himself. He'd witnessed just about the worst thing he'd ever seen in his entire life—military included.

The rape itself had lasted 11 grueling minutes; Cassidy screamed the entire time until one of the militants wrapped her own belt around her throat. Her shredded clothes had been tossed in a pile close to Saxon's feet. Cassidy had not spoken a word in the hours after the incident. Saxon had heard her crying softly to herself, but he was just too shocked to say anything.

His anger was reaching a breaking point and he refused to let Cassidy endure any more torture at the hands of these monsters. Stretching out his leg as long as he could, Saxon quietly kicked Cassidy's ACU pants over to him. Maneuvering the pants behind him so his hands could reach, he began feeling through every pocket to try and find anything he could break a lock with. His heart skipped a beat when he felt a hairpin in the pocket. He pinched the hairpin between his thumb and pointer finger before stuffing it into the lock on his chains. Praying that it would work, he desperately tried to pick the lock.

After several attempts and almost ten minutes, the lock snapped open. Saxon breathed a sigh of relief and ripped the chains from his wrists; he stood up and ran over to Cassidy. Her face was bloodied, bruised, and she was shivering badly. Saxon fetched the blanket and wrapped her tightly in it.

"Cass, can you hear me?" Saxon asked softly. Cassidy's eyes fluttered but she nodded.

"Yes," she whispered in a shaky voice. She sounded like she was on the verge of crying again.

"Good," he said, then quickly went to work picking the locks on her wrists and ankles. Both locks were opened with relative ease. "Can you walk?" he asked, helping her sit up. Again, she nodded.

"I need my boots and clothes," she said in a small voice. Saxon got her everything she needed and helped her get dressed. He was utterly impressed by her courage and determination, but there was no time to compliment her.

They had to get out. Now.

As soon as Cassidy finished tying her boots, Saxon inched the steel door open and peered out into the hallway. They appeared to be in an old office building, desks and tables were pushed up in the corner on top of one another.

The first priority was to secure weapons, then find the means to call in an extraction. Gesturing for Cassidy to follow him, Saxon headed down the hallway. He moved in such a way that his boots didn't make a sound over the old wood floor. He heard Arabic chatter coming from one of the offices at the end of the hall. Crouching down, Saxon peered into the office.

Three men stood around a small TV—they were watching a soccer game. Saxon recognized them as part of the group that had attacked Cassidy. There, in the corner of the small office, were Saxon's weapons and gear. He would have to take these three down without alerting anyone else in the building. Difficult, but not impossible.

"Stay here," Saxon whispered to Cassidy. Moving in a crouch, he slowly stalked into the room. He noticed the man on the right had a large knife sheathed on his hip.

Saxon stood up and grabbed the man on the right by the collar of his tunic. At the same time, he swiped the knife from the sheath and stabbed the man in the middle; Saxon drove the blade through the man's chest. Adjusting his grip on his first man, Saxon wrapped his sturdy arm around the man's neck, squeezing as hard as he could. The third man reached for his AK-47, but Saxon kicked right at the man's knee. His leg bent in an awkward angle and the man buckled. Saxon expelled the knife from the other man's chest and drove the bloody blade through the third's throat, killing him instantly. He turned his attention back to the man caught under his arm and snapped his neck with ease.

"All clear," Saxon muttered. Cassidy appeared in the doorway, pleased to see her attackers had died the most violent of deaths. Saxon knelt beside his gear and picked up his rifle. He checked the ammo before passing it off to Cassidy.

"Cover the door," Saxon ordered before returning to his gear. He fished through his vest, looking for his satellite phone. He had memorized the number to call and quickly punched it in as soon as he found it. On the third ring, a man answered.

"Hello?" Major Hadley answered in a panicked voice. Major Hadley had been the only other man, aside from the pilots, who knew about the mission to rescue Cassidy—he'd approved his men to go with Saxon.

"Command, this is Echo 3-1. I have rescued package with me. I say again, the package is in hand. Need immediate extraction."

"Jesus Christ, we thought you were dead," Hadley said, the relief present in his stressed voice. "Where are you?"

"Unknown," Saxon responded.

"Stand by, tracking your SAT phone," the man said. After what felt like an eternity, his voice came back over the line. "We got your location, Echo 3-1. QRF is en route. I repeat, QRF is on the way."

"Copy. I'll try to reestablish comms. Stand by," Saxon said. He connected his SAT phone to his comm system and put the earpiece back into his ear. "Command, come back, over."

"Lima Charlie, 3-1," Hadley answered. "QRF is spinning up now."

"Copy."

Saxon slithered back into his vest and took his rifle back from Cassidy. He drew his sidearm, a Heckler and Koch Mark 23, and held it out for Cassidy. She accepted the weapon and racked the slide.

"Stay behind me," Saxon said as they moved back into the hall. He thumbed the safety off of his rifle and started creeping down the hallway, carefully checking each office as they passed them. They went through a set of double doors and found the staircase; they were on the fourth floor.

Silently, they stepped into the staircase and began descending down the rickety stairs. The floorboards creaked with each step, but they appeared to be moving unnoticed for the time being. Saxon knew their best chance would be to get outside of the building and try to find a solid landing zone for the QRF (Quick Reaction Force).

Saxon paused before the door that led to the first floor. He heard several men talking loudly from behind the door.

"Get back," he said to Cassidy, warily. Gripping his rifle, he booted the door open and came face to face with five militants. The five fighters were shocked to see their American prisoner standing before them, and their pause gave Saxon all the time he needed. He unleashed an automatic burst of supersonic rounds, cutting down the men with ease. As the last man fell back, he inadvertently squeezed the trigger of his AK-47, firing a burst of fire into the ceiling.

"Fuck!" Saxon yelled as he heard the yelling from the floor above. "C'mon, we gotta move!"

Saxon and Cassidy sprinted down the hall and finally saw the exit door. Bullets started flying down the hall as a group of fighters gave chase to the escaped prisoners. Saxon booted the door open and shoved Cassidy outside. Before the door closed behind them, Saxon turned around and emptied his magazine, killing three fighters.

He looked around for a good place to hunker down and wait, but the building was the only structure that provided significant cover. They were in a part of the country that had been decimated by civil war, so most of the buildings were nothing more than piles of rubble.

"Echo 3-1, this is Warbird 2-2," the familiar voice of the Osprey pilot said. "We're five mikes out. I repeat, five mikes out. I have two Apaches on station to provide air support, Thunder 2-1 and Thunder 2-2."

"Good, copy!" Saxon said. He reached for a cylinder clipped to his vest and pulled the pin, then tossed it against the building and a vibrant purple smoke began to spray from the tube. "Thunder 2-1, I've popped smoke on the target building. Anyone coming out is considered hostile! Stand by to engage on my mark."

"Roger that, solid copy," the Apache pilot answered.

Taking Cassidy's hand, Saxon ran for the closest structure, a half-destroyed house. The familiar sound of helicopter rotors came over the city; the two Apaches soared over the destruction and saw the purple smoke.

"Echo 3-1, we have your target. Ready to engage."

"Engage!" Saxon yelled into the radio.

The Apaches fired off rocket after rocket at the office building, which exploded in a brilliant eruption. Saxon felt the ground shake beneath him. Swinging back around, the Apaches unleashed another hellish barrage at the burning building, surely killing any of the fighters that remained inside.

Suddenly, gunfire erupted behind Saxon and Cassidy. A group of at least 50 fighters were rushing towards them, firing their weapons wildly. Saxon spread out and began engaging, switching his selector-switch to semi-auto to conserve ammo. Accurately and precisely, he returned fire, killing six fighters with six rounds. Cassidy hunkered down next to him, knowing her pistol wasn't of much use at a longer range.

"Echo 3-1, we're gonna set down north of the burning building. We're seeing a mess of bad guys heading your way," the Osprey pilot informed. Overhead, Saxon saw the Osprey fly into view.

"Acknowledged, just put the fucking bird down! We'll be there!" Saxon cursed. He stopped firing and looked at Cassidy right in the eyes. "You have to run, now! Don't stop until you get to the Osprey!"

"Gray, I'm not leaving you," she argued.

"Goddammit, Cassidy, if you don't make it out then this was all for nothing," Saxon urged. "I'm gonna lay down fire and when I do, you run like hell."

"I can't leave you!" she cried.

Both of them froze when they heard the unmistakable sound of a mortar.

Without hesitation, Saxon threw his body over Cassidy and covered her. The mortar hit the ground about 15 feet away, jarring them. Shaking his head, Saxon got to his feet and leveled his rifle, popping off another series of shots, and killing four more fighters. Cassidy raised the Mark 23 and began firing, killing a fighter loading an RPK machine gun. Saxon jumped back on the radio.

"Thunder 2-1, Thunder 2-2, we are under heavy enemy fire! Be advised, large enemy force moving in from the south of our position. Need you to service targets, over."

"Roger, 3-1. Moving to service targets to the south of your position," the Apache pilot said calmly. Saxon switched channels to the Osprey pilot.

"Evac, have a squad on the ground to cover the exfil of the package!" Saxon said sternly. "As soon as you have the package, get the fuck out of here."

"Copy, Echo 3-1," the Osprey pilot responded, the uneasiness was evident in his voice.

"Listen to me," Saxon said to Cassidy, reloading his MK18 as fast as he could. "Once those Apaches engage, you're gonna run. I'll provide cover and be right behind you. Don't stop running and don't look back, ok?"

"Ok, ok," Cassidy nodded.

Saxon dropped down behind cover and grabbed Cassidy, embracing her tightly. He held her until he heard the Apaches roar overhead and the familiar sound of the 30mm Boeing M230 chain gun.

"Go!" Saxon yelled, leaping to his feet and shouldering his rifle. Cassidy took off running as fast as she could. She looked up and saw the Osprey flying toward the extraction point. Saxon squeezed the trigger on his MK18, killing a few stragglers who were seeking cover from the Apaches. He ducked down and ran after Cassidy; he was about 200 yards behind her. Off in the distance, he saw the Osprey come to a hover and start descending. Saxon smiled as the rear door to the Osprey opened and he saw a squad of Army Rangers waiting to jump out and secure the landing zone.

Cassidy was panting and heaving by the time she reached the Osprey. A young Army Ranger wrapped his arm around her and helped her into the Osprey. He strapped her into the seat and gave her a thumbs up.

"She's secure!" the Ranger yelled up to the pilots.

"Where's Saxon?" the pilot yelled back, not wanting to leave anyone behind.

Saxon sprinted toward the Osprey. He felt a great sense of pride seeing Cassidy safe and sound. The squad of Army Rangers were taking a knee around the rear platform, waiting for Saxon to board. The Apaches had all but decimated the enemies in the area. Anyone who was still alive was too scared to continue fighting—that was the power of the Apaches.

He was less than 50 yards from the Osprey when he slowed to a jog. A second later, he heard the distinctive crack of a Russian Dragunov SVD sniper rifle. The round cut through the back of his vest and blew out through his chest; he dropped to the ground instantly, falling on his face like a tree that had just been cut down.

"Gray!" Cassidy shrieked. She watched in horror as Saxon hit the ground hard. At that moment, the area opened up with gunfire as more fighters appeared from the wrecked buildings, seemingly from out of nowhere.

"Contact!" the Ranger Captain yelled, raising his M4A1 carbine. The Rangers engaged immediately.

"We gotta get outta here now!" the pilot screamed. "Get everyone on board, we're getting out of here."

"Get on board!" the Crew Chief screamed at the Rangers.

"No! We still have a man out there!" the Ranger Captain retorted, firing away at a large group of hostiles moving towards them.

Saxon hadn't moved a muscle since being shot, the fall had taken the wind out of him completely. He was breathing in clouds of sand, but he didn't have the strength to roll over. Bullets were crashing all around him, kicking up dirt and dust. The Rangers were doing their best to hold off the onslaught. Painfully and slowly, Saxon rolled over onto his back and switched on his radio.

"Get... the fuck... out of here," he growled into his mic.

"Fall back, fall back!" the Ranger Captain regrettably yelled at his squad. One by one, the Rangers ducked back into the Osprey.

"Gray! Gray!" Cassidy screamed, holding her hand out toward him. "We can't leave him!"

"We don't have a choice!" the pilot shouted. "We're lifting off."

The Osprey slowly ascended, its rotors kicking up clouds of dust around Saxon. Using every last ounce of strength he could muster, Saxon was able to get to his feet and reload his MK18.

"Echo 3-1, do you copy?" the Apache pilot asked.

"Copy," Saxon said groggily.

"We're at bingo fuel, we've got to refuel and rearm," the pilot was audibly upset about having to leave him, but there was nothing he could do about low fuel and ammo. Saxon chuckled.

"Don't worry. Just make sure Cass gets back to base in one piece. I'll be fine."

"You got it," the pilot answered. "Good luck, Saxon."

Saxon switched off his radio and gripped his rifle in both hands as the large swarm of enemy fighters closed in—they were yelling boisterously. Finding cover was a useless endeavor against a force as large as the one coming straight at Chief Petty Officer Gray Saxon. He was going to stand his ground and fight until they cut him down.

He waited until they were well within range before he started firing, mowing down the first line of fighters with ease. They returned fire, but their erratic aim proved ineffective. Saxon calmly switched from target to target, killing any man who crossed into his rifle sight. He conserved ammo, firing only one round at a time.

Saxon was feeling confident all the way up until a butt of an AK-47 was smashed over his head. His body went limp almost instantly and he dropped to the ground.

Yusuf stood over the unconscious SEAL, smiling with evil pride.

"Take him back to the trucks," he said in Arabic to three of his soldiers. The three men picked up Saxon with significant effort and hustled back to a battered truck with a machine gun mounted on top.

As he walked back to his own vehicle, Yusuf flipped open his cell phone and dialed the only number programmed into the phone.

"Yes?" the man answered in Arabic.

"We've captured the American soldier," Yusuf boasted.

"Good," the man sounded pleased. "Bring him to me."

Yusuf hung up the phone and hurried back to the truck, hopping in the back next to the American. He leaned in closely and kept his voice low.

"Now you will understand suffering, American."

Chapter Four
Chicago, Illinois - Four Years Later

The music and flashing lights were both mesmerizing and bothersome to Sulieman Khatib. He stood at the window of his Lakefront Suite at the Congress Plaza Hotel overlooking the massive *Lollapalooza* music festival. On average, nearly 400,000 people flock to Chicago's Grant Park for the iconic music festival each summer. While Sulieman still considered himself to be a young guy, the insane crowds and loud music was something he wasn't interested in anymore. Those days were long gone for the 36-year-old Saudi man.

He chuckled to himself as he watched a large group of scantily-dressed teenagers vomiting into trash cans. He took another sip from the glass of Jim Beam he was currently enjoying. Since moving to America when he was 18, Sulieman had enjoyed most of America's splendors. He was a big fan of Las Vegas and tried to visit at least once a month. Vegas was full of everything Sulieman enjoyed most about America—liquor, gambling, and women.

The two other men with him were sitting on the couch, whispering into the ears of a pair of high-end escorts. Bottles and empty condom wrappers took up most of the surface area on the large coffee table. Sulieman poured himself another glass of Jim Beam, checking his expensive Rolex watch as he gently poured.

Although Sulieman liked to consider himself a businessman, some people would consider him a terrorist. His profession that had made him rich beyond his wildest dreams was simple—selling weapons. In fact, he was one of the most notorious arms dealers in the Middle East, having dealt extensively to the ISB, ISIS, Taliban, and Al-Qaeda.

His most loyal customers were the men of the ISB, or Islamic Syrian Brotherhood. The ISB were extremist rebels who had grown exponentially over the last ten years. Operating mainly in Syria and the surrounding countries of Iraq, Jordan, Turkey, and Lebanon, the ISB preyed on the fear and terror of others. Over the last ten years, they had claimed responsibility for almost 30 suicide bombings, a dozen mass shootings, and the murder of hundreds of US troops. Most notably, though, was the capture and torture of Warrant Officer Cassidy Minor almost five years prior. After the horrific video had been made public, the ISB had become a household name, especially in the United States.

That was the reason he was in Chicago, to meet a potential new client. The two had only ever spoken through dark web chat rooms, but the client provided enough information that Sulieman felt at ease meeting the man to make the sale. In the master bedroom were dozens of weapons cases, ranging from long rifles to handguns and plenty of ammunition. The client had been specific that he wanted "Good guns, none of that cheap shit" and Sulieman had delivered on his promise. He'd acquired 30 AR-15 rifles from a variety of manufacturers—Salient Arms International, Daniel Defense, and Noveske.

Sulieman checked his watch again; the client would be at his door any minute. He turned to his two subordinates.

"Clean that mess up," he scolded. His voice was heavily accented, but he spoke perfect English. The stockier of the two men, Abduhl, grunted and got up, retrieving a black garbage bag. He pushed all of the bottles and wrappers into the bag, clearing the table of the mess before returning to his escort. Sulieman shook his head. Abduhl was reliable and trustworthy, but his growing affinity for drugs and prostitutes was concerning to Sulieman.

The hand on Sulieman's watch hit 6 PM. Simultaneously, there was a crisp knock at the hotel door. Sulieman stood up a little straighter and hissed at Abduhl and the other man, Khaled. They both straightened out their suits and tried to appear professional. Sulieman walked over to the door and opened it.

Three men stood in the hallway, all wearing jeans, tan boots, dress shirts, and sport coats. Two men were clearly Caucasian, while the third man was of Middle Eastern descent. Sulieman held the door open and gave them a friendly smile. They entered without paying him much attention.

One of the white men stopped in the center of the suite and looked around, grunting slightly at the sight of the two escorts on the couch. He was tall and muscular, his biceps were stretching the material of the sport coat. His sand-colored hair was cut short, but long enough to comb over. The sides and back of his head were shaved clean; he sported stubble and a close-cropped mustache. There were significant creases in his forehead and dark bags under his grey eyes. The man was certainly intimidating, but also darkly handsome. He wore a large Diesel watch on his left wrist and a thick bracelet on his right. A nasty scar ran across his face all the way from under his left eye to his chin. Sulieman shuddered as he studied the scar, wondering what could've happened to leave such a grisly mark.

"You're Sulieman Khatib?" the man asked. Sulieman correctly assumed this was the man he'd been in contact with.

"At your service," Sulieman said, sticking out his hand. The man did not shake it. Sulieman chuckled nervously and put his hand down. "And who might you be?"

"You can call me Saxon," the man said. He didn't bother introducing his two colleagues. They looked at Sulieman's two goons with vague looks of disapproval.

"Pleasure to meet you, Mr. Saxon," Sulieman smiled again. "May I offer you a drink?"

"I'm here to buy guns, not make friends," Saxon growled. Sulieman gulped but maintained his composure. He was not used to such aggression from a client. Even his more extreme clients were at least polite to a fault.

"Fair enough," Sulieman squeaked. "Abduhl, let's show our guests the merchandise."

Abduhl and Sulieman led the three men into the master bedroom. Gun cases were stacked all over the room. Saxon and his colleagues exchanged a pleased look with each other. Abduhl heaved a case onto the bed and flipped it open, revealing a pristine Daniel Defense M4 V7 assault rifle. The rifle was fitted with a Trijicon ACOG Sight and a Vertical rifle grip.

"Daniel Defense M4," Sulieman introduced, gesturing to the rifle. "One of the best, a precise and deadly rifle. I've fit it with a sight and grip, but you can attach whatever accessories you please."

Saxon suppressed a smile and picked up the rifle, checking over the weapon. Pleased with what he saw, he set the rifle down and wiped his hands on his jeans.

"How many more of these do you have?" Saxon asked.

"Eight," Sulieman said proudly. "With 300 rounds of ammunition per rifle. I can offer you 12 Salient Arms AR-15s and 12 Noveske Arms rifles. With ammo and attachments as well."

"Well, your reputation precedes you," Saxon grunted. "What do you have in terms of sniper rifles?"

Sulieman snapped his fingers and Abduhl fetched two long cases and set them on the bed. He opened the cases and stepped back, letting Saxon take a look.

"I'm very pleased to offer you two of the finest sniper rifles in the world," Sulieman boasted.

The first case contained a Remington Modular Sniper Rifle, or MSR. Saxon couldn't hide his pleasure—the MSR was one hell of a rifle and he had no idea how a schmuck like Sulieman Khatib had gotten his hands on it. The rifle was kitted out with a Harris Bipod, a Leupold Mark 4 scope, and an AAC Titan suppressor. The magazine was separated from the rifle and was topped off with .338 Lapua Magnum rounds.

Saxon turned to the second case. It held a McMillan Tac-300 sniper rifle, fitted with an 8x40mm scope. In addition to the scope, Sulieman had attached a Harris HEBR swivel bipod. The Tac-300 was chambered to fire a .300 Winchester bullet.

Stepping back from the cases, Saxon crossed his arms and nodded approvingly.

"I must say, I'm impressed. You didn't disappoint," Saxon complimented. Sulieman stuck his nose up and smiled arrogantly.

"I've never disappointed any of my customers before," he said proudly. He waved Abduhl out of the room.

"Oh, I'm sure," Saxon said. There was a slight sarcasm in his tone. He leaned in closer to Sulieman and lowered his voice. "But then again, terrorists normally aren't too picky about where their weapons come from."

Sulieman pulled back in disgust. His dealings with terrorists were not publicly known to many people, especially not to Americans like the one before him.

"I don't appreciate the accusation. I'm a simple armorer. What people choose to do with the weapons after is entirely up to them," Sulieman countered defensively.

"You and I both know that's a lie," Saxon scoffed, unimpressed with Sulieman's holier-than-thou routine.

"You know nothing about me, American," Sulieman spat, his eyes narrowing with anger. Saxon chuckled and stepped back toward the bed. Following Sulieman's suit, he waved his two men out of the bedroom as well.

"Oh, I know nothing about you?" Saxon challenged once the two men were out. "Let's see, Sulieman Khatib. You were born in Saudi Arabia, basically royalty... your father and the Prince were good friends. You came to America when you were 18 to go to college, stayed for the women and the drugs. I know you have a standing room at the Bellagio in Vegas and a favorite dancer at the Spearmint Rhino. Her stripper name is 'Krystal' but her real name is Teisha Jennings; she has a two-year-old son. You suspect it is your kid, but you're too much of a pussy to go and find out. You do, however, have a daughter in Atlanta by a woman named Jennifer Mills. You write a check every month for $3,800 but you haven't seen her in years," Saxon paused, pleased with the haunted look on Sulieman's face. It was a true mix of absolute shock and horror. "Need I continue?"

"Who... who are you?" Sulieman stuttered. Saxon grabbed Sulieman by the throat and pulled the man in closely; Sulieman's feet were almost off the ground.

"I'm fate, motherfucker," Saxon snarled. Sulieman tried to call for help, but Saxon squeezed even tighter, closing the airway. "By now, those two hotties out there will have knives to their throats. You should be more careful who you let into your hotel room, Mr. Khatib."

Saxon loosened his grip on Sulieman's throat and the man dropped to his knees, coughing and gasping desperately for air. He tried to get up and run, but Saxon swung his foot and delivered a vicious kick to the side of Sulieman's head, knocking him out.

He stepped into the living room and saw Abduhl and the other man quivering in fear. Each of the escorts was holding a razor-sharp karambit knife against their jugulars. Sweat dripped from Abduhl's forehead and his eyes were wide with panic.

"Please," he choked out. The escort pressed harder with the blade of the knife, drawing blood. Abduhl yelped and his bladder gave out and he pissed all over himself.

"Fucking amateurs," Saxon shook his head in disgust. "Kill them."

Simultaneously, the escorts slashed the knives across the men's throats, cutting them open from ear to ear. Blood erupted and sprayed all over the table and couch as they fell over—dead before their heads smashed onto the glass table. The escorts got up silently and placed the karambits on the table without a word.

"There's a black Ford Econoline van in the garage," Saxon said to the two escorts. "Take as many cases as you can carry and toss them in the van."

"Should I help them?" the Middle Eastern man, Rahman, asked. Saxon shook his head. The two escorts quickly picked up several cases each and headed for the door.

Saxon went back into the bedroom and opened a rifle case, it contained a Noveske N4 Diplomat. The rifle was fitted with a Surefire M900 weapon light foregrip and an M68 Aimpoint red dot scope. Reaching into another case, Saxon fetched two Surefire casket magazines; they held 60 rounds instead of the traditional 30-round magazine.

"Ryan, take that window," Saxon pointed to the far window in the hotel room. "Rahman, you got the bedroom. I'll take the living room."

Ryan and Rahman both armed themselves with Salient Arms AR-15s and took up their positions. They both turned toward Saxon, waiting for his signal.

Gray Saxon flipped the safety off the rifle and brought it up to his shoulder. He peered through the scope and saw the sea of people dancing and cheering to the music down below. The loud EDM music was approaching its crescendo, Saxon had timed everything to perfection. Inhaling deeply, Saxon relaxed every muscle in his body and wrapped his finger around the trigger.

Just as the beat dropped, Saxon squeezed the trigger, dropping a young man where he stood. Ryan and Rahman opened up as well, spraying rounds into the crowd. It took several seconds before the concert-goers understood what was happening, giving Saxon more time to gun down a cluster of five people. Calmly, Saxon moved from person to person, firing single rounds and making every shot count.

The music stopped abruptly and the screaming overtook the park. There was a mad rush to get to cover, people trampling over each other and tripping over the bodies of the dead or wounded. Left and right, people were hit by bullets as the entire park turned into a kill zone.

Saxon emptied the 60-round magazine and reloaded; he lowered his rifle, watching the chaos ensue down below. He heard the distant echo of sirens.

"Grab the rest of the weapons and get to the van. Meet at the safe house," Saxon ordered. "I'll cover."

"You got it, boss," Ryan said. He and Rahman gathered up the rest of the weapons. Before they left, they made a point to wipe their AR-15s down and toss them near the bodies on the couch. Weapon cases in hand, Ryan and Rahman hurried out of the room as Saxon began firing again. He adjusted his aim to the frenzy of people trying to climb over the gates and unloaded, carefully counting the number of bullets he fired. When he'd fired every bullet except for the last, Saxon lowered the rifle and went back into the bedroom.

Sulieman lay on the ground, still unconscious. Saxon grabbed the man and positioned him sitting upright against the bed before turning the rifle on him and blowing his head apart. Reaching into his sport coat, Saxon pulled out a small bottle of cleaning solution. He methodically wiped down the rifle before dropping it next to Sulieman's corpse.

Before leaving, Saxon carefully grabbed each of the karambit knives with a towel he found in the bathroom. He closed each blade and slid them into Khatib's pockets—one in the left and one in the right.

Ten seconds later, he was closing the door to the hotel room behind him and heading for the staircase. He hit the lobby and saw nothing short of pandemonium. Slipping past the screaming concert-goers, the shocked travelers, and the overwhelmed hotel staff seeking refuge, Gray Saxon stepped out of the hotel and onto Michigan Avenue. A trio of ambulances rushed past him, followed by more police cars than he cared to count.

Chapter Five
Chicago, Illinois

Special Agent in Charge Riley Hanna, flipped through the dossier on Sulieman Khatib while she waited for the elevator in the Congress Plaza Hotel. She was flanked by her partner, James Gutierrez. James was still technically a rookie with the FBI—he hadn't even had one full year under his belt.

The FBI had been mobilized mere moments after the shooting stopped. Chicago Police and SWAT had done their best to lock down a ten-block radius around Grant Park. Almost instantly, the hospitals in the city were overwhelmed with over 600 victims with gunshot wounds and other injuries. The death total had already reached 55 people.

Since Riley had arrived at the scene, everything she'd been told felt off to her. Sulieman Khatib had been identified shortly after a SWAT team had kicked the door down and discovered the bodies. A thorough investigation into his life had turned enough red flags for concern, but Riley wasn't convinced. And then there was the fact that the security cameras had been disabled all throughout the Congress and the neighboring streets. She was convinced this wasn't just your run-of-the-mill terror attack, no matter how much Gutierrez tried to convince her it was.

Riley Hanna was 32 years old, relatively young for a Special Agent in Charge, and she looked much younger than her age. She always wore her brown hair in a ponytail and her tanned skin was perfect, not a wrinkle to be seen anywhere. She accredited this to her rigid skincare routine and good genetics—her dad was Italian while her mom was German and both looked great for their age. Despite having the smarts to go to Harvard, Riley had been drawn to law enforcement her entire life. When the opportunity came to her to work for the FBI, she pounced, never stopping to look back.

Riley and Gutierrez ducked under the yellow tape and stepped into the hotel room. Cops and Forensic Experts were everywhere. Three blue tarps were draped over the bodies of the dead men. A shorter cop in a blue suit broke away from the throng of cops.

"I'm Mike Jefferson, Superintendent for the CPD," he said, sticking out his hand. Riley and Gutierrez both shook it.

"Special Agent in Charge Riley Hanna. This is my partner, James Gutierrez," Riley introduced.

"Glad you guys are here," Jefferson sighed, putting his hands on his hips.

"Of course," Riley nodded. "I've been reading up on Sulieman Khatib."

"He's right over here," Jefferson pointed to the tarp against the bed. "Single gunshot to the head, self-inflicted by the looks of it."

"How much do you know about him?" Riley asked, opening the dossier once again.

"Next to nothing. My guys have told me bits and pieces, but we're all still trying to wrap our heads around this," Jefferson admitted.

"He's a well-known arms dealer in the Middle East. Most notably, he sells millions of dollars of weapons to the ISB, Islamic Syrian Brotherhood. They're a vicious group of extremists and were the ones responsible for that video a few years back of the female pilot."

"Oh fuck," Jefferson breathed. He'd seen the video when it first leaked to the public and was abhorred by what he saw.

"These other two, Abduhl Wardak and Omar Naeem, are ISB enforcers. Sulieman hired them as his personal bodyguards when he traveled," Riley continued.

"Everyone I've talked to is thinking this is terrorism." Jefferson hung his head. "That Khatib guy, he must've slit their throats after the shooting," Jefferson gestured to Abduhl and Omar.

"What makes you say that?" Riley asked. Jefferson pulled a clear evidence bag from his back pocket.

"Two karambit knives. Found in Khatib's pockets. I have to get them tested, obviously, but I'll bet you my house that this is what killed those two," Jefferson said confidently, tucking the bag back into his pocket.

"How many guns did you find at the scene?" Riley inquired.

"Three. Forensics is running some tests on them."

"I'd like to see the weapons at some point," Riley said politely.

Everything that Jefferson was telling her was adding up to it being terrorism. Khatib and his goons opened up on the concert-goers, trying to kill or wound as many as possible. Khatib kills them before turning the gun on himself. It wouldn't be the first time that terrorists have taken their own lives. In fact, that theory made the most sense to Hanna.

But she kept coming back to the CCTV cameras. The entire block had been down at the time of the shooting. Sure, it was possible for Sulieman Khatib to have someone else helping, but Riley didn't buy it. Terrorism was loud and public. Terrorists didn't care about being seen on security cameras.

"You're still not convinced?" Jefferson broke the awkward silence. The expression on Hanna's face told him that she was on the fence about his theory.

"No," Riley said simply, shaking her head. "Everything I've read about Sulieman Khatib points to him being a businessman. He's not a killer and he's certainly not going to open up on a bunch of civilians. He's not an extremist."

"What about these two?" Jefferson gestured to the bodies of Abduhl and Omar.

"It's possible, but very unlikely. These two are muscle, not killers. Whoever did this is a killer and a damn good one. Majority of the dead were shot through the head. Terrorists aren't that accurate or methodical, at least not in my experience."

"Ok, so then what?" Jefferson asked, getting frustrated that his detectives appeared to have dropped the ball.

Riley gestured for him to follow her out of the hotel room. With Gutierrez following close behind, they stepped into the hallway.

"My gut is telling me someone wants us to think this was terrorism," Riley said. "Nothing about these three guys points to them doing something like this. But all of the evidence points right at them. I don't know, it feels staged. Like, the way his body was positioned is too damn convenient. And then what, you're telling me Sulieman kills these two with knives and then shoots himself? Why not just shoot them? Plus, from what I can tell, there's no motive, nothing in Sulieman's past leads me to believe he is this dedicated to any of the terror groups he deals with."

"Well, you're throwing my main theory out the window," Jefferson grunted. "If it's not terrorism, then what is it?"

"Someone else had to have been here," Riley said. "Someone else shot those people and wanted all of us to think it was these guys."

Jefferson sighed heavily and rubbed his temple. In all of his police career, any time the feds got involved, the case just became more and more complicated. Agent Riley was making good points, as much as Jefferson hated to admit it. Terrorism was a demon in and of itself, but if someone had staged it to look like terrorism, that was almost worse.

Jefferson walked back into the hotel room, visibly annoyed by the young FBI agents. Gutierrez scratched his beard and shook his head.

"Why do you do that?" he asked.

"Do what?"

"Annoy everyone like that? You can be really condescending," Gutierrez criticized. This wasn't the first time Gutierrez had made these comments, he'd thought Riley was a know-it-all from the moment he'd met her.

"James, are you really telling me you think it's terrorism? You remember the Las Vegas shooting?"

"That guy was white and had no known affiliates to terrorists. These guys were Muslims and they were involved with the ISB!" Gutierrez hissed. "That sounds like terrorism to me."

Riley flipped open the dossier again and pulled out a piece of paper. She handed it to Gutierrez aggressively.

"Read that," she insisted. Gutierrez skimmed the paper. "How many of our 55 victims were shot through the head?"

"41, according to this," Gutierrez muttered.

"What does that sound like to you?" Riley pressed. Gutierrez rolled his eyes and relented.

"It sounds like our shooters were military, if you ask me. That kind of shooting has to be learned... trained. And terrorists aren't known for their accuracies."

"Exactly," Riley smiled, pleased that Gutierrez was finally coming around. "So, that means we have work to do."

"We're gonna need a military expert or something, right?"

"Right again, James," Riley patted him on the shoulder. "But don't worry, I know just the man for the job."

Chapter Six

Emeryville, California

Rain fell steadily on Riley Hanna and James Gutierrez as they stepped out of their police-issued Suburban. Both agents were wearing their black FBI windbreakers. They popped their umbrellas and strolled up to the gates cordoning off a massive construction site. Men in high-visibility jackets were moving all over the site. Heavy equipment and dump trucks moved synchronously. It was nothing short of chaos, but Riley could tell it was well controlled.

"So, who is this guy exactly?" Gutierrez asked as they headed into the site.

"John Shannon," Riley said. "I met him a few years ago when he was still in the Navy. He got kicked out, not sure why. But he was one of the best."

"Oh, great," Gutierrez grunted.

"Can I help you with something?" an annoyed voice asked. Riley turned and saw a grumpy-looking man approaching them. He wore concrete-stained boots and jeans, a flannel shirt with an orange vest, and a white hard hat that read 'WALSH CONSTRUCTION'.

"Special Agent Riley Hanna, FBI," Riley introduced, shaking hands with the man.

"David Spencer, I'm the Superintendent here," the man said, relaxing the frown on his face slightly.

"I'm looking for John Shannon," Riley said. "I was told he was working here."

"Yeah, he's here," David grunted. He pointed to the far side of the construction site where a large Caterpillar 320 excavator was loading dirt into Peterbilt dump trucks. "He's running the backhoe. Just be careful!" David warned before walking away.

Carefully avoiding a moving Caterpillar D8 bulldozer, the two agents crossed the site and slowly approached the excavator. The door to the machine was locked open and Riley could clearly see John Shannon at the controls of the machine.

He was wearing tan Timberland boots that were caked with mud, dirt, and concrete. His blue jeans had a noticeable rip on the left knee. The green high-visibility Carhartt t-shirt was stained with machine grease, motor oil, and mud. His hands were dirty and rugged—dirt was even smeared on his cheek. His black Pit Viper sunglasses had specks of dirt and mud all over them. A Marlboro Gold was pinched between his lips. He puffed on the cigarette as he expertly operated the excavator.

John Shannon had lost some of the toned muscles he had when he was in the SEALs and had put on close to 20 pounds. He was nowhere near the good shape he was in during his military days. At just under six feet tall, Shannon had been solid muscle in his fighting days. Now, he was pushing 215 pounds and had taken up smoking again, almost up to a pack a day.

As he spun the excavator around to dump a bucket full of dirt into an awaiting articulated dump truck, John spotted Riley Hanna and paused. He was shocked to see her, but that also meant bad news. It was always bad news when it came to Riley Hanna. John dumped the dirt into the truck before setting the bucket down on the ground and turning the throttle down on the excavator. He flicked his cigarette into the dirt before throwing the master brake on and carefully stepping out of the machine, groaning in discomfort. His back had been giving him consistent issues for almost a year.

"Hello, John," Riley smiled as she approached. John ran his hand through his short brown hair and chuckled to himself.

"How's it going, Hanna?" he asked in his deep baritone. He and Riley hugged, which caught Gutierrez off guard.

"This is my partner, James Gutierrez," Riley gestured toward Gutierrez. John merely nodded at the man.

"So, what brings you to Emeryville?" he asked, leaning against the tread of his excavator.

"You heard about what happened in Chicago?" Riley asked. John nodded.

"Of course. It's all over the news. Chris Cuomo's calling it 'possible terrorism'. So is Blitzer and Cooper and Tucker Carlson."

"Yeah, I know," Riley said bitterly. The media had been pushing the terrorism narrative since the names of the dead men in the hotel room were leaked. "The death toll is up to 58, we lost three more at the hospital."

"Couple more and you'll have a new record," John muttered cryptically. "I didn't think Vegas would get beat for a while."

"Let's pray it doesn't," Riley shifted on her feet. "John, I'm here to ask for your help."

John laughed like it was the funniest thing he'd heard in a long time. He shook his head and reached back into the cab of the excavator, grabbing his Yeti and taking a sip of black coffee.

"That's a good one, Riley," he chuckled.

"I'm serious, John," Riley narrowed her eyes. John stopped laughing. "John, I don't think that was terrorism. There's enough evidence to support the theory, but I don't buy it. Something else is going on here, I can feel it," Riley insisted. John sighed heavily as he popped another Marlboro Gold into his mouth.

"Why are you smoking again? I thought you quit," Riley commented.

As he grabbed his lighter, Riley finally noticed the silver wedding band on his left hand. She did a double-take, hoping neither Gutierrez nor John would notice. The last time she had seen John Shannon, the two had spent the night in a hotel just outside Disneyland in Anaheim. Whenever John was in Coronado, they would spend a weekend in some fancy hotel, drinking wine and having wild sex. When John was kicked out of the Navy, he'd fallen off the face of the earth. Although Riley would never admit it, she had fallen for him and was deeply hurt when he became a ghost. That was enough for her to request a transfer and land the SAC job in Chicago.

John scoffed and lit the cigarette, blowing a cloud of smoke at Hanna. "You're such a dick," she chuckled.

"Were you two a couple or something?" Gutierrez blurted out, causing Riley to wheel around and give him a heated glare. John chuckled and exhaled another cloud of smoke.

"Or something," he said, winking at Hanna. She rolled her eyes and tried to change the subject, too shy to ask about the wedding ring. That was something she hadn't expected to see.

"Look, we're wasting time here. Will you help us or not?" Riley pressed.

"No can do," John shook his head. "I'm on the Navy's shit list. No way they'd reinstate me."

"John, the three bodies in that hotel room were linked to the ISB. I know you have experience with them. I read most of your file, you hunted those guys for a while before the Navy gave you the boot," Riley admitted.

"I didn't hunt them," John puffed. "I just killed them. That's what happens when you kill an entire Delta team and rape a pilot. They send guys like me after you."

"That's why I need your help, John! You have an eye for this stuff. I'm just asking you to take a look at everything and tell me what you think. If you think it's terrorism, that's good enough for me. Please, for old time's sake," Riley lowered her voice.

John finished off the cigarette and tossed it into the dirt. He looked at Riley and could see in her eyes that something had her genuinely spooked. She was still just as beautiful as she was when they were sleeping together. Deep down, John figured she was probably onto something. Riley Hanna was the smartest woman he'd ever met. And if she was seeking him out after all these years, then there was a lead.

"Alright," John relented. "But if I agree to this, I'm gonna need access to everything. Crime scene, bodies, physical evidence, witnesses... all of it."

"You got it," Riley nodded, suppressing her smile as best she could.

"Glad we got this sorted out," Gutierrez rolled his eyes, feeling as if his time had been wasted. "I'll be in the car."

Gutierrez turned on his heel and walked back toward their Suburban, Riley and John followed a few paces behind. When no one was looking, John smacked Hanna's ass and laughed hysterically.

"Excuse me!" Riley squealed.

"What?" John shrugged, stifling laughter. "Can't blame me, we had some good times, Hanna."

"Yes, we did, but that ring on your finger tells me those days are behind us," Riley crossed her arms. John's smile vanished.

"Yeah... I guess they are," he muttered.

John walked away from Hanna, lighting another cigarette as he went to speak to the foreman.

Chapter Seven
Jefferson Estates, Illinois

Ryan Bueshay slipped out of the mansion onto the back cobblestone patio; the sun was just rising over the horizon. He closed the door quietly behind him and sat down in a comfy deck chair, propping his feet up on the table. The mansion he was currently residing in was a thing of wonder to a small-town guy like Ryan.

Located just outside the Downtown area, Jefferson Estates was a small neighborhood of recently built mansions. The house was worth just around $2.15 million and was over 5,800 square feet. It included five bedrooms, six bathrooms, a beautiful back patio and pool deck, and a large fish pond behind the pool.

In all his life, Ryan Bueshay had never seen a nicer house. Then again, he didn't have much to compare it to. Having grown up in rural Kentucky, Ryan never had much. His dad had taken off before he was born, abandoning him and his mother without so much as a cent to their name. His educated mother worked odd jobs in diners and bars, trying to make ends meet. It was after she'd gotten hooked on crack cocaine that Ryan knew he needed to get out of Kentucky.

That led him to the military, more specifically, the Army. By his 21st birthday, Ryan was a Ranger in the 75th Battalion. He had loved every second of his career in the Army, but a knee injury got him a one-way ticket to a medical discharge. The discharge had left a stale taste in his mouth, but that wasn't what drew him to Gray Saxon. Mere months after his discharge, Ryan's old team had been killed in a terror attack—an attack that the ISB had taken credit for.

Ryan Bueshay looked a lot different than he did during his military service. He'd grown his brown hair out before shaving the sides and back, the top of his head was filled with long, flowing locks—he normally gelled and combed his hair back to keep it out of his face. After his discharge, he had become enamored with piercings and tattoos. He had gauges in both ears and an industrial piercing in his left ear, along with several smaller rings along the cartilage. Each side of his nose had a ring, and a spectrum piercing completed the picture. Additionally, he had a tongue piercing and a silver ring through the center of his bottom lip. His tattoos were numerous and plentiful, the most notable being the Army Ranger star and crossed rifles on his right hand. His left hand displayed a detailed view of planet Earth. The piercings and tattoos distracted people from the fact that he was handsome and friendly, his blue eyes were always bright behind a pair of glasses.

Leaning back in his chair, Ryan took out a pack of Newports and a Bic lighter. He pulled a smoke from the pack and lit it, taking a long pull from the cigarette. The past few days had been filled with taking inventory of the small arsenal in the basement of the mansion. Aside from the weapons acquired from Sulieman Khatib, Saxon had gotten his hands on at least 40 more weapons, thousands of rounds of ammunition, and tactical equipment.

Just as Gray Saxon had anticipated, pretty much everyone was under the suspicion that the Chicago shooting had been the work of ISB extremists. Leaving the bodies, guns, and knives at the scene only perpetuated the theory.

"Care if I join you?" Rahman Saleh asked, peeking his head through the door. He was carrying a small joint and a lighter of his own. Ryan waved him off, puffing on the cigarette. Rahman sat down across from Ryan and torched his joint, sighing in relief as he felt the marijuana enter his system.

"Didn't know you smoke," Ryan commented.

Rahman chuckled. "There's a lot you don't know about me, southerner." He blew a thick cloud of smoke across the table.

Rahman Saleh was a 35-year-old Iraqi Army veteran who had spent most of his 20s combating terrorism alongside US troops. He had considered himself a true patriot up until his wife and two small children were murdered by ISB insurgents—a deliberate move as retribution for Saleh's allegiance to the Americans. After that, Saleh left the Iraqi Army.

"So," Ryan said, bringing Rahman back to reality. "What do you think his grand scheme is?"

"Hmm, he hasn't told you either?" Rahman retorted. He didn't hide his surprise. For someone as intelligent as Gray Saxon, he wasn't very chatty.

"Secrets, secrets," Ryan chuckled, finishing off the cigarette and mushing the butt into a small ashtray sitting on the table. "I'm gonna go make some breakfast. Do you want anything?"

"Eggs, if you don't mind," Rahman smiled appreciatively. "I'm gonna finish this and be inside in a few."

Ryan walked back into the kitchen. Gray Saxon was leaning against the counter, sipping a piping hot cup of coffee and scrolling through his iPhone. He was dressed casually in a pair of shorts and a baggy sweatshirt. He looked up at Ryan and nodded respectfully, not offering any words.

"Morning," Ryan muttered, opening the fridge and grabbing the carton of eggs. Saxon grunted, picked up his mug, and left the kitchen, returning to his office. He locked the door behind him without speaking a word.

After close to three months of living in the house with Saxon, Ryan had gotten used to his personality. Saxon kept his distance, which was fine with Ryan. Although he would never admit it, Ryan was respectfully fearful of Saxon... anyone with half a brain would be.

"What's for breakfast?" a woman asked as she walked into the kitchen. Ryan cocked his head behind him and saw Ilsa, one of the 'escorts'. In reality, Ilsa was no escort, but a former British Intelligence Operative—a trained and lethal killer. It was easy to be disarmed by her pretty face and kind smile, but beneath her beautiful exterior was the heart and soul of a fearless warrior.

"Eggs and bacon," Ryan said, smiling at Ilsa.

"Delicious," she returned the smile, her smooth English accent sounded as entrancing as ever. "Alaina will be down soon."

Alaina Nilsson had played the role of the second 'escort'. A striking woman of 29, Alaina had lived most of her life in Stockholm, Sweden. A career in the Swedish Air Force allowed her to cross paths with Gray Saxon.

"Good morning, Ilsa," Rahman waved, coming in from finishing his joint. Ilsa smiled and poured herself a glass of water, offering one to Rahman. He accepted the glass and took a small sip. It was no secret that Rahman had his eyes on Ilsa. Ryan laughed under his breath and turned his attention back to the food on the stove.

Alaina appeared in the kitchen, drying her long blonde hair with a large towel. She smiled casually to the group and sat down at the kitchen table.

"Good morning, everyone," she said in her thick Swedish accent. "I trust you all are well-rested."

"Of course," Ryan said sarcastically. Alaina ignored him and headed for the fridge.

The door to Saxon's office opened and he reappeared, sipping his coffee. He carried several thick manila folders in his left hand.

"Good, you're all here," he said quietly. He handed each of them a folder before refilling his coffee cup. "Study the folders. That's our next target. Any questions, ask. If you're uncertain about anything, ask."

"Where did you get all of this?" Ryan asked as he flipped through the detailed folder. He was hard-pressed to hide his astonishment at the sheer amount of information on their next target. "This is a lot of information."

"You let me worry about that. Full briefing later this week, but look over everything," Saxon responded. "Ilsa, I need to speak to you outside."

Alaina gave Ilsa a concerned glance as she got up and headed to the back door, following Saxon outside. Once the door was closed, Saxon sat down at the patio table, gesturing to the seat across from him.

"Don't look so worried," Saxon said in a more relaxed tone. Ilsa chuckled and sat down. Saxon thumbed a cigarette out of the carton and offered one to Ilsa; she politely declined and waited while he lit the smoke and took a puff.

"You and I are going out tonight," Saxon said. "Simple gun buy. Nothing exciting. We'll meet the seller at his house and be back here within two hours."

"Ok," Ilsa said simply. "Just let me know what time."

"I trust you, Ilsa," Saxon continued. "If you have hesitations, I want you to tell me."

"I don't. Not even a little bit. I believe in what we're doing and I mean that," Ilsa nodded. Saxon took another pull from the cigarette and looked at her intently.

"Keep an eye on Rahman," he lowered his voice. Ilsa raised an eyebrow. This was the first time Saxon had hinted at a sense of distrust for anyone in the house.

"Any particular reason?" Ilsa asked.

"Just keep an eye on him please," Saxon smiled.

Saxon didn't feel it necessary to divulge everything he knew and suspected to Ilsa. He trusted her more than anyone else in that house, but there was still a level of secrecy he needed to hold on to.

Chapter Eight
McCormick Place, Illinois

Overnight, the McCormick Convention Center had been trans-
formed into an FBI command center. The largest convention center in
North America, McCormick Place was located on the shore of Lake
Michigan and right outside downtown Chicago. The spacious innards of

the convention center allowed the FBI to set up computers, evidence tables, and have tactical teams on standby.

Crime scene and computer techs were busy at work, combing through security footage and the abundant physical evidence left behind in the hotel room. Since arriving at the command center, John Shannon had been confined to a small office. Hanna's superiors were less than thrilled with her for bringing him back.

The door to the office opened and Riley Hanna appeared in her blue FBI Jacket. John looked up and smirked.

"Didn't really expect a hero's welcome," he chuckled. Riley shook her head and gestured for him to get up.

"Follow me," she said ominously. John jumped up and followed Riley through a hallway to the large evidence room. Almost 20 techs were pouring over the evidence and thoroughly studying everything. A man in a black suit saw Riley Hanna and hurried over, bumping past a duo of technicians.

"Agent Hanna," he said, his annoyance clear from his aggressive tone. He was an older man with graying hair and a wrinkled face. His dark eyes were narrowed at the young Special Agent in Charge. Riley stiffened as he approached.

"Director McGrady," Riley nodded respectfully. She gestured to John Shannon. "This is Master Chief Johnathan Shannon."

"Sir," John offered his hand. Deputy Assistant Director Tom McGrady shook John's hand but didn't take his eyes off of Hanna.

"Former Master Chief," McGrady clarified. "Hanna, the FBI will not allow you to bring disgruntled Navy personnel into this investigation."

"Director, please hear me out," Riley jumped to defend herself. "Master Chief Shannon has extensive experience with the Islamic Syrian Brotherhood. He's extremely knowledgeable and I think an outside opinion would be paramount for our investigation. I do not believe this is an act of terrorism, sir."

"I don't care what you think this is," McGrady lamented.

"With all due respect," John interrupted before McGrady could continue his verbal lashing. "You need answers. Quickly. Every minute that passes without answers leads to more unease among civilians. It also increases your chances of having viable information leaked to the press and creating a fucking panic."

"I have been doing this for a long time, son," McGrady snapped. "I know how this works."

"You do?" John challenged. "Good, then you'll let me take a look at everything and help you guys as best I can."

"Sir, John will only act as an advisor. I just want to hear what he has to say once he's looked at all the evidence. It can't hurt anything," Riley urged. She knew McGrady well enough to know he didn't want to do anything to hurt the investigation, but he was a rule follower at heart.

McGrady was quiet and looked at his shiny black shoes, sighing loudly. He resented Riley bringing a man like John Shannon so close to such sensitive material. But both of them made good points, McGrady couldn't deny that.

"Ok," he relented. "He can get access. Hanna, you are entirely responsible for him while he's here acting purely as an advisor. Is this understood?"

"Of course, sir," Riley nodded. "Thank you, sir."

"Don't make me regret trusting you," McGrady said to Riley as he walked away.

Riley breathed a loud sigh of relief and rubbed her temple. John chuckled and popped a cigarette into his mouth.

"Come on," Riley said. "Let's get to work."

"I'll follow you," John mumbled, lighting the smoke and taking a drag.

John Shannon was given immediate access to everything after signing a nondisclosure agreement and went to work. He skimmed through witness reports and coroner reports, absorbing as much information as he could. The physical evidence was next. He spent almost an hour inspecting the guns and knives collected from the hotel room. He jotted notes down in a small notebook as he worked. Riley Hanna chose to let him work, leaving him alone for much of his initial investigation. She trusted John, there was no need for her to babysit the man.

Riley was sitting next to a trio of FBI technicians watching a cell phone video of the shooting when John Shannon came up behind her. She could smell the cigarettes as soon as he walked up to them.

"You really need to stop smoking," she said, not taking her eyes off of the monitor.

"We should talk," John mumbled quietly, ignoring Hanna's comment.

"Ok, give me a few minutes."

"What are you watching?" John asked, pulling up a chair next to the group.

"One of the people at the concert was taking a video when the shooting started," one of the techs muttered. She restarted the video, letting John watch from the beginning.

The video started with two young girls jumping up and down, singing along with the blaring music. The girl on the right was clearly holding the phone. Not even five seconds into the video, gunfire could be heard and the girls started looking around in confusion. The music stopped and that's when the screaming started, almost drowning out the concussive gunfire.

"Jesus," John grumbled. He got up and walked away, Riley followed close behind. She led him into her small, makeshift office and closed the door.

"Alright, John," she put her hands on her hips.

"Tell me if I'm wrong about any of this," John said, opening his notebook. "There is no security footage of anyone other than Sulieman Khatib and his two guys coming or going into that hotel room, correct?"

"That's correct. The cameras were disabled 27 minutes before the shooting started and came back on almost 20 minutes after."

"And the knives found in Sulieman's pocket were used to kill Omar and Abduhl. That's a fact?"

"Yes," Riley nodded. John then bit his lip and nodded.

"Well, if I'm Sulieman Khatib, I'm not going to slit the throats of my two cohorts. They outweighed him by almost 50 pounds each, so he didn't hold both of them down and murder them. There's a chance they did it themselves and then he took the knives, but no other fingerprints were found on the blades except for Sulieman's," John explained. He paused, waiting for Riley to ask any questions she may have.

"Continue, please," she urged, anxiously awaiting his assessment.

"The security cameras are the biggest clue," John said. "Terrorists do not care about cameras. They know they're going to die. So, if it really is Sulieman and his guys, then why disable the cameras? Especially if they're already in the hotel room and have no intention of leaving? It just doesn't make sense."

"I know, I know," Riley agreed. John shook his head.

"You don't have enough to prove it, but I'd bet money someone else was in that hotel room," John concluded, much to Hanna's approval.

"So, you agree with me?" Riley asked.

"Yeah, I think something else is going on. But proving it is going to be hard."

"Well, how do we prove it?"

John was quiet, staring at Riley intently. He had an idea, but it involved using about every favor he could possibly call in.

"Have you heard of Khaled Al-Khatib?" John spoke after almost 30 seconds. Riley shook her head. "I'm not surprised, the man is a ghost. That's Sulieman's older brother, he's a ranking member of the ISB. Much more radical than our boy Sulieman."

"Ok," Riley raised an eyebrow, wondering where John was going with this.

"Logically speaking, if Sulieman was making a move on behalf of the ISB, Khaled would know about it. He would also know if Sulieman was planning to meet anyone," John kept his voice low.

"John, what are you suggesting?" Riley urged him on.

"I think we need to have a chat with Khaled Al-Khatib."

Chapter Nine
Al Karak, Jordan

The wind rushed past John Shannon as he flew gracefully over the darkened Jordanian night sky. He tried to breathe as calmly as he could from the oxygen tank attached to the front of his body. Smoking nearly a pack of cigarettes a day for the last couple of years had taken a toll on his lungs; he was starting to feel lightheaded. In addition to the oxygen tank, John had almost 100 pounds of equipment fixed to his body. Carefully angling his head to the right, John saw the rest of the ten-man JSOC team freefalling with him and felt a wave of excitement surge through him. He had missed this more than he cared to admit. The instant adrenaline rush blocked his concerns about his physical condition and he smiled behind his mask.

The Joint Special Operations Team, made up of the Army's 1st Special Operational Detachment-Delta, had been mobilized after receiving actionable intelligence from John Shannon on Khaled Al-Khatib. Master Chief John Shannon was well known among the Special Operations community, so his call was taken seriously. He'd gotten onto the team after calling in a favor with US Army General, Bill Abernathy. The two went way back and John had saved Abernathy's butt on more than one occasion. Despite John's blacklisted status within the US Armed Forces, Abernathy had secretly gotten John in the country and onto the team.

John yanked on the ripcord and his chute popped from the rucksack on his back, slowing his descent dramatically. The rest of the JSOC unit deployed their chutes and the team landed within 100 yards of each other. Shredding his jump gear, John strapped on his helmet and shouldered his rifle, an M4A1 rifle fitted with a suppressor, Trijicon ACOG sight, and a foregrip.

"Tomcat Lead, this is Outlaw," John whispered into his mic, his breathing was labored and heavy. "Standing by, over."

"Copy that, Outlaw. Target location is half a click to the west. Rally up on my position," the Delta leader, Jameson, called back.

Getting to his feet, John cleared the distance between himself and the rest of the JSOC team. Hurrying past the other Delta operators, John came to a stop and took a knee next to Jameson. Jameson looked up and saw John's sweat-covered face.

"You good, Shannon?"

"I'm good," John nodded, settling his breathing and heart rate.

"We'll take point," Jameson said in a low voice. "Keep it tight and don't get killed, please. I'd hate for a celebrity to be killed on my mission."

"Fuck you, Jimmy," John snapped. Jameson sniggered and signaled for his team to move out.

The team moved out in silence, moving like ghosts in the darkness. They came over a ridge and saw that the complex consisted of a single-story house and two barns. In the darkness, the team could see three roaming sentries outside the barn. Jameson held up his fist and the team took a knee. The sniper of the team, Davenport, laid down in the sand and propped up his Heckler and Koch 417 rifle. The 417 was fixed with a Night Scope, allowing Davenport to see clearly through the pitch black.

"Eyes on target," Davenport said, flicking the safety off.

"Weapons free," Jameson responded.

Taking a relaxing breath, Davenport centered the first armed guard in the crosshairs of his rifle. Without hesitation, he pulled the trigger and the hushed round blew apart the guard's head. Slowly swinging right,

Davenport fired again and killed the second guard with a round through his neck. He adjusted once again and fired one last round, dropping the third guard before he even knew what was happening. The team waited for a few seconds to see if anyone had heard the shots, but it was clear that Davenport had killed the three guards without raising any alarms.

"Davenport, provide overwatch," Jameson ordered. "Team, let's move."

Quickening their pace, the team moved across the desert terrain and closed in on the main house. John shouldered his rifle as they approached the house; he scanned the property calmly. Deciding it was just too dark, John folded the night vision goggles attached to his helmet over his eyes. His field of vision illuminated around him. He chuckled to himself as he saw the rest of the Delta team follow suit.

The team moved around the house, hugging the wall tightly. Jameson led the team to the front door and held just before. John broke out of formation to take up position on the other side of the door, nodding to Jameson to signal he was ready. Jameson reached over and tested the door—it was unlocked. He pushed the door open and John stepped inside, turning around to check behind the door. The rest of the Delta team filed into the house. With John now leading the team, they moved down the hallway. A sleepy man stumbled into the hallway carrying a Norinco Type 56 rifle. He looked to his right and his eyes widened. Before he could shout a warning or raise his rifle, John shot him down with two pinpoint bullets to the man's face.

He froze for a second, staring at the dead body in front of him. In his prime, he wouldn't have hesitated, but John hadn't killed a man in many years. He'd forgotten the intense emotion that came with taking a life in such proximity. The most excitement John had had in recent memory was getting to run his company's demolition excavator—a massive CAT 349 fitted with a hydraulic hammer.

Shaking those thoughts from his head, John gestured for a Delta to follow him. John and the other Delta poured into the room the dead man had come from, coming face to face with two more armed terrorists. The two men didn't stand a chance, they were cut down in a nanosecond by John and the Delta.

Clearing the rest of the rooms, the Delta team linked up and moved as a complete unit toward the back bedroom. Jameson booted the door down and rushed in, activating the flashlight on the end of his M4A1. The woman in the bed jumped up, screaming wildly. Khaled Al-Khatib reached for the AK-47 lying next to his bed. John leaped across the room and delivered a vicious kick to Khaled's head, knocking the man unconscious. Two operators subdued the woman, tying her hands and feet. John and Jameson tied Khaled's hands and pulled a black bag over his head.

Less than ten minutes after Davenport fired the first shots, the Delta team was retreating over the ridge toward the awaiting extraction helicopter.

Chapter Ten
Mashabim Air Base, Israel

Alongside Jameson and Davenport, John Shannon strode through the Israeli-based Air Base toward a small brick building. Most of the US soldiers stationed at the Air Base hadn't been aware of a JSOC unit coming in, so the team's arrival had been met with a certain amount of surprise. Luckily for John, no one seemed to know or care who he was.

The trio walked into the building and locked the door behind them. Inside the building was only a single room, and Khaled Al-Khatib was zip-tied to a chair in the middle of the room. Groggily, Khaled looked up at the men and smirked.

"I already told the other man... I won't talk," he said. His English was good but heavily accented. "You can torture me all you want, but you Americans have too many rules. You have nothing to threaten me with."

"Well, unfortunately for you," Jameson pulled up a folding chair and sat in front of Khaled. "That's not entirely true. My friend over here has some questions for you. You're going to answer them or he's going to do some really awful shit to you."

"Go ahead and try, pig," Khaled spat. Jameson chuckled and looked over to John.

"He's all yours," Jameson got up and stood next to Davenport by the door.

John sat down in the chair and pulled out his pack of Marlboro Golds, pulling one out with his teeth. He stared hard at Khaled, narrowing his eyes on the man. Khaled withered under the iron gaze, shifting nervously in his chair. He'd been interrogated for information in the past, but the look in John's eyes was something he had not seen before.

"My name is John," he introduced, lighting the cigarette. "I have some questions about your brother, Sulieman Khatib."

"Ask him yourself," Khaled answered. "I won't talk to you."

"Well, I would if I could," John shrugged, puffing the smoke and pulling out his phone. He opened a picture of Sulieman's dead body and turned the phone for Khaled to see. Khaled's face dropped when he saw his brother's lifeless corpse.

"Sulieman is dead?" he asked in a quiet voice. John tucked the phone away and blew a dark cloud of smoke in Khaled's face. The surprise from Khaled wasn't shocking to John.

"Your little brother and two of his goons shot up a music festival. In America. Killed almost 60 people before they killed themselves," John explained. "I was hoping you could shed some light on why your brother might've wanted to do that."

"Sulieman sold weapons, he wasn't a killer." Khaled shook his head. "He never had the stomach for it."

"So, you didn't know what he was planning?" John asked. Khaled shook his head.

"All Sulieman told me was that he was making a large sale to a..." Khaled's voice trailed off before he could finish his thought. John leaned forward, taking the cigarette out of his mouth.

"To a what?" John growled.

Khaled kept his mouth shut and stared back at John, anger in his old eyes. He was not going to say another word if it meant helping the Americans.

"He knows something," Jameson said ominously. John turned around and nodded. He put the cigarette out on the floor and took a knee in front of Khaled.

"Make sure no one comes and interrupts us," John said. Jameson nodded once and crossed his arms, knowing what was about to happen.

"Tell me what you know, Khaled," John urged. "Or I swear on my wife, things will get very ugly for you."

"You're bluffing. You Americans have too many rules. I won't talk," Khaled responded. John leaned in closer to Khaled and lowered his voice to a low growl.

"I want nothing more than to be back in my air-conditioned home, going to my union job and getting benefits for pulling levers. I'm not military, fucker. I can do whatever I want to you and no one will bat an eye," John growled.

John opened the pocket on his thigh and pulled out a pair of pliers. Khaled's eyes widened slightly at the sight of the tool.

"Tell me what you know about your brother or I'm going to break your fingers one at a time," John snarled, opening the pliers and pinching Khaled's pointer finger on his right hand.

"Fuck you!" Khaled cried. Sweat started streaking down his bushy face. His breathing increased dramatically as he waited for the inevitable pain to come.

John Shannon yanked the finger back, breaking it and the joint with a sickening crunch. Khaled screamed in pain as John twisted the broken appendage. Taking Khaled's middle finger between the pliers, John repeated the process. Tears streamed down Khaled's face as he cursed wildly in Arabic.

John almost made it through Khaled's entire right hand before the battered man held up his left hand, begging for mercy.

"Please," he croaked. "No more."

"Tell me what I want to know," John said, taking the pliers off of Khaled's pinky finger. He sat back down across from Khaled and tucked the pliers away. "This was just a warm-up, Khaled. I have much worse shit planned for you if you refuse to talk."

"I'll talk, I'll talk," Khaled said weakly. He was ashamed of himself, but he hadn't anticipated the excruciating pain that John inflicted on him.

"Who was your brother going to sell weapons to?" John asked.

"An American. Sulieman was making the sale to an American," Khaled revealed. John raised an eyebrow as it was clear Khaled was not lying.

"An American?" John clarified. Khaled nodded slowly.

"Yes. An American soldier. This man contacted Sulieman, wanted a lot of weapons, and wanted to make the sale on American soil. Sulieman said that New York and Chicago had been discussed."

"You are telling me that an American soldier contacted your brother?" John tried to hide his shock. Again, Khaled nodded.

"The man was knowledgeable about weapons and told Sulieman he had fought in many battles. They talked through email extensively before the meeting."

"Alright," John lit another cigarette. "What else do you know?"

"I swear, that's all I know. Sulieman didn't know anything else about him, just that he was American. He didn't even know a name."

A few minutes later, John and the two Delta men left the building. Jameson had given Khaled some food and applied ice to his hand. As they walked back toward the runway of the base, Jameson asked, "So, what does that mean? Sulieman was killed by a soldier? An American?"

"Honestly," John puffed nervously on his cigarette. "It means that this just got a lot more complicated."

Chapter Eleven
Lincoln Park, Illinois

Riley Hanna was deep in REM sleep when her phone buzzed loudly on her nightstand, startling her awake. It took a few seconds before she was aware enough to look at the phone—it was John Shannon.

"John?" she answered, rubbing her eyes with the back of her hand.

"Sorry to wake you," he said. "Is your line secure?"

"Yes. Is yours?" Riley sat up in her bed. John scoffed and she could hear him take a long puff from a cigarette. "John, you really need to stop smoking. It's a disgusting habit and it's just plain bad for you."

"Save the health lesson for another day," John quipped. "I had a talk with Khaled Al-Khatib."

"And?"

"Sulieman was in Chicago to make a sale. His brother would've known if he was there to kill people. Khaled was pretty adamant that he wasn't," John said.

"Well, that just confirms what we've been thinking."

"I'm not finished," John blurted. "Khaled told me that Sulieman was going to sell guns to an American... an American soldier."

"Wait... what?" Riley was sure she'd heard John wrong. "Sulieman Khatib was in Chicago to sell guns to an American soldier?"

"That's what Khaled told me," John puffed.

"How reliable is this information?" Riley asked.

"Very," John said. He had interrogated his fair share of men back in his SEAL days and he was willing to bet his life that Khaled was telling the truth.

"Alright, John, be honest with me. What do you think that means? I mean, I'm already having thoughts, but I want to know what you think."

"Whoever Sulieman met with killed him and then killed those people to cover their tracks and throw us off. Sulieman Khatib is not a killer. Whoever killed him and those people is extremely smart. Putting 60 bodies on a terror organization is a great way to distract people. Everyone is worrying about terrorism when, really, it wasn't. And if it was a soldier, that could explain why the shots were so accurate and the lack of surveillance footage," John explained.

Riley could hear the anxiety in his voice. If a US Soldier was responsible for this attack, that was an entirely different beast. And it no doubt was going to make things messier. That would change the entire narrative as well. Instantly, it would no longer be an issue of growing terror activities. Blame would be pointed back at the United States government and military.

"Ok," Riley rubbed her forehead. "We have to take this seriously and start looking into it. I'll have James start looking through flight manifests for US soldiers flying into Chicago. It's at least a place to start."

"Start with soldiers who aren't on active duty," John suggested. "Check any military installation in Illinois and the surrounding areas for anyone who was unaccounted for or off-base at the time of the shootings."

"Good idea," Riley agreed. "I'm going to the office now and I'll get things started on my end."

"Isn't it like two in the morning there?" John asked. Riley yawned obnoxiously, getting a laugh from John.

"Not like I'm going back to sleep anyway," Riley muttered.

"Sorry about that. Figured I shouldn't wait," John said. There was a brief moment of silence between the two of them.

"Do you ever miss it?" Riley blurted out. She instantly regretted saying it and rolled her head back in annoyance.

"Which part?" John chuckled. "The fancy dinners, Disneyland dates, amazing sex? Of course I miss it."

"Yeah, me too," Riley admitted quietly. She thought of the ring on his finger. "I didn't know you were married."

This time, John was quiet for a lot longer, making Riley extremely anxious. He had figured the subject would come up at some point, but he still wasn't sure he wanted to get into all of it. Riley had been a great friend for many years, even more than just a friend when he was home.

"Yeah," John sighed. "I'm married, but it's not for the long run."

"Wh-what do you mean?" Riley asked.

Another long pause. Riley wasn't sure if John was lighting another cigarette or just breathing super heavily, as if trying not to get emotional.

"My wife, Anna, was diagnosed with an inoperable brain tumor," John choked out. "She's got maybe a month or two."

"Oh my god, John," Riley gasped. "Why aren't you at home with her? Why didn't you say anything? I wouldn't have asked you to help me if I knew that."

"I've watched her wither away for years, Riley," John said grimly. "This was always going to be the outcome. Me being there or not being there won't change a fucking thing. If she's got days to live, her sister is going to call me so I can be there for the end. Not the way either of us planned it, but what else can we do?"

"Sorry," Riley muttered, taken aback by his sudden aggressive attitude.

"I'll be on the next flight back to Chicago," John grumbled before hanging up.

Riley put her phone down, feeling horrible for asking John about the ring. She pushed her thoughts of embarrassment away and got dressed, made a coffee to go, and headed to the parking garage.

Chapter Twelve
North Potomac, Maryland

North Potomac was one of the nicest suburban neighborhoods in Maryland, with the average household income just above $160,000. The beautiful homes were what had drawn Walter Nichols to settle in North Potomac with his family. He'd been married for over 20 years and had fathered four kids—two boys and two girls—with his elegant wife, Chrissy.

For the last ten years of his life, Walter Nichols had served as the Special Envoy to the Middle East, more specifically, Syria. Because of his line of work, Nichols had traveled all over the world and had the privilege to bring his family along for most of his travels. But he was getting older and so were his children; traveling all of the time was becoming less and less realistic.

Since the Chicago shooting, Nichols had been on call after call with his contacts in Syria, trying to verify the media claims that the ISB was behind the attack. He'd spoken with the director of the FBI multiple times and got confirmation that the bodies found in the hotel room had connections to the ISB. He had no way of knowing the SAC Riley Hanna had reason to believe that a US serviceman was responsible for the attack.

Walter Nichols pulled into his driveway, exhausted after a day of non-stop meetings and phone calls, trying to help in any way he could. He was surprised to see that there were no outside lights on. Chrissy was religious about turning the outside lights on once the sun set. Walter shrugged it off and grabbed his briefcase before heading through the front door.

"Hello," he called into the huge home. There was no response. Again, Walter didn't overthink it. Maybe his family was in the basement. He kicked off his loafers, loosened his tie, and headed into the kitchen to set his briefcase down.

"Good evening, Ambassador Nichols," Gray Saxon said. He was sitting at Nichols' kitchen table, across from his wife. Saxon had a suppressed Para-Ordnance Black Ops 1911 in his right hand, aimed right at Chrissy Nichols.

Chrissy Nichols had obviously been crying, her cheeks were streaked with tears that had ruined the small amount of make-up she usually wore. Her hands were cuffed with zip-ties. There was a strip of duct tape over her mouth. Walter's lip quivered as he looked at the stranger in his home pointing a gun at his wife.

"Take whatever you want," he said in a shaky voice. Saxon chuckled and kicked out one of the chairs.

"Have a seat," he said calmly. Walter did as he was told, sitting down next to his wife.

"Are you ok?" Walter asked Chrissy, kissing her on the head. She nodded feverishly and her eyes welled with tears.

"She's fine," Saxon answered.

"Who are you? What do you want?" Walter asked, turning to face Saxon.

"I want you to help me," Saxon said simply. "If you do that, then you'll never see me again. But if you refuse, I'll be forced to kill your family members one at a time until you do."

"Please, please don't hurt my family," Walter shuddered. "Wait... where are my children?"

"They're upstairs," Saxon said. "One of my guys is watching them. He won't hurt them, I promise."

"What do you need?" Walter asked, trying to remain calm. Saxon set the gun down on the table and stood up.

"It's quite simple. All I need you to do is tell your contacts in The White House that the attack in Chicago was perpetrated by members of the ISB. A terror attack committed by a Syrian terror group is sure to spark debate about engaging the ISB," Saxon stated calmly.

"The implications of that are very dangerous," Walter explained, trying to remain calm.

"More dangerous than me pointing a gun at your wife?" Saxon challenged, picking the 1911 up and pointing it at her again. Chrissy cried loudly, shaking nervously and desperately trying to free her wrists.

"Put the gun down!" Walter yelled. Saxon flipped the weapon around and pistol-whipped Walter, drawing blood from his forehead. Walter fell onto the floor, seeing stars.

"You'll find I am not a very patient man, Mr. Nichols," Saxon snarled, pressing the gun to Walter's eye. "I suggest you make up your mind. Or I'm going to put a bullet in your wife's head."

Saxon stepped over to Chrissy and put his arm around her neck. He pressed the gun to her forehead and cocked the hammer slowly.

"You have three seconds," Saxon growled. Walter struggled to get to his feet.

"Please..." he begged, raising his hands up in surrender.

"Three," Saxon counted.

"Please don't shoot my wife!"

"Two."

"I'm begging you! Please!"

"One," Saxon wrapped his finger around the trigger.

"Ok! I'll do it! Please, just stop aiming that gun at my wife!" Walter sobbed; tears were in a freefall down his cheeks.

Saxon safetied the gun and lowered it away from Chrissy. He knelt down next to the weeping man and grabbed him by the collar.

"Please don't waste any more of my fucking time."

"I won't," Walter panted, trying to steady his elevated heart rate.

"Good. Now let's get to work, shall we?"

Chapter Thirteen
O'Hare Airport, Illinois

When John Shannon stepped off the gangway into O'Hare airport, his phone was bombarded with hours' worth of delayed notifications. He groaned and began scrolling through them, deleting the ones that were irrelevant. John stopped dead in his tracks when he saw the Twitter notification.

"Syrian-based terror group claims responsibility for Lollapalooza shooting" - the notification read. Hurrying over to an empty seat at a random gate, John opened the lengthy article and began reading it.

During his flights from Tel Aviv to Chicago, the ISB had taken credit and claimed responsibility for the attack in a letter released to Al-Jazeera. In the letter, the ISB's leader, Yusuf Bakar Akhmedi, praised Sulieman's actions and threatened more violence on American citizens. John recognized Yusuf's name instantly. Yusuf had been involved in the kidnapping and rape of Warrant Officer Cassidy Minor. During his last year in the SEALs, John had been killing his way through the ISB, with Yusuf being the prime target. But time and time again, the slippery terrorist had gotten away.

Once John was back in an FBI-issued Chevy Tahoe, he called Riley Hanna. After she didn't answer, he left a brief voicemail and started driving into the city. A few minutes later, his phone started ringing.

"Hello," John answered.

"Sorry I missed your call," Riley said. "It's been complete chaos over here."

"So, the ISB took credit, huh?" John was hoping Riley had more information than a Twitter article.

"Yes. And that's changed everything. The US Special Envoy to Syria confirmed that it was ISB as well. No one is going to listen to our theory anymore," Riley sounded defeated.

"Riles, it's not a theory. We have a lead now. All we have to do is pull on it and something will come loose, I guarantee it."

"No one has called me 'Riles' in years," Riley laughed. "John, no one here is going to give me the time of day. As far as everyone is concerned, this was terrorism. The FBI's job now is to make sure there aren't any more attacks, not chasing down leads from some SAC and a disgraced SEAL."

John swore softly, wishing he had another pack of Golds. Riley was right, the FBI would be changing their entire game plan. A mass shooting was one thing... terrorism was a whole different ball game. But Riley had pulled John into this and he wasn't about to give up that easily. After all, he didn't work for the FBI or the United States government. There was no reason he had to keep helping, but John knew he couldn't walk away. He was in the prime of his life when he'd been run out of the Navy; he had years more to give to his country and his superiors knew that. Forcing him to retire was the worst possible punishment they could've handed him. And now, bitter as he was, John still felt that same pull to help that had led to his enlistment.

"Riley, you and I both know that something else is going on. We have to find out who Sulieman was meeting with," John stressed.

"I know that," Riley paused. "I'll see what I can do from my end. Do you have any contacts that could help us?"

"No one in the Navy is going to talk to me," John chuckled. "But it's worth a try. I'll get on the phone and let you know what I come back with."

"Good plan. And hey, don't come back to McCormick or the Field Office. I told McGrady we were done investigating, so the last thing we need is you to be seen by him. Just head back to my place, there's a spare key above the door frame," Riley said.

"Sounds good. Talk soon," John hung up and headed for Lincoln Park.

Chapter Fourteen
North Potomac, Maryland

Gray Saxon sat in the family room of the Nichols home, watching in satisfaction as all of the major news networks were discussing the ISB taking credit for the Chicago shooting. The 'letter' that had been sent to Al-Jazeera had been written by Walter Nichols, with some encouragement from Saxon. Yusuf Bakar Akhmedi would get his, soon enough. Ever since he captured Saxon a second time, Yusuf had been on borrowed time.

"Well, congratulations, Walt," Saxon said, standing up and heading over to Walter, who was tied to one of the kitchen chairs. Chrissy was asleep in her chair next to him. Ryan Bueshay was leaning against the sink, sipping a Heineken he'd found in the fridge. Ilsa and Alaina were upstairs, keeping the four children under control. The last 24 hours had been stressful for the kids especially. Rahman sat at the kitchen table, typing away on his laptop.

"You did exactly what I asked of you," Saxon took a seat across from Walter and his wife. "And who said diplomacy was dead?"

"I did what you asked," Walter spat in disgust. "Please, just let me and my family go."

"I'm a man of my word," Saxon said. He propped his feet up on the table. "But here's the deal. I'm going to have to hold onto you for a while. A United States Special Envoy is granted certain privileges. And that is too valuable to pass up."

"What are you talking about?" Walter asked. He looked nervously at his wife.

"Our business is not done," Saxon narrowed his dark eyes. "You're coming with us."

Saxon stood up and grabbed Walter by the collar, dragging the man to his feet. Chrissy began screaming hysterically, only stopping when Ryan bounced her head off the table, knocking her unconscious. Using his pistol, Saxon clocked Walter on the head and his body went limp.

"What about the kids?" Rahman asked. Saxon looked up and saw the hesitation in Rahman's eyes.

Saxon flipped his pistol around and offered it to Rahman. Rahman shook his head in disgust, pushing the gun back to Saxon.

"Are you fucking nuts?" Rahman asked. "No way, I'm not doing that."

"No witnesses, Rahman," Saxon snarled. "You understand that?"

"Saxon…" Rahman protested.

Saxon rolled his eyes and flipped the safety off his Para-Ordnance 1911. Rahman watched in horror as Saxon walked over and fired one suppressed round into the back of Chrissy's head, blood splattered all over the kitchen table. Glaring at Rahman, Saxon handed the pistol off to Ryan.

"Go get Ilsa and Alaina. No witnesses," Saxon snarled. Ryan nodded and accepted the gun before walking upstairs. Saxon bent over and grabbed Walter Nichols, hoisting him up over his shoulder.

90 seconds later, their black Chevy Suburban sped out of the Nichols' subdivision. With Saxon behind the wheel, the Suburban soared toward the interstate. Ryan, Rahman, Ilsa, and Alaina exchanged nervous glances, horribly disgusted with what Saxon had just done. He'd changed the plan mid-mission, something that didn't sit well with the rest of the team.

Chapter Fifteen
Lincoln Park, Illinois

John Shannon popped the cap off two chilled Redd's hard ciders and handed one to Riley Hanna. She smiled and accepted the drink, taking a small sip. Although John preferred something much stronger than the fruity cider, he knew they were a guilty pleasure for Riley. During many of their nights together, they could drink a 12-pack, no problem. The two had hundreds of files, flight manifests, and travel logs spread out over the kitchen table. Both Riley's personal and FBI laptops were running programs trying to find any current or former US servicemen that had been in Chicago during the shooting.

"This is always the frustrating part," Riley commented, referring to the waiting game they were playing. Until something came up or they found anything solid, they were in a limbo state of the investigation. Not having the backing of the FBI was going to be difficult, but not impossible. Riley was determined and having John there made her feel more confident and relaxed.

"Yeah, I'm not used to this," John laughed, sipping his cider. "They used to give me two or three targets a week to hit. I never waited for anything."

"Can I ask you something?" Riley said, looking up at John with her beautiful, kind eyes.

"You can ask whatever you want. Can't promise I'll answer, but go ahead," John winked.

"What happened to you? With the Navy, I mean. I never saw you again after that," Riley said, struggling to hide how much it bothered her that John had disappeared on her. John hung his head and reached into his pocket for a fresh pack of cigarettes.

"No," Riley said firmly. "No smoking in my apartment."

"Alright, alright," John threw his hands up and tossed the pack on the table.

"Just talk to me, John," Riley urged, putting her hand on his knee. "Please."

John took Riley's hand in his own and held it tightly. He looked at her intensely and it was the first time that Riley saw the deep sadness in his hard eyes.

"I'm sorry, Riles," John whispered. "For disappearing like I did. I didn't know what to do after I got ran out of the Navy. I loved being a SEAL."

"I don't need an apology," Riley said.

"You want an explanation," John smirked. Riley nodded seriously. His smile vanished instantly.

"Yes, I do. Just tell me what happened," Riley pressed.

John's phone started ringing and he lunged to pick up the call. Riley shook her head and turned back to her files, mumbling something under her breath. Swiping his cigarettes from the table, John stepped out onto the patio of Riley's apartment.

"Hello?" he answered, popping a smoke into his mouth and lighting it with his Bic.

"How's it hanging, Johnny-boy?" a familiar voice laughed on the other line.

"Little to the left, how about you?" John sniggered, blowing out a dark cloud of smoke.

"Still going, haven't had to use pills yet," the man said, laughing hysterically at his own joke.

"You haven't changed at all, Smitty," John chuckled.

Tommy "Smitty" Smith was a former Green Beret out of Fort Bragg. He had been honorably discharged after an ankle injury in a jump exercise. Smitty could still run and fight, but not quick enough for the Green Beret standards. Since being retired, he'd found work as a security consultant, opening his own firm based in Coyote Springs, Nevada. Always at the center of every prank or joke, Smitty had met John during his third tour to Afghanistan. Despite being a few years younger than John, they got along very well.

"So, what's the deal, man?" Tommy asked after he stopped laughing. "I haven't heard from you in a long ass time and I get out of a meeting and see a missed call from Ares himself."

Ares was the Greek god of war, a nickname that Tommy had given John after the second time they met. John had come by the moniker honestly.

"Is your line secure? I don't want anyone listening in on us," John asked warily.

"My line is always secure. Fuck Big Brother," Tommy scoffed.

"Alright, I assume you've heard about the Chicago shooting?" John asked. Tommy confirmed that he had, which wasn't surprising. "Everyone is saying it's terrorism, but I'm telling you, it isn't."

"What do you mean?" Tommy asked. "The ISB claimed it. The stiffs were all ISB associates."

"Tom, I know. I'm working the case with an FBI agent."

"Is it that sexy little thing from back in the day?" Tommy blurted. John rolled his eyes.

"Yes," he said through gritted teeth. Tommy laughed wildly.

"Attaboy! Good for you, my man."

"Would you shut up and listen to me?" John asked, exasperated with Tommy's never-ending antics. "Look, it was not terrorism. The three guys were arms dealers, they were in Chicago to offload some weapons."

"Where did you get this information?" Tommy asked skeptically.

"Khaled Al-Khatib," John responded coolly.

"Holy fucking shit," Tommy breathed. "How the hell did you talk to him?"

"C'mon, you know I can't tell you that. But Sulieman Khatib was one of the dead guys in the hotel room. His brother told me that Sully was going to meet a buyer in Chicago. An American soldier."

"Khaled Al-Khatib told you that his brother was selling guns to an American troop?" Tommy repeated.

"Yes," John confirmed. "He was positive. And he wasn't lying, I can guarantee you that."

"Fuck," Tommy exhaled. "What's the FBI doing about that?"

"Nothing," John grunted. "As far as they're concerned, this is terrorism. ISB confirmed that."

"Yeah, that complicates things," Tommy agreed. "So, what do you need from me?"

"Access to your databases and mainframes. We need to find out who Sulieman was meeting with. Every day we don't, we risk another attack. I've just got this sick feeling that more people are going to die before this is over."

"You got it. Can you get up to Nevada?"

"I can leave tonight."

Chapter Sixteen
Coyote Springs, Nevada

After virtually driving without stopping, John Shannon pulled his Chevy Tahoe into the parking lot of Patriot Security Incorporated. Riley Hanna was fast asleep in the passenger seat, snuggled up with a blanket and a pillow. She'd been rather quiet during most of the drive, still annoyed at John for dodging her questions. As much as John would've loved to be honest and come clean with her, he just couldn't bring himself to tell her everything.

"Hey," John whispered, rubbing Riley's shoulder. "We're here."

Riley stirred and slowly opened her heavy eyes. She looked up at John and grunted. John hung his head dramatically, getting a small snicker out of Riley.

"I'm still mad at you," Riley grumbled sleepily. She tossed the blanket and pillow into the backseat.

"Yeah, I know," he said. He pulled a bottle of mouthwash from the console and took a sip, swishing the liquid around in his mouth before opening his door and spitting onto the pavement. "Come on. Tommy will be waiting for us."

Tommy Smith was waiting for John and Riley at the entrance to his security firm. He had two large coffees and a bag of donuts. John smiled at the sight of his old friend.

"Good to see you, buddy," John said, graciously accepting the coffee. "This is Riley Hanna."

"Pleasure to meet you," Riley smiled, stifling a yawn.

"Glad you guys are here," Tommy said. "Come on, I've got you set up in one of our control rooms."

John and Riley tried not to ogle at the impressive facility as Tommy led them to the second floor. The inside of the facility was decorated with famous war paintings, relic guns, and old military vehicles. Turning down a hallway, Tommy opened the door to one of his control rooms.

The room itself was tired, like a college lecture hall. Brand new Apple computers lined the top two tiers. A large screen was at the front of the room, a small projector on a table sat in the middle of the room.

"These computers have access to every Fed database in the country," Tommy said proudly.

"Is that legal?" Riley asked.

"Eh, mostly," Tommy sniggered. Riley shook her head, she couldn't help but chuckle.

"I can't thank you enough, Tom," John said, sitting down in one of the chairs.

"Stop it," Tommy waved his hand dismissively. "Make yourselves at home."

20 minutes later, Riley was tapped into two separate databases. She was searching through CCTV footage from O'Hare Airport when her

search algorithm came back with a hit. Turning to the second monitor, Riley opened the file that the algorithm had spat up.

It was a CCTV still image from just outside O'Hare Airport. Two men standing next to a black GMC Denali. One of the men was distinctly Middle Eastern, while the other was Caucasian. The Caucasian had several piercings in his ears, nose, and lip.

"John!" Riley exclaimed, waving him over. Hurrying over, John slid into the chair next to Riley.

"What's up, Riles?" he asked, looking at the picture.

"I used an algorithm to scan faces for Military IDs. I got a hit on these two," Riley explained, pointing to the picture. She opened a side-by-side tab to read the files on the two men.

"I still don't understand how you do this shit," John shook his head in disbelief.

"It's not that hard," she shrugged. "You just never cared to learn anything about technology."

"Fair enough," John shrugged. Riley knew well enough that John pretty much despised the crazy technology advancements—his iPhone was at least three years old.

"Ok, so the white guy is Ryan Bueshay, a former Army Ranger. He was discharged honorably after a knee injury. Since then, he's worked odd jobs at Waste Management and Amazon, but nothing as of ten months ago," Riley read off Ryan's file.

"Army, huh?" John breathed, impressed that they had actually found someone that met their vague description. "Who's the other guy?"

"Rahman Saleh. 35 years old. Former Iraqi Army. He came to America about three years ago," Riley said. Rahman's file was significantly shorter than Ryan's. Riley couldn't stop staring at the picture, wondering if those two men were the real culprits behind the Chicago shooting. Both men were former military, fitting the description that Khaled Al-Khatib had given John.

Leaning back in his chair, John ran his hands through his brown hair and exhaled loudly. He pulled his carton of cigarettes out of his breast pocket and lit one up, taking a deep drag. Riley was too focused on the picture to reprimand him for his filthy habit.

"What do you think?" Riley asked, turning to look at John. He flicked the ash off the end of his cigarette and held the smoke between his pointer and middle fingers.

"Riles... I think we just found our guys," John said, gaping at the picture. "Please tell me there's a way to figure out where these guys are?"

"Hold on," Riley said, turning back to her computer. She copied the picture into a facial recognition search and let the computer do the rest.

"The program will take a few minutes to run," she explained as the progress bar popped up on her screen. John sat up and took another puff, trying to blow the smoke away from Riley.

"So, why didn't you ever get married?" John blurted. Riley laughed at his impeccable timing.

"Really? You want to get into that now?" she asked. John shrugged and gestured to the progress bar, which indicated that the program wasn't even halfway done.

"I don't know, John," she sighed. "I never got any closure with you. I kept waiting for you to come back or show up somewhere. Kind of hard to move on with anyone when you're waiting for someone else."

"I'm sorry," John said softly, feeling like shit for having put Riley through that.

"I couldn't just move on like you did," Riley continued, folding her arms.

"I don't know if I ever truly moved on, Riles," John whispered. He put the cigarette out and stared into her intoxicating eyes. She matched his gaze with the same fiery passion that had always been there. John leaned in with every intention of kissing Riley, she leaned in as well.

The computer dinged, the program having finished running and coming back with a result.

Riley immediately looked away to the computer and opened the new file. She moved over slightly so John could see.

"Holy shit," John gasped. "That fucker is heading for Creech."
"What do you mean, Creech?" Riley asked.
"I need to find Tommy," John ran for the door. "Get ready, we're leaving!"

Chapter Seventeen
Creech Air Force Base, Nevada

Special Envoy Walter Nichols was sweating bullets as he drove toward the front gates of Creech Air Force Base. The base itself acted as the operations center for most of the drone missions in the Middle East. Ryan Bueshay sat in the passenger seat, dressed in Army fatigues. He had a Beretta M9 holstered on his thigh. Gray Saxon sat in the backseat, also clad in Army fatigues. He had his Para-Ordnance pressed against the back of Walter's seat.

"We're approaching the gate," Saxon whispered into the mic he had hidden under the collar of his shirt.

"Acknowledged. We are standing by to move in," Ilsa's smooth voice responded. Saxon tucked his weapon away as they got into line behind an Army Hummer.

"Just keep calm and this will all be over soon," Saxon said quietly to Walter. He eyed the intimidating soldiers in the guardhouse, each one of them looked like they had been forged from granite.

Their car was still, waiting for the Hummer in front of them to get cleared into the base. Before leaving for the base, Saxon had modified the backseat of the BMW X5. He had removed most of the cushioning, allowing a human to slip inside the leather and have the seat retain form. To anyone looking in, the seats were just fine aside from the slight wrinkles. When the Hummer moved forward, Saxon slipped inside the backseat, disappearing from view.

Walter rolled down the window and came to a stop at the guardhouse. One of the soldiers came over and leaned into the window.

"IDs please," he said in a deep voice. Walter handed over his ID and Ryan produced a military ID. The soldier looked at Walter's ID and back to the man in the car. "I wasn't aware we were having a Special Envoy on base today."

"Yes, well it was last minute," Walter said, trying to hide his fear as best he could.

"Just hold here for one second," the soldier said, giving Walter a small smile.

Walter's hands were sweating profusely as the soldier entered the guardhouse once again. Ryan looked over at him and shook his head.

"Calm the fuck down," Ryan whispered harshly. Walter shuddered and took a couple of deep breaths, trying to calm his nerves. He had always been a little skittish when it came to danger, but this was another level of fear he never thought he'd experience in his life.

The soldier peaked his head out of the guardhouse, a look of skepticism on his strong face. He adjusted the gun holstered on his hip and walked back to the car.

"Hey, I don't have you on the guest list," he said. Walter gulped as Ryan Bueshay leaned over.

"We cleared it with the State Department earlier this morning," he said, giving the soldier a friendly smile.

"I can check again," he said quietly. Ryan could tell the soldier's gut was telling him something was off.

"That would be great. Thank you," Ryan said graciously.

After going back to the guardhouse, the soldier picked up the phone and called his supervisor. Ryan watched as the soldier talked on the phone for almost a full minute. The soldier hung up and came back to the car, holding the two IDs.

"Sorry about that, Ambassador Nichols. You and your bodyguard are clear to enter the base. General Levinson will meet you at the administrative building," the soldier handed back the IDs and waved for the gate to be raised.

"Thank you," Walter said, waving respectfully to the guards.

"That was close," Saxon muttered in the backseat. "Alright, head for the administrative building. Ryan, you're up. I need at least 15 minutes to get into the control building. The diversion has to be big and it has to be loud."

"I know, I know," Ryan said. He unsnapped his holster and checked his Beretta, racking the slide and chambering the first bullet.

"Well, Walt," Saxon clapped Walter on the shoulder. "This is where we say goodbye."

"Wh-What about my family?" Nichols asked, still ignorant to the fact that his family had been murdered in cold blood. Saxon took his hand off Walter's shoulder.

"Don't worry, Walt," Saxon reassured him. "You'll be seeing them soon."

As Walter came to a stop in front of the administrative building, Saxon withdrew a long piece of piano wire from his pocket. He wrapped it around both his hands and lunged forward, strangling Walter Nichols from behind. Walter struggled at first, but Saxon's iron grip was too much for him to handle. The thin wire cut through the ambassador's neck like a knife through butter—he died less than a minute later.

"Move," Saxon hissed, jumping out of the car and tucking the bloody wire into his back pocket. He pulled a hat over his face and hurried toward the Ops Center. Ryan was slower to get out of the car; he moved around to the trunk and popped it open. Inside was a tactical vest, an M249 SAW machine gun, and a stand-alone M203 grenade launcher; with the launcher came a bandolier of ten grenades.

Ryan slipped the vest on and fastened it to his fit. He attached the machine gun to his combat harness and threw the bandolier over his shoulder. Before slamming the trunk, Ryan grabbed the M203 and hurried away, keeping his face down to avoid eye contact with any suspicious soldiers.

Chapter Eighteen
Creech Air Force Base, Nevada

Gray Saxon moved around the backside of the Ops Center without raising any alarms. He had memorized the route to the center and knew the guards' rotations well enough to know when to move. Using a forged ID card, he swiped the door and it buzzed. Saxon pushed the door open and slipped inside. Taking a knee in the small corridor, Saxon opened his left cargo pocket and produced a handheld EMP device. The device could knock out security cameras and phones, but left computers operational.

Saxon activated the device and tossed it by the door. He pulled on a black balaclava and drew his Para-Ordnance.

"Hey!" Saxon heard a voice call out from down the corridor. "The phones are dead!"

"So are the cameras," another voice yelled. Saxon smiled underneath the balaclava, the EMP had worked to perfection. He moved down the hallway, crouching down to slip past the three Airmen who were trying to figure out what was happening.

Taking a right down a long hallway, Saxon spotted the door at the end of the hallway and darted across the hall, stacking up on the door. He swiped his badge and the door unlocked. Pushing it open, he reemerged outside; he was starting a small green building.

The building itself resembled a large shipping container, much like the ones seen on barges or trains. However, there were no markings or anything on the sides of the container. Saxon knew from experience that those containers were used to pilot UAV Drones thousands of miles away.

Saxon crossed over to the container, taking extra caution to make sure he wasn't spotted. Using the bottom of his gun, he knocked on the door three times. Almost immediately, the door cracked open.

Before the Air Force Mission Commander could see who it was, Saxon planted his boot right on the door, kicking it open forcefully. The Airman was thrown back, crashing on the carpeted floor in a heap. Saxon slipped inside and quickly closed the door behind him. Turning back to the small room, he aimed his Para-Ordnance at three unarmed Airmen. The man on the ground groaned in pain, his nose was gushing blood.

"Nobody make a sound," Saxon whispered. "Hands up where I can see them."

Slowly, the Airmen raised their hands. Working quickly, Saxon zip-tied each of the Airmen and put a strip of tape over their mouths. He forced them on their knees in the back of the small room and lined them up. Satisfied that they were subdued, Saxon turned to the large screen at the front of the room. The controls were on either side of the screen. Gray Saxon was standing in the control room for an MQ-9 Reaper Unmanned Aerial Vehicle, or UAV.

"Alright," Saxon said beneath the balaclava. "Right now, there is a Reaper on station in Syria providing intel for our troops. I also know that that particular Reaper has attack capabilities. So, which one of you is the pilot?"

The young African American man at the far end of the line raised his head. His name patch said "Hopkins". Saxon crossed the room and helped Hopkins to his feet. He cut his zip-ties and sat Hopkins down in the pilot chair.

"You're gonna divert the drone to these coordinates," Saxon said, setting a piece of paper in front of Hopkins.

"I need clearance to divert," he responded, not breaking his military bearing. Saxon nodded. He knelt down next to Hopkins and spoke in a low voice.

"You need clearance, huh? Ok, here's your clearance. If you don't divert that drone, I am going to execute your friends one by one until you do," he threatened.

Hopkins didn't budge. Saxon stalked over to the man with the bloody nose and pressed the barrel of his Para-Ordnance to the man's forehead. He flipped the safety off the 1911.

"I need clearance!" Hopkins hissed. Saxon looked down at the man with the bloody nose and saw that he was a captain. Dragging him up to his feet by the collar of his ACU, Saxon forced the captain over to Hopkins.

"Tell him to move the drone," Saxon snarled, pressing the 1911 to the back of the captain's head.

"Move the drone, son. Do what he says," the captain mumbled, the blood leaking into his mouth.

"Sir?"

"Just do it, goddammit."

Reluctantly, Hopkins grabbed the controls and began moving the drone to the coordinates that Saxon had instructed. Saxon grabbed the captain and threw him back in line. He tucked the 1911 in his waistband and folded his arms, watching the live feed of the drone. Saxon checked his watch and took a deep breath.

"Come on, Ryan," he thought to himself.

Hopkins expertly piloted the drone over a small village in Jordan. He looked back at Saxon for some direction.

"Stay in a holding pattern until I tell you," Saxon ordered, checking his watch again. "Prep missiles and get ready to engage."

"Are you serious?" Hopkins gaped. "I have no idea who I'm shooting at!"

Saxon whipped out his 1911 and pressed it to Hopkins' temple. Hopkins closed his mouth and turned back to the controls, then prepped the missiles on the drone to engage and entered a holding pattern over the village.

Everyone in the room immediately tensed up at the distinct sound of gunfire outside the Ops Center.

Chapter Nineteen
Creech Air Force Base, Nevada

Hiding underneath an Army flatbed truck, Ryan Bueshay pulled a camouflage shemagh over his face. He then slipped a pair of sunglasses over his eyes and checked his watch. Just a few more minutes.

He was staring at the runway, lined with various types of aircraft. The hangars on either side were filled with soldiers and aircraft alike. As quietly as he could, Ryan pulled out the M203 and loaded the tube with a 40mm grenade. He slung the SAW around his back and crawled toward the front of the flat bed.

The timer on his watch went off and he shut it off immediately. There was no time to waste, Saxon was depending on him to do his part. Ryan brought the launcher up and aimed at one of the helicopters parked on the runway. He took a deep breath and squeezed the trigger, the grenade detonated and exploded, severely damaging the helicopter. Large chunks of steel from the chopper shot violently into the air.

Sirens blared loudly as the base immediately went into lockdown. Ryan rolled out from under the truck and fired another grenade, blowing up a second chopper. He took off running as a group of soldiers ran towards the inferno.

"Hey! Stop right there!" one of them yelled upon seeing Ryan darting off. The soldier yanked out his radio. "Attention! We have a saboteur on base. Repeat, enemy on base! He's heading towards the hangars!"

Keeping his legs moving, Ryan reloaded the M230 as fast as he could before firing again and destroying a Humvee. He reloaded the launcher and kept running, knowing he couldn't stop for even a second. He turned behind him and saw a small group of armed soldiers running after him. Ryan threw himself aside, firing the grenade at the wall of the nearest building. It detonated and, as hoped, the debris from the wall slowed his pursuers down.

Gunfire bombed all around Ryan as the gunners in the watchtowers zeroed in on his position. He ducked behind a hangar, dodging the bullets as best he could. He was running out of grenades for the launcher but didn't want to unleash the SAW just yet. The SAW was his backup plan. Dropping to a knee, Ryan peered around the corner of the building and raised the launcher toward the watchtower. He squeezed the trigger and watched as the tower exploded in on itself—whoever had been inside the tower was dead.

Getting back to his feet, Ryan took off running again; more bullets flew around him, getting closer and closer to hitting him. He had a substantial group of soldiers chasing after him and they were getting a little too close for comfort.

From out of nowhere, a bullet smashed into Ryan's left shoulder—the momentum of the round spun him around like a top. The M203 launcher fell from his grip and slid out of reach. Ryan ducked behind a Black Hawk helicopter and cocked the SAW; he needed to buy Saxon a few more minutes. Ignoring the blood dripping out of his shoulder, Ryan spread out on the ground under the nose of the Black Hawk, propping the machine gun up on the bipod. He brought the gun into his shoulder and squeezed the trigger.

The fiery barrage of rounds from the SAW forced the team of soldiers behind cover. Ryan didn't let up, firing the entire drum of ammo before he stopped shooting. Ducking back behind the chopper, he struggled to reload the massive weapon with only one good arm. He heard the soldiers yelling to each other, calling out Ryan's position to other teams.

Finally, after almost a full minute of struggling with the weapon, Ryan hauled the weapon over his back and took off running. He spun around and fired a burst from the SAW, hitting one of the soldiers in the legs. Whipping back around, Ryan fired a ten-round burst at an approaching Humvee. By now, the runway was flooded with military personnel. Ryan smirked underneath the shemagh—Saxon's plan was once again working to perfection.

Ryan knelt down in the middle of the runway and pulled the trigger, shredding a second Humvee and forcing the soldiers inside to bail out. Rounds kicked up at his feet, the group behind him was gaining on him. Ryan looked around and realized he was getting boxed in. He cursed under his breath for having dropped the M230. Sprinting back for the cover of the Black Hawk, he checked over his gear. He was down to one more drum of ammo for the SAW and two magazines for his Beretta.

Before he could get into position to use either weapon, another round struck him in the stomach. He instantly felt his breath get sucked away; Ryan fell onto his back, the SAW landed on top of him. Drawing quick breaths of air, he tried to roll onto his side. Tossing the SAW aside, he painfully rolled over. Blood poured out of the grisly stomach wound.

"Target down!" one of the soldiers yelled.
"Take him!" another one yelled out.

Ryan Bueshay fell back onto his back and sighed as the two teams of soldiers slowly moved in on him, encircling him with their drawn rifles. Since he had joined up with Gray Saxon, the thought of dying never entered Ryan's mind. Even though he knew they were doing bad things, he always thought he'd live to see the good come out of it. Ryan had been a true believer in what Saxon was trying to do, the thought of not being able to see it through to the end bothered him more than dying. But he felt at peace knowing his distraction had allowed Saxon to finish this part of his plan.

Before the soldiers realized what was happening, Ryan pulled the Beretta and stuck the barrel of the gun under his chin. He winked at the closest soldier before pulling the trigger.

Chapter Twenty
Creech Air Force Base, Nevada

As soon as the gunfire kicked off, Saxon jumped into the chair next to Hopkins. He knew Ryan's diversion would only buy him a few minutes and there was no time to waste.

"Alright, missiles are prepped?" Saxon asked, pressing the barrel of the 1911 into Hopkins' gut. The Airman nodded. Saxon looked up at the screen and recognized the village instantly.

That village was a place Gray Saxon was far too familiar with. He had sworn to himself that he would never return there. Even looking at the village on the screen sent a chill down his spine.

"Oh my god," the captain muttered as he watched the screen. Everyone in the structure could clearly make out the group of small kids playing on the outskirts of the village.

Saxon saw it too and bit his lip. The kids were innocent in all of this. He had nothing against them, despite the fact that he knew most of them would grow up hating Americans. His war was not with them. Silently, he prayed that they would move just a few hundred yards away.

"Arm missiles," Saxon ordered. Hopkins shook his head firmly.

"You're gonna have to shoot me because there is no way I'm firing on kids," Hopkins glared at Saxon, not backing down this time. Saxon jammed the gun harder into the man's sternum.

"I'm not asking you to shoot on the kids," he snarled, trying to push any thought of the kids out of his mind. He couldn't allow himself to falter on things as trivial as morality—he had a mission to finish.

"You can't do this," the captain spoke again. Saxon glared at the man.

"You have no idea what I'm doing," Saxon spat.

With Saxon distracted for half a second, Hopkins lunged at him, grabbing for the 1911. The two fell to the ground, wrestling over the handgun. Saxon jerked his knee upward, trying to catch Hopkins in the stomach or groin, but all he caught was air. Winding up, Hopkins landed a solid punch right in Saxon's gut. Saxon's eyes watered as he struggled to catch his breath and keep his hand on the Para-Ordnance.

"Drop the gun!" Hopkins screamed, landing another punch. He grabbed Saxon's wrist and twisted, desperately trying to force the gun out of his hand.

Saxon kept his hand sealed around the gun, but he knew he couldn't withstand another punch like that without losing the gun. He caught a quick glance at his hostages—they were wrestling with their restraints, trying to get free to help Hopkins.

As Hopkins reeled back to throw another punch, Saxon wrapped his finger around the trigger and pulled it. The 1911 cycled, firing a .45 caliber round through Hopkins' face. In slow motion, Hopkins fell onto his back, most of his face had been blown away by the round.

The captain and the other Airmen cried out as they watched their comrade topple over, dead before his head hit the carpeted floor. Taking in huge gulps of air, Saxon got to his feet and rushed back to the controls of the Reaper. Someone surely would have heard the gunshot and he knew he didn't have long.

Sitting down behind the controls of the Reaper, Saxon visualized how Hopkins had been flying the drone. He grabbed the joysticks and carefully flew the Reaper into position, making sure the missiles were primed and turned to view the screen one more time.

The kids were running toward the small creek, almost 200 yards from the village. Gray Saxon breathed a sigh of relief.

Saxon pressed the trigger and fired the Hellfire missile at the village. The captain and two other Airmen watched in shock as the missile struck and blew apart a structure. The villagers ran in all directions and the entire village erupted into chaos.

Gray Saxon fired a second missile, destroying another couple of buildings that were built on top of each other. As if he'd been flying drones his whole life, he expertly flew the Reaper around for another run. He flew the drone a little lower, targeting a mass of villagers running from the burning buildings, and fired another missile. The third Hellfire vaporized the group of villagers in a blink of an eye, leaving a crater where they had stood.

Saxon released the final Hellfire and watched as another home was decimated by the missile. Smoke encapsulated the whole village, obscuring the drones' view, but the job was done. A large chunk of the village was destroyed and that was enough for Saxon to feel proud.

He got up from the chair and checked his watch before heading for the door. Everything was perfectly on schedule, just as Saxon had planned. Reaching for the radio on his hip, he opened his frequency and spoke into the mic under his balaclava.

"Mission accomplished. Say again, mission accomplished," he growled.

"Standing by for exfiltration," Ilsa responded.

"Copy, move in," Saxon ordered. He adjusted his grip on the 1911 and reached for the door.

"You'll never get away with this," the captain growled, shooting Saxon a disgusted look.

Saxon smirked and raised his 1911.

Chapter Twenty-One
Creech Air Force Base, Nevada

The convoy tore down the road, kicking up dust all around the four black Sport Utility Vehicles. As they approached the gates, John Shannon watched in awe as another explosion erupted inside of Creech Air Force Base.

"Holy shit," Riley gasped from the backseat. "You were right."

"Yeah," John grumbled. He racked the charging handle on his M4A1 and attached the rifle to his harness. "Drive through the gates, they know we're coming," John said to the driver—a former Delta operator currently on the Patriot Security Inc. payroll.

"Got it, sir," the driver responded, pressing the gas pedal.

Sure enough, the gates to Creech Air Force Base were raised, allowing the convoy to move through without stopping. They slammed down the second the final vehicle was through.

Before leaving Patriot Security with a ten-man team, John had Tommy call his military contacts. The name Tommy Smith carried tremendous weight in the military community—getting clearance to the base for his team, an FBI agent, and an advisor was a small feat. Additionally, Riley had been in contact with the FBI and had a team mobilized almost immediately.

The convoy rolled to a stop outside the administrative building, where a team of soldiers had cordoned off the car with Walter Nichols' dead body inside. John and Riley jumped out of the SUV and hurried over to the car; the soldiers backed away upon seeing Riley's FBI jacket. She peered inside and saw the dead body, the ligature marks on his neck were fresh and raw.

"Do you know who that is?" Riley whispered to John. She vaguely recognized the man but couldn't think of his name.

"Special Envoy Walter Nichols," a soldier standing guard said.

"He's the Ambassador to Syria, right?" John asked. The soldier nodded.

Another burst of gunfire cut through the air and everyone instinctively ducked. John gripped his rifle and signaled for the Patriot Team to follow him.

"Stay here," John said to Riley, putting his hand on her shoulder.

"You're not sticking me on the sideline, John," Riley said, shrugging off his hand.

"That's not what I'm doing," he responded, then turned to the soldier. "Where's all that coming from?"

"The runway," the soldier pointed. "Major Wilson is trying to cut off the attacker right now."

"Tell Wilson he's got backup coming!" John called as he ran toward the runway, the Patriot Team hot on his tail.

By the time, John and his team reached the runway, Ryan Bueshay lay dead with a self-inflicted bullet in his skull. John broke off from his team and ran over to Major Wilson. He was already sweating profusely and panting heavily—exercise was not something he'd been particularly passionate about since leaving the Navy.

"Major!" John called, letting his rifle hang from the harness as he approached him.

"You the backup?" Wilson asked, sticking out his hand. John shook his hand and nodded.

"John Shannon, sir. Former DEVGRU."

"Shannon? Yeah, that name sounds familiar," Major Wilson said, eyeing him skeptically. John disregarded the Major's look. Plenty of people in the military community had heard the rumors about John Shannon, but few knew the true story. John wasn't about to explain himself to Major Wilson.

"Yeah, I'm sure it does," John scoffed. He gestured for the Major to follow him and walked toward the body. John knelt down next to Ryan, studying his tattoos. The Ranger symbol on his hand was the same one in the picture that Riley had found.

"See his hand?" John asked, pointing. Major Wilson nodded.

"He was a Ranger?"

"Yeah. His name was Ryan Bueshay," John said, getting back to his feet.

"How do you know that?" Wilson raised a grey eyebrow.

"Look, sir, I've been working on a possible connection between that dead guy and the shooting in Chicago."

"I heard Chicago was terrorists."

"Yeah… well, it wasn't. And this attack here proves something else is going on. There could be more attackers or infiltrators on base. We need to lock down the base and verify everyone immediately."

"I know this," Major Wilson said, slightly annoyed. "I already have teams securing every building on base."

"Well, how can we help?" John asked, ignoring the Major's tone.

"I have a team going to the Ops Center, but they didn't check in yet. Go make sure everything is alright," Wilson ordered, wishing he could have gotten rid of John sooner. John saluted lazily and hurried off toward the Ops Center.

The abandoned Humvee was still idling in front of the Ops Center, broken glass and shell casings encircled the vehicle.

"Eyes up, boys," John warned his team. He peered inside the vehicle and saw a wounded soldier in the backseat—he was bleeding profusely from a wound in his chest. John threw open the door and jumped inside.

"Hang on, kid," John groaned, searching the Humvee for a medical kit.

"He was so fucking fast," the young soldier croaked. John had no luck finding anything to stop the bleeding and silently cursed himself for bullshitting with Major Wilson for as long as he had. He leaned out of the truck and called over his team.

"Get a medic over here right now!" he yelled. He turned to another one of his guys, "You four, go secure the Ops Center. Now!"

The soldier grabbed John's collar, not wanting to be left alone.

"It wasn't supposed to end like this," he grumbled, banging his head against the seatback in frustration.

"I got you, kid. Just take it easy," John said, feeling his stomach turn... the kid was on borrowed time. He had unfortunately seen too many people die and was all too familiar with the last couple of minutes of someone's life.

"My girlfriend, she's—"

Before the young soldier could finish his sentence, a bullet blew his head apart, covering John in brain matter and blood. He fell out of the Humvee onto his back, his team immediately raised their weapons to look for the shooter.

John crawled toward the back of the Humvee and peered around the tail. At the far end of the runway, he saw a man climbing into a pickup truck with a brunette woman behind the wheel. The man had a long rifle in his right hand. The shemagh was wrapped loosely around his face, but John got a glimpse of the man's face and his eyes went wide with recognition.

"Holy fuck!" John gasped.

John Shannon was still in shock when he got to his feet, just in time to watch the pickup speed off, leaving a cloud of dust in its wake. The truck smashed through a gate in the back of the base and sped away before anyone could stop it.

One of the Patriot guys, Lucas, jogged over to John, panting heavily.

"I gotta stop smoking," Lucas groaned, breathing in as much air as he could.

"You and me both," John said. He reached into his pocket and pulled out his pack of Marlboros, offering one to Lucas. Chuckling, Lucas took a smoke. John lit both cigarettes and inhaled, sighing loudly.

"Ops Center is fine but the drone control building is a mess," Lucas said, blowing out a cloud of smoke. "Looks like a damn massacre in there. Those Airmen didn't stand a chance."

"What do you mean?" John asked.

"Our attacker hit the drone building," Lucas shrugged, not sure what else to say.

John finished off the smoke and headed back to find Riley, the shock of what he'd witnessed was still weighing heavy on him.

"Oh my god, John! Are you ok?" Riley shrieked and ran over to him. He was still covered in gore.

"Don't worry," John muttered. "It's not mine."

"What happened?" Riley asked, forcing John to sit down against a Humvee. John fumbled for another cigarette, but Riley snatched the pack from his hand.

"C'mon," John groaned. Riley shook her head.

"Talk."

"I know who's doing this," John whispered. Riley's eyes went wide.

Chicago had not been terrorism. No, it had been something much worse; the curtains had finally been pulled back. Chicago had been the start of something truly horrible. And the mastermind of what was to come was John Shannon's former commanding officer. A man he'd thought dead long ago.

Gray Saxon.

Outside Damascus, Syria

The smell of gunpowder and cordite was still ripe in the hot desert air, it was so strong that John Shannon could almost taste the combination or propellants. It made his throat itch something awful. He knelt down next to a pool of vivid red blood, shell casings were mixed in with the plasma and sand. Reaching a gloved hand into the puddle, John pinched one of the casings between his thumb and forefinger. Although the ISB was known to use a multitude of weapons, their primary arms were AK-variants, which commonly were chambered in a 7.62 millimeter round. The casing, however, was from a 5.56 NATO cartridge.

"Command, Viper Main," John muttered through his mic. "I'm at the last known sighting of Petty Officer Saxon. No sign of him, I repeat, no sign of him,"

"Acknowledged, Main," the answer came back from Command. "Gather any intel you can. If you find anything that could give us a lead on his whereabouts, grab it. Extract will be on station in ten mikes,"

"Ten mikes. Copy that, Main out," John signed off.

Three other Navy SEALs from John's team were spread out around the abandoned and destroyed village. The trip to the wrecked town had been a quiet one. All four of the SEALs had no doubt been having similar thoughts. Gray Saxon had defied orders and gone out on his own to rescue Warrant Officer Cassidy Minor. It was one of the bravest and most noble things John had ever seen someone do in his extensive career in the Navy. Like the three other SEALs, it bothered him immensely that Saxon hadn't come to him first. If John had had any inkling of a suspicion that Saxon was planning on going off reservation, he would've been right there with him.

"Check in," John switched to the team channel. "Anyone got anything?"

"Negative, just a fuck load of blood," an older SEAL everyone called Stick grunted. "Wish there was a way to tell who's it was,"

"ISB usually takes the bodies of their dead," the second SEAL, Mack, chimed in. He credited himself as an expert on all things ISB, having spent the most time in Syria dealing with them out of anyone else on the team. "Saxon must've done some serious damage before they took him,"

"The Rangers thought they did quite a bit," Valdez, the final SEAL on the team, commented. "Still, I'm just glad they brought Cassidy back in one piece. Terrible what she had to go through,"

"Did you see her?" Mack asked no one in particular. He'd helped unload Cassidy and get her to a medical bed as soon as she and the Rangers had landed back at base. He shook his head in absolute disgust. "My god, those savages did a fucking number on her. Imagine what the hell they're going to do to Saxon,"

"Hey, wiseguy, shut the fuck up," Stick scolded.

"Just saying," Mack shrugged.

"Cut the bullshit, boys," John ordered. He stood back up, dropping the shell casing back into the blood and sand. "Let's keep moving, I want to clear this town before extract gets here,"

After a thorough and exhaustive search of the village, John took a knee in front of his SEAL Team. He hung his head slightly. John didn't need to remind his team that this was personal for all of them. A brother SEAL was missing in action and more than likely in the hands of the enemy. But Gray Saxon was more than just another missing serviceman. He'd been a larger than life personality in the community, someone that John had always looked up to and respected. For all intents and purposes, Gray Saxon had been thought to be utterly indestructible, as if forged from a slab of granite. To know that someone like him could be taken alive by the enemy was extremely discomforting. The ISB had proven their capacity for torture with Cassidy Minor. John and the rest of his team could only imagine what Gray Saxon was being subjected to.

"John, we'll find him," Stick reassured him. He had known that John had looked up to Gray Saxon, it was obvious. Saxon had been that role model for a lot of the younger SEALs, too. But as much as Stick wanted to believe his own words, he knew that Saxon's chances of survival were slim. Mack and Valdez remained silent. Neither of them had really known Gray Saxon. While it was still awful to lose another Team guy, they didn't have the personal connection to Saxon that John and Stick clearly did.

John looked up as if he was going to say something, but stopped himself. He looked at his team sadly and grabbed his radio.

"Command, this is Viper Main. The village is clear, I repeat, village is all clear," John grumbled. "No sign of Saxon,"

"Understood, Main," the voice on the other end sounded equally discouraged. "Extraction will be on site in about two mikes,"

"Copy," John stood up and walked away toward the landing zone.

Mack and Valdez stood up and started after him; Stick held up his hand.

"Let him go," he whispered, narrowing his eyes to make sure the two younger SEALs understood he meant it. Mack and Valdez nodded and stayed where they were.

They watched John come to a stop and take a knee. He reached into his pocket and pulled out a cigarette and a lighter from seemingly nowhere. Valdez gave Mack a funny look.

"Didn't know Johnny smoked," Valdez commented. Mack nodded his head in agreement.

Chapter Twenty-Two
The White House, Washington D.C., Maryland

The president of The United States was a patient and virtuous man who'd made a name for himself as a daring prosecutor before turning to politics. Although he was technically a Democrat President, he tried to be as independent as he could be. That was one of the main reasons he'd gotten elected—his bipartisanship had won over more than enough Americans. He was known for being fair and kind, but equally as strong with foreign powers. The president was not known for getting upset, but as he sat before a select group from his Cabinet, he could feel the smoke coming out of his ears. He'd chosen to have the meeting in the Oval Office as opposed to the usual Situation Room. He needed his people to understand the severity of the situation.

"Gentlemen," he spoke loudly so everyone could hear him clearly. "We all sat here two weeks ago and you all told me that the shooting in Chicago was a terrorist attack, that the attack had been perpetrated by members of the Islamic Syrian Brotherhood. But now, you're telling me that the attack was actually the work of a former Navy SEAL, who you all thought was dead. Not only that, but this SEAL killed a US Ambassador, hijacked a US drone, and used it to destroy an entire Syrian village of mostly women and children. Am I missing anything?"

"That is what we believe at this moment, sir," Secretary of Defense Bill Alders said. He bounced his leg nervously as the president glared at him.

"Mr. President," the Director of National Intelligence, Linda Penton, spoke up. "We're just as surprised as you are. The reports from Creech Air Force Base are extremely new and we haven't had a chance to corroborate everything."

"I'm having trouble discerning whether you people are lazy or incompetent," the president spat. He stood up from his chair and did a loop around the room, his gaze meeting everyone seated around the office.

"I want to make something absolutely clear. This is not some domestic issue that we can brush under the rug. So, if any of you are not up to this, leave now. I have no patience for incompetence," the president waited to see if anyone would be bold enough to step down. No such luck. He smirked and sat back down.

"Secretary Alders, I want a file on this Gray Saxon in front of me yesterday. Get to it," the president ordered, dismissing the Secretary of Defense with the wave of his hand. Alders jumped up and pulled out his cellphone, eager to leave the ass chewing. The president turned to his Director of National Intelligence. "As for you, I want you to bring the SEAL and FBI agent who have been working on this case. It appears they are the only two people who thought outside the box in this case. I want them in the Oval Office by the end of the day. Is that understood?"

"Of course, sir," Linda Penton nodded. "I can get them on a flight immediately."

"Good, you're dismissed," the president said, slightly friendlier than he'd been with the Secretary of Defense.

The Vice President, Chief of Staff, Director of the CIA, and the Chief of Naval Operations were the only men still sitting at the table. Relaxing now that he'd gotten his point across, the president sat back down.

"Admiral, what can you tell me about this Gray Saxon character?" the president asked, focusing on Admiral Daniel White, the head of the US Navy. White sighed and adjusted in his chair.

"Well, up until a few hours ago, I was under the impression that Chief Petty Officer Saxon was dead. He went rogue about four years ago and led an unauthorized mission into Syria to rescue a female pilot, Warrant Officer Cassidy Minor," Admiral White explained. The president nodded, remembering the incident. He had been a senator from California at the time, the incident happened a year before he was elected to office.

"The mission went awry and we lost an entire Delta Force team," White continued. "Almost a week later, Saxon made contact with our forces and successfully evacuated Warrant Officer Minor. But in the process, he was wounded and taken captive by the ISB. That was the last time anyone heard or saw Saxon. Over the next couple of months, our forces tried to locate him but came back empty every time. Officially, he is listed as MIA, but we all assumed he'd been killed. After the video the ISB released of Warrant Office Minor, Saxon's chance of survival seemed nonexistent."

"So, Saxon goes off reservation to rescue another soldier and is taken captive after?" the president clarified. Admiral White nodded. "Why did Saxon have to go out on his own to rescue Warrant Officer Minor?"

"At the time, sir, we didn't have solid intelligence of where she was being held. We had suspicions, but nothing concrete. Saxon heard the rumors of where Minor was being held and sprang into action," Admiral White informed.

The president shook his head and suddenly felt nauseous. The account from Admiral White was a heroic tale, it pained the president to think that someone like Saxon could do the horrific things that he'd supposedly done.

"Well, Saxon sounds like he was a hero," the president muttered, then chuckled softly.

"By all accounts, he was," Admiral White agreed sadly.

"So, has he turned? Are he and the ISB working together?" the president asked.

"There is nothing to confirm that he is working with the ISB. The village he targeted in the drone strike is an ISB stronghold so I think it's safe to say he's not working with them."

The president ran his hands through his greying brown hair and took a deep breath. He was truly unsure of how to handle this situation, which was a new feeling for him. Being the president was an impossible job, but he always seemed to find a way to do the right thing. He'd avoided major criticism and hadn't been faced with anything nearly as challenging as what lay in front of him.

"I can't help but wonder," the president said quietly, "if we brought this all on ourselves."

"How do you mean, sir?" the vice president asked.

"Gray Saxon was a hero. We left him in that godforsaken country to endure who knows what. It doesn't surprise me a man like that is looking for retribution."

"We can't blame ourselves," Admiral White countered. "Saxon knew the risks when he went off reservation."

"Maybe so... but we need to make damn certain that kind of thing doesn't happen again."

Chapter Twenty-Three
Los Angeles, California

The Windows Lounge at the Four Seasons was busy as usual, nearly filled to the capacity with patrons. It was past midnight, but the bar was still open for business for at least another two hours. At the far end of the bar, Gray Saxon sat alone, sipping a glass of Johnnie Walker Black Label. His eyes were glued to the TV, watching the newscast on the Lollapalooza shooting. He smirked as he heard the anchor call it an "act of apparent terrorism".

"Can I get you another one?" the bartender asked, gesturing to Saxon's empty glass.

"Sure," he nodded, sliding the glass toward the bartender. Saxon's attention was briefly taken by a group of four women at the opposite end of the bar. They were all dressed fairly similarly, although Saxon didn't have an ounce of fashion knowledge. They were all beautiful enough to draw attention to them. He caught the eye of one of the women—she was the best looking in Saxon's mind. She smiled at him and waved discreetly; her group was being hit on by a pair of fancy-dressed businessmen.

As the bartender turned to pour Saxon another drink, the woman broke off from the group and slid into the empty barstool next to him. She was strikingly attractive and clearly much younger than Saxon. He stole a quick look, checking her out up and down. She wore black stiletto heels and black leather pants that looked like they were painted on. Her silver-grey crop top was backless and exposed a heavy amount of cleavage; her light brown hair had blonde highlights running through it and was lightly curled.

"This seat taken?" she asked, giving him a small smile. He noticed her stare a second too long at his scar, but she didn't appear to be scared off. Saxon shook his head.

Gray Saxon had not been with a woman in a long time. In fact, the last person he'd been with was Warrant Officer Cassidy Minor. Things like lust and sexual desire disappeared when he was a prisoner of the ISB. The only thing he thought about was survival. After he'd escaped, his mind was solely focused on revenge. Weeks, months, years had gone by and he was finally realizing how much he'd missed human interactions and connections. His relationship with his team was purely business; he sought no pleasure or friendship with them. While the death of Ryan Bueshay had been a blow to their team, Gray Saxon fully expected him to die while creating the diversion. It was all part of the plan. They were just pawns. Pawns that thought they knew everything and were too ignorant to realize they were being kept in the dark.

"It's all yours," he said quietly. She got comfortable and hung her purse around the back of the stool.

"What're you drinking?" she asked, resting her elbows on the bar top.

"Johnnie Walker Black," he answered simply.

Right on cue, the bartender returned with his drink, sliding it back over to him. Saxon nodded at him in appreciation and took a sip.

"Can I get you anything, ma'am?" the bartender asked. Saxon chuckled to himself, watching the bartender struggle to keep his eyes off of the woman's chest.

"I'll have what he's having," she said, smiling her bright smile and pointing to Saxon. The bartender hurried away.

"I bet you he's going to be thinking about you tonight," Saxon muttered, taking another sip of his drink. The woman laughed and shrugged.

"I've got it, might as well show it off," she said. Her voice was smooth and sexy.

"More power to you," he said, raising his glass in her direction.

"So, are you here for work or pleasure?" she asked, leaning closer towards him.

"Bit of both, I guess. I've got business here in Los Angeles."

"Aren't you mysterious?" she commented, playfully pushing his shoulder. He laughed to himself, finding it hard not to be interested in her.

Their chemistry was instantaneous, something Saxon had never experienced with his first wife, Jayne. Sure, there had been love and affection, but at the end of the day, they were still high school sweethearts who got married way too young. The initial flames between them had been completely snuffed after Saxon's multiple deployments to the Middle East. The only other woman he'd been with was Cassidy Minor, but even in the heat of the moment, Saxon knew nothing could ever come of it, despite wanting nothing more. Cassidy had been the perfect woman in his mind.

Saxon sat listening to the woman tell him about the businessmen trying to get her group of friends to go to a nightclub with them, his mind wandering to places that it hadn't gone in eons. He felt his hands start to sweat, which rarely happened because he almost never got nervous. He thought he'd conquered fear during his internment with the ISB, but as Taylor continued talking to him, he could feel his nerves acting up.

The bartender returned with her drink and asked if they wanted anything else, although he paid no attention to Saxon. After he left to tend to the rest of the patrons, she raised her glass towards Saxon.

"Cheers," she smiled. Saxon returned her smile and clinked his glass against hers. "I'm Taylor, by the way. Taylor Lavine."

"Conner," Gray lied, feeling slightly weird about lying to her.

"Are you from around here, Conner?" she asked, taking a large sip from her drink. Saxon shook his head and shrugged at the same time.

"I grew up in Sausalito, California. Not too far from here, but not right next door or anything. How about you?" he asked, leaning towards her so he could hear better. The years of gun fighting had given him a case of tinnitus that acted up at the least opportune times.

"Florida. Born and bred," Taylor said proudly. "I live in Jacksonville at the moment, but I'm looking to move."

"Any particular reason?"

"Just looking for a change of scenery," she said, forcing a smile. Saxon could instantly tell there was more to the story there, but he didn't pry. "My friends and I came up here to blow off some steam and have fun. Stopped in Vegas for a few days before coming here."

"Having fun is important," Saxon chuckled, downing his drink.

"If you don't mind me saying, you don't look like you've had fun in a long time."

"Probably because I haven't. My life is… a little complicated."

"Everyone's is complicated," Taylor said. Saxon could hear the lust in her voice. She put her hand on his thigh and looked deep into him with her penetrating brown eyes.

Less than 20 minutes later, Gray Saxon was feeding the key into his hotel room while desperately trying to keep his lips pinned against Taylor's. He swung the door open as soon as he could and kicked it closed behind them. Saxon grabbed Taylor by the shoulders and pinned her against the wall, kissing her neck passionately. She reached down and fumbled with his belt, moaning loudly as he continued to kiss her neck. He instinctively grabbed her wrists when she tried to pull his jeans down; he had his 1911 tucked in the small of his back.

"What's wrong?" Taylor asked, breathing heavily. She looked concerned, wondering if she had pushed him too far. Saxon grinned and picked her up, planting his lips on hers once more. He carried her to the bed and lay her gently on top of the comforter.

"Everything is perfect," Saxon whispered into her ear. She threw her arms around him and kissed him as hard as she could.

With Taylor focused on the foreplay, Saxon pulled the gun out of his waistband and gently slid it under his king-sized bed, making a mental note to grab it as soon as they finished.

Taylor was snoring softly under the covers, her hair a mess and her clothes scattered all over the room. Saxon peered over Taylor's naked body and saw the sun was barely bleeding through the curtains, the clock had been knocked off the nightstand during the previous night's extracurriculars. As quietly as he could so he wouldn't wake her, Saxon slipped out of bed and snatched the 1911 from under it. He hurried back toward the closet, opened the small safe, and tucked the Para-Ordnance inside.

He then slipped back into bed alongside Taylor, maneuvering his arm under her to hold her close to him. She continued to sleep peacefully. He was about to fall asleep again when his phone buzzed loudly on the dresser.

"Goddammit!" Saxon hissed. He leaped up from the bed and snatched the phone, relieved that Taylor was still sound asleep. Stepping onto the deck of his hotel room, he finally answered the phone.

"Saxon," he answered quietly.

"Hardware for phase two has been acquired," Rahman Saleh reported. "I've secured an apartment in South Pasadena, it's approximately one hour from LAX."

"Good work. That'll do just fine," Saxon responded, pleased that Rahman had come through on his part of the mission. "Ilsa and Alaina are on their way and should be there later tonight. I will be there in the next couple of days."

"You're not coming with them?" Rahman asked, surprised that Saxon had changed the plan again without letting them know. Now that Ryan was dead, Rahman had assumed that he was Saxon's right-hand man. Being left in the dark didn't sit well with Rahman, and he was beginning to realize that Saxon was very good at leaving them in the dark.

"No," Saxon simply said. "Have you contacted our new recruits?"

"Yes, I have," Rahman said hesitantly. "They're young. Young and completely brainwashed."

"Perfect. I'm assuming they've left quite the trail on the internet."

"Of course they have. They've even traveled to the Middle East a few times. I'm meeting with them this week to explain the job."

"Keep it vague. Be smart about it. I'll be in contact soon," Saxon cut the call and went back inside, eager to get back into bed with Taylor.

Once again, he cuddled up next to her and fell fast asleep with his body pressed warmly against hers.

Chapter Twenty-Four
The White House, Washington D.C., Maryland

John Shannon and Riley Hanna waited anxiously in a large conference room in the East Wing of The White House. They had been jetted directly from Creech Air Force Base to Andrews Air Base. From there, they were driven to the White House and given a spare change of clothes. Riley and John took turns showering and then waited for a Secret Service agent to come and get them.

John was laying on the couch with a pillow over his face, snoring loudly. Laughing, Riley picked up a pillow from another chair and threw it at him. He gagged and shot up, his hair all messed up from sleeping.

"What was that for?" he asked groggily. He squinted his eyes a few times and shook his head, trying to wake himself up.

"You're snoring like a bear, Shannon," Riley folded her arms, giving him a sassy look. John rolled his eyes and fell back onto the couch.

"You've never complained about my snoring before," he muttered before shutting his eyes again.

Riley shook her head and stood up, feeling the need to stretch her legs. In less than two minutes, John was back to snoring just as loudly as he had been before. It always amazed Riley how he could fall asleep almost instantaneously. He had told her many times it came from his time in the military and learning to sleep wherever, whenever.

The door to the room swung open and a trio of Secret Service agents walked in; they all looked like they had been molded from steel. John shot up and fixed his hair as best he could.

"The president is ready for you two," the lead agent said. John and Riley followed the agents out of the room and through the White House. Neither of them had ever been to the official office of the president, they looked around admirably, taking in everything as they made the journey to the Oval Office.

They were met by another group of Secret Service agents before they were allowed to enter the Oval Office. The lead agent opened the door and escorted John and Riley inside. Behind the Resolute Deck, the president of the United States looked up from a file he was reading. He smiled brightly and got up, buttoning his suit as he crossed the room.

"Pleasure to meet you both," he stuck out his hand. John and Riley each took turns shaking the president's hand.

"It's an honor to meet you, sir," Riley said. She was completely star-struck; John did a much better job of hiding it.

"Nonsense," the president waved his hand, gesturing for them to sit at the couches. "The honor is all mine. I want to thank you two for all the work you've been doing on this case."

"No need to thank us, sir," John said, sharing a quick smile with Riley. "We're a good team."

"I can tell. I've been reading up on the case, but I wanted to hear everything from you two directly. I hope that is ok," the president propped his leg up on his knee.

"Of course," Riley nodded.

Riley and John took turns telling the president everything, from her initial suspicions to John's mission to Jordan, and finally, the incident at Creech Air Force Base. John concluded by telling the president that he was 100% sure he'd seen Gray Saxon leaving the air base. The president listened intently; he didn't interrupt or ask any questions.

"Well, you two have done some outstanding work," he said after a few seconds of silence. "First off, I want to apologize for the lack of support, Ms. Hanna. I assure you things will be different starting immediately."

"I appreciate that, sir," Riley smiled appreciatively. The president turned to John.

"I read your file too, Mr. Shannon," he said. There was a hint of mystery in his voice. "I also feel it necessary to apologize on behalf of the United States military. The way you were forced to retire is utterly unacceptable."

"Thank you, sir," John said quietly. The president smiled.

"Now that we've got that out of the way, here is what I propose. We need to find this Gray Saxon yesterday. The way I see it, you two are my experts on this entire situation. So, Ms. Hanna, I'd like you running the investigation from here. You can have access to anything you need and I will see to it personally that the CIA, DIA, and NSA are all working with you. Mr. Shannon, I want you on the ground, knocking down doors. Whatever drama you had with the Navy is forgotten. Effective immediately, you are reinstated and given the rank of Master Chief. Whatever you need, tell me and I'll make it happen."

Riley and John were visibly shocked. They looked at each other and back to the president with open mouths. The president chuckled and leaned back in his chair.

"Thank you, sir," Riley chirped.

"One other thing," the president interjected. "I need to keep this quiet for the time being. If anything about Gray Saxon gets out to the press... well, I'm sure you can imagine how that would go over. For the time being, everyone needs to think this is terrorism."

"I understand, sir," Riley nodded.

John, however, shook his head and laughed to himself. Riley raised an eyebrow at him as they made eye contact. His entire mood had changed in a split second.

"Mr. President, with all due respect, I'm not sure I want anything to do with the Navy. I appreciate the gesture, but that's going to be a no from me. I run an excavator now, the Navy is the last thing I want to be a part of," John said, much to Riley and the president's surprise.

"John..." Riley hissed, shooting daggers at him. She knew better than to disagree with the Commander in Chief. John ignored her, keeping his eyes on the president.

"Is there any particular reason you feel that way, Mr. Shannon?" the president asked.

"Plenty of reasons. I am happy to help as much as I can with this situation, but I'm not going back to the Navy."

"Can you give me a reason why, son?"

"I don't know what you know, sir," was John's response. The president chuckled softly.

"Probably not the whole story," he admitted. "If you want to say anything, know that it'll stay between the three of us."

John tapped the side of his leg nervously, itching for a cigarette. He didn't care about spilling his story to the president, in fact, John figured the president should probably know the true story. But he never thought he'd come face to face with his past and Riley Hanna. He couldn't help but find it ironic that he was more anxious for Riley's sake than his own.

"Sir, the Navy asked me to do certain things," John began, looking at Riley hesitantly. "Things that I was not ok with and I stated that many times. But I did them because that was my job. But they pushed it too far, and when I refused a mission, I wasn't just forced to retire; it cost me my job, my rank, my retirement... it cost me everything. I had to take a job at my brother-in-law's construction company and join a fucking labor union to be able to pay my wife's medical bills. So, with all due respect, I want nothing to do with the Navy," John concluded.

His hands started sweating profusely as the president looked him up and down. He waited for the president to say something, but the man was silent. The president folded his hands, looking at John intently.

"I am very sorry for that, Mr. Shannon," the president finally spoke. "I cannot force you to do anything you're not comfortable with."

"I will help in any way I can," John insisted. "Just not with the Navy."

"We'll see what we can do," the president smiled. "For now, you two get to work and I will have a unit assigned to assist you by the end of the day,"

Five minutes later, John and Riley were being driven away from the White House to their hotel. They hadn't spoken since they left the office—Riley was still shocked at John's behavior in front of the president. But she could see when he spoke to the Commander in Chief that he was still bitterly angry at the Navy.

"I'm sorry," John said, turning to look at Riley. She looked at him and touched his hand.

"What happened, John? I wish more than anything that you would tell me."

Just as John opened his mouth, his phone began ringing. Reaching into his pocket, he flipped his phone over to see who was calling. His heart skipped a beat when he saw his sister-in-law's name.

Chapter Twenty-Five
Los Angeles, California

It was well into the afternoon by the time Gray Saxon rolled over onto his stomach. With his eyes still shut, he ran his hand over the bed, trying to blindly find Taylor. He opened his eyes and looked around blearily when he didn't feel her next to him. Saxon sat up in bed, hearing the shower running in the bathroom; Taylor's clothes were still scattered across the room.

He climbed out of bed and walked over to the bathroom, carefully opening the door without making a sound. The glass shower door was steamed and foggy, but he could still see Taylor, washing her arms in the water. He kicked off his shorts and tip-toed over to the large shower, opening the glass door without a sound. Slipping inside, Saxon reached out and pulled Taylor into him.

"My god!" she yelled, startled by Saxon. She immediately started laughing and threw her soapy arms around him.

"I thought you left for a second," he whispered as he leaned in for a kiss. Taylor kissed him, slipping her tongue inside his mouth.

"You're not getting rid of me that easily, Conner," she smiled. Saxon's eyes dropped. Taylor cocked her head to meet his gaze. "What's wrong?"

"Nothing, nothing," Saxon lied. He moved closer to her, letting the hot water hit his back and shoulders.

"Good," Taylor purred, running her hands over his chest and abdomen. She leaned up and kissed him as her right hand gripped his groin.

Saxon flinched unintentionally and Taylor gave him a strange look. "Ok, what is wrong?" she pressed.

"Nothing." He shook his head and snickered to himself. "I'm just not used to this. I haven't been with anyone in a very long time."

"You seemed to know what you were doing last night," Taylor bit her bottom lip. Saxon laughed and kissed her forehead.

"It's been a long time," he shrugged.

"How long is a long time?"

"You wouldn't believe me if I told you," Saxon said, trying to hide his embarrassment. She kissed his neck, a move that made his toes curl.

"Try me," she said, looking up at him with her seductive eyes.

"Four years," he said flatly. Taylor gaped at him.

"You're lying!"

"I'm not," Saxon laughed. "I've been busy."

"So, you haven't been with a woman in four years?"

Saxon nodded and shrugged. "I can't even comprehend that."

"Sorry to disappoint."

Taylor yanked Saxon into her and kissed him passionately.

"You're anything but a disappointment," she breathed.

"You wanna go back to bed?" he asked, grinning at her. Taylor shook her head and spun around, bending over at the waist. Saxon laughed. "You're gonna be the end of me, baby."

Saxon stared into Taylor's eyes, running his hand through her beautiful hair. She slowly ran a finger over the grisly scar on his face. Saxon's body was covered in a maze of jagged scars, Taylor couldn't begin to imagine what had happened to him, but his body told a horrific story. She touched a thick scar on his shoulder. He gently grabbed her hand and set it on the pillow they were sharing.

"That was amazing, Conner," she whispered, giggling softly. Saxon smiled at her and rolled onto his back. She rested her head on his shoulder, ignoring the scars.

"Gray," he said quietly, shutting his eyes. He couldn't keep lying to her.

"What?"

"Gray," Saxon repeated, opening his eyes and staring at her intently. "My name is Gray. Gray Saxon."

Taylor didn't respond immediately, she was studying him closely. She'd certainly given people she'd met in bars fake names before. But the man before her felt different; his reasons for the secrecy weren't as simple as one would've thought.

"Why'd you give me a fake name?" she asked. Saxon sighed and brushed a strand of hair away from her face.

"Because," he began. "If anyone asked, you would never have to lie for me."

"What are you talking about?" Taylor sat up, debating whether or not she should just walk out on him.

He saw the shift in her mood and cursed himself. For the first time in years, he'd allowed himself to indulge. He'd allowed himself, for a minute, to envision a future where he could be with a woman. A life that didn't end with violence and death. A life where he could be happy. But as quickly as they had come, those dreams were fading away.

"I've done things," Saxon admitted. "Things that will catch up to me at some point, I know they will. I didn't want to involve anyone else, but you... you made me rethink things. I felt like shit lying to you. I'm sorry, I really am."

Taylor was quiet. She was definitely annoyed that he had lied to her, but she knew all too well that she was keeping plenty of things from him. He had no idea why she'd really come out to California, nor did she ever think she'd consider telling him. If Gray Saxon wanted to be called Conner, then what did she care? They had been brought together by fate, of that she was certain. She'd never been one for religion, but she was a firm believer in fate and the philosophy that everything happens for a reason.

"You don't need to apologize," Taylor said after close to a minute of silence. "We've all got stuff. But, I do appreciate the honesty, Gray."

"You're not mad?"

"How can I be?" Taylor shrugged. "But, can I ask you something?"

"Sure."

"You've killed before, haven't you?"

Saxon nodded slowly.

"How could you tell?"

"You've got the same eyes that I saw in my dad. And my brother. They were both soldiers and killed a few too many people. My dad was in Vietnam and my brother was in Afghanistan," Taylor explained, running her fingers over the scar on his face once more. Saxon winced slightly as she touched him.

"And this?" she asked softly.

"Knife," he answered. "I was tortured for almost a year. That's how I got most of them. A few of them are from bullets too."

"Tortured?" Taylor gasped.

"I was in the military, too." He sat up a little higher, resting against the headboard. "Towards the end, I got myself into a pretty bad situation. I was captured and held for a little over a year."

"My god," Taylor whispered, unsure of what to say. "I can't even imagine that, I'm so sorry."

"Like you said, no need to apologize," Saxon smiled sadly. "The truth is, I haven't been able to enjoy much of my life since then. The military, the government all think I'm dead and that's the way I want to keep it."

"I'm not going to say anything," Taylor said strongly. "I understand... wanting to disappear, I mean. I'm almost jealous, that's got to be very freeing."

"It can be," Saxon smiled and kissed her.

"I'm hungry. Care to grab breakfast with me?" he offered. Taylor responded by kissing him. "I'll take that as a yes," Saxon chuckled.

Chapter Twenty-Six
Oakland, California

John Shannon had been chain-smoking since he and Riley landed in Oakland. He smoked the entire drive from the airport to Alta Bates Summit Medical Center in Oakland, only a few minutes from where John resided in Emeryville.

His heart stopped when he'd seen his sister-in-law, Carmen, had called him. It was a phone call he had figured would be coming, but it didn't make it any easier. Thankfully, Riley chartered an FBI plane and got them to California as fast as possible.

The elevator doors opened and John rushed out and hurried down the hallway of the hospital, slipping past nurses and doctors. He knew the way by heart, rounding a corner and jogging down another hallway. Riley was a few paces behind, understanding John didn't need her at the moment.

John slowed down and came to a stop outside a hospital room; he bent over, hands on his knees, and took deep breaths. He peeked inside through the four-by-four glass window; his in-laws were surrounding the hospital bed, there was a nurse and a doctor off in the corner. John looked back and saw Riley walking towards him.

"Are you ok?" she asked. He nodded and stood back up, wiping the sweat from his brow.

"You can wait out here," he muttered. "I don't want anyone to have the wrong idea."

John Shannon opened the door and stepped into the hospital room. Immediately, all eyes were on him. His sister-in-law, Carmen, smiled sadly and waved him over. Her husband, David Spencer, was next to her; David was John's boss at Walsh Construction. His mother and father-in-law gave him a warm hug—they had always liked him. He hugged them back.

"It's nice to see you," his mother-in-law, Annie, croaked. She was fighting back tears.

"Always, mama," John smiled, giving her another quick hug.

John stepped aside and dropped to a knee on the right side of the bed; Anna opened her eyes and smiled weakly. John chuckled and smiled back at her, he wrapped his hand in hers, their wedding bands touching.

"Let's give them some space," Carmen said, ushering her husband and her parents out of the room. The nurse and doctor stayed behind, carefully monitoring Anna.

"Hey, baby," John whispered as soon as her family was gone. Anna tried to sit up, but her strength was all but gone. The defeat in her eyes nearly made John burst into tears, but he was determined not to cry, no matter how much he wanted to.

"It's good to see you," Anna said, her voice was ragged and shaky. "How's the case going?"

"Oh, it's going," John smiled. It never failed, Anna was always curious about his day, whether he'd been chasing rogue Navy SEALs across the country or digging holes in Emeryville. "Between you and me, the guy we're looking for used to be a SEAL."

"A SEAL? Did you know him?" Anna asked, lifting her head up curiously. John nodded.

"A long time ago," he admitted. John moved closer to his wife and kissed her. "But don't you worry about that, I'll have it all taken care of and then you and I can go back to Hawaii. Renew our vows, walk on the beach, that kind of thing."

"Don't tease me, Johnny," Anna smiled, gripping her husband's hand tighter.

Her smile suddenly vanished and her eyes began welling. John couldn't bear the sight and lowered his gaze, he didn't want her to see him cry. The entire time they'd known each other, John had never cried in front of his wife.

"John, you don't have to be brave for me," Anna whispered, it was getting increasingly more difficult for her to talk. He looked up at her as the first tears fell down his stubbly cheeks.

"I'm sorry, Anna," John muttered, squeezing her hand. "I'm sorry I was such an angry son of a bitch. You deserved so much better than me."

"John, I loved you. Angry son of a bitch or not, I loved you for you. It wasn't fair what the Navy did to you, but we made the best of it. We had some good times together," Anna smiled, her eyes were starting to glaze over.

"We had a lot of good times, honey," John agreed. Anna took both of his hands and pulled him close to her.

"I need you to promise me something, John," she whispered.

"Anything," he said, blinking away more tears.

"Don't waste the rest of your life. I don't want you to be alone, people aren't meant to be alone," Anna said, starting to cry. "Do what you want in life, do what makes you happy. And please, John, find someone that's forever. I don't want you to be alone."

"I promise, baby," John cried softly; the tears were in a freefall. "I love you so much, Anna. I'm sorry I didn't say it enough."

"It's ok, Johnny. I never doubted it. I love you too. Always."

John cuddled up to his wife and held her until she took her last breath; the ECG monitor flatlined.

Chapter Twenty-Seven
Oakland, California

Riley Hanna found John Shannon outside, sitting against the hospital with a cigarette in his mouth. There were at least half a dozen cigarette butts around his feet. Ignoring the foul smell of nicotine, she sat down next to him. He looked at her sadly; his eyes were bloodshot and the streaks of dried tears were visible on his rough cheeks.

"I'm so sorry, John," Riley comforted, putting her arm around her friend. Her mom had died of cancer a few years back, so she knew all too well the pain of losing a loved one like that.

"You know what's funny?" John asked, taking a massive drag from the cigarette. "In all the years I was with Anna, all I wanted was to be back overseas with my team. With the good old United States fucking Navy. And now? Now, I wish I had taken her out to dinner more. Taken her to Paris like she always wanted. But no, I just smoked and worked and was a miserable prick."

John dropped his head into his hands and started crying again, something Riley Hanna never thought she'd see. The John Shannon she had known was forged from steel, he'd never allowed his emotional side to come out. Riley hugged him, letting him rest his head on her shoulder as he cried softly. She took the cigarette from his hand and put it out on the concrete; John didn't even notice. Her heart broke for him. As she listened to his raspy sobs, Riley wished she'd never thought to ask him for help. Not that it could've changed the outcome, but at least he would've had more time with Anna. But John didn't even mention it when she asked. He accepted and walked off the job site after making one phone call, which Riley now figured had been to his sister-in-law.

After about ten minutes of silence, John finally sat back up and rested his head against the building. He had a strong headache by now from crying.

"Riles," he sputtered.

"I'm here, John," she whispered, holding his hand.

"I think... I think I'm ready to tell you what really happened... with me and the Navy," John whispered. He reached into his pocket and pulled out his half-empty pack of Marlboros. Before he could light one, Riley yanked the pack away and stuffed it in her jacket.

"If you're going to tell me, tell me," Riley said sternly. "But enough with the cigarettes."

"Ok, ok," John said, chuckling softly.

"I'm all ears," Riley held his hand. "You can tell me anything."

"Gray Saxon was my Commanding Officer when he went rogue to rescue a female Air Force pilot," John started, bouncing his leg nervously. "He went MIA after rescuing the pilot; her name was Cassidy Minor."

"I remember that," Riley said, having recalled the news coverage following Minor's rescue.

"We were working around the clock trying to find Saxon," John continued. "But some of the big shots in the Navy and the CIA thought of a more dramatic approach. They needed to show everyone that the rape and torture of a US servicewoman wouldn't stand. That's where I came in."

Chapter Twenty-Eight
Al-Kawm, Syria - Four Years Ago

The sandstorm was nearly on top of Master Chief John Shannon, the wind was picking up substantially. Dust and sand swirled around the flat terrain, but John could still see the village clear enough for the mission.

"Viper Actual, this is Viper Main," John said into his mic. He spoke in a low voice instead of a whisper. "I have eyes on the village, over."

"Copy, Main," the Mission Commander, Joe Weingardt, answered. "Hold position, we're adjusting our satellite. Our drones can't fly in that sandstorm."

"Roger," John muttered.

"F-35s are inbound, I repeat, F-35s are inbound," Weingardt said.

"Acknowledged," John echoed.

John was dug in on the flat terrain of the Syrian desert, almost 300 yards away from the village of Al-Kawm. He was dressed in all black camouflage and carried a Remington Modular Sniper Rifle as his main weapon. In addition to the MSR, John had a suppressed M4A1 on his back and a H&K Mark 23 on his hip. The MSR was propped up on the bipod and was fixed with a Night Owl scope, allowing John to see in the pitch-black darkness.

On the other end of the comms was Joe Weingardt, a CIA agent attached to John's SEAL team. He was a 50-year-old man from Southern Mississippi who had earned a grim reputation among the Special Forces community, known for using SF operators as his personal hitmen. The exploitation of Warrant Officer Cassidy Minor had essentially given

Weingardt free reign to take out as many ISB targets as possible. Ever resourceful, Weingardt had been following John Shannon's career for some time, and chose him immediately to join his Black Ops unit. John had already carried out half a dozen ops, eliminating or capturing every single target he'd been given so far.

"Viper Main, overwatch is up and we have visuals on the village," Weingardt said. "Activate your strobe."

"Stand by," John responded. He reached behind his back and flipped on his infrared strobe. "Strobe is on."

"Copy, we see you," Weingardt confirmed. "You have executive authority. Actual, out."

"Copy, Actual," John switched his comm channel and peered through the scope of his MSR. He adjusted the zoom variable and located the target house.

The house was at the far east end of the village, surrounded by several smaller huts. As he watched the house through his scope, John could see several roaming sentries, all armed with AK variant rifles. According to the briefing given by Joe Weingardt, guards were to be expected. They were prepared to die for their boss, Muhammed Bakar Akhmedi. Muhammad was the brother of Yusuf Bakar Akhmedi—the one who was responsible for the Cassidy Minor incident and the kidnapping of Gray Saxon. The CIA and SEALs had been after Muhammad for months, knowing he was Yusuf's right-hand man.

"Tiger 2, this is Viper Main, come back," John growled into his mic. He wrapped his shemagh over his mouth to avoid swallowing sand.

"Viper, we read you loud and clear, over. Flying towards you, get ready to laze the target for drop," the pilot of the Lockheed Martin F-35 Lighting II said calmly.

"Copy that," John responded. "Moving in to laze target."

Getting to his feet, John moved in a low crouch, hurrying toward the village. He was aware of the possibility that there would be look-outs on the roof. As he got closer to the village, he dropped back to his prone position. Angling his rifle at the tops of the huts, he scanned each one, looking for anyone who could give away his position. He saw nothing and was on the move again. It was missions like this that always excited John; him against everyone. He'd gotten used to the solo missions having been Weingardt's go-to for the last two months.

John lay back down in the sand and drew his M4A1 assault rifle. He had fixed an AN/PEQ-2 laser designator on the top rail of the rifle. The PEQ-2 allowed John to use a wide infrared beam to mark targets for aerial strikes. The beams were only visible through night vision goggles, giving the users the ultimate advantage over the enemy. John dropped his NVGs over his eyes and aimed the PEQ-2, marking the house at the end of the road. It was the largest house in the small village.

"Tiger 2, target marked," John almost had to yell as the wind began blowing even harder.

"Copy, time on target, two minutes," the pilot responded, her tone as cool as ice.

"Roger, you're clear and hot," John said.

John brought up his MSR and peered through the scope, watching the house intently. The guards were huddled together by the front gate, trying to avoid the relentless wind. Clearly, they were more concerned with the adverse weather than a United States fighter jet. Out of the corner of the scope, John spotted movement in the house. He adjusted and zoomed in as much as he could, focusing on the large windows on the second floor of the home.

His eyes went wide behind the sniper scope when he saw a little girl looking out of the window. An older woman came into view and picked up the small girl. John recognized the woman as Muhammad's wife—her photo had been included in the pre-operation briefing. The idea of calling in an airstrike on the village had not sat well with John, but he eventually relented after Joe Weingardt insisted that Muhammad's family wouldn't be in the home. Weingardt had either lied to get John to comply or hadn't done a thorough enough job. John wasn't sure which one of those options was worse.

"Viper Actual, come in!" John yelled, switching the channel back. There was a long pause before Weingardt answered.

"This is Actual," he answered, almost annoyed that John was contacting him.

"His family is in the house, I repeat, his family is in the house!" John cried. "Disengage the jets!"

"Negative," Weingardt said without hesitation. "Target is in the house, mark the target, and vector the F-35s in."

"Did you hear what I fucking said?" John yelled back. "There's a little girl in the house. Call off the jets!"

"And risk letting the target get away? Negative, complete the mission," Weingardt cut the communication.

John frantically switched his channel back and tried to hail the F-35 pilot.

"Tiger 2, Tiger 2, come in, over!" John screamed, getting to one knee. His eye was glued to the scope of his MSR, watching the mother and daughter through the window.

"Viper Main, bombs away," the pilot said after a few seconds of silence.

Overhead, John heard the roar of the F-35 as it screamed over the desert floor; the engines whining loudly. John dropped his MSR and stood up, watching in horror as the F-35 released the Joint Direct Attack Munition (JDAM) bomb.

The house erupted in a massive explosion, absolutely destroying the structure and killing everyone inside instantly. John felt like he was going to throw up; the inferno illuminated the dark sky around the village in a brilliant hue of orange and red.

"What the fuck?" John muttered.

Chapter Twenty-Nine
Al-Tanf, Syria - Four Years Ago

Less than two hours later, John was sitting on the floor outside the Command Center at the Al-Tanf military installation. He could hear a few different voices yelling from inside the Command Center, but he couldn't seem to find a fuck to give about that. He popped a cigarette into his mouth and lit it, ignoring the rules to not smoke inside buildings on base.

During the mission briefing, John had asked Joe Weingardt point-blank if Muhammed's family was going to be in the house at the time of the mission. John had no problem taking out terrorists, but he was not about to be compliant in the killing of women and kids; he was yet to have to cross that line during his military career. Weingardt had sworn up and down that the family would be gone, but a man like Weingardt also knew John's sense of morals. Morals that he himself lacked. There was no doubt in John's mind that Weingardt knew the family would be there and sent him in to mark the target regardless.

"John, please come in," Commander Richard 'Rick' Garrison barked, throwing the door to the Command Center open forcefully. "And put that goddamn smoke out, sailor."

"Yes, sir," John muttered, smashing the cigarette on his boot. He tossed the ruined smoke on the floor and swayed into the Command Center. Joe Weingardt had both hands on the long table and an expression mixed with disgust and disdain. There were a handful of other Naval officers, including Commander Garrison, and a duo of CIA agents that were a part of Weingardt's attaché. Weingardt looked up at John and scoffed; he shook his head in disgust and chuckled.

"Do you realize that you almost jeopardized that mission, Shannon?" Weingardt spat.

"Master Chief Shannon," John corrected, balling his fists. Commander Garrison rolled his eyes, already tired of the pissing contest between his SEAL and the CIA agent.

"Master Chief, I'm afraid he's right," Garrison said. "That kind of reaction is not what we brought you on for..."

"Commander, whose job was it to brief me on the mission?" John asked, not taking his eyes from Weingardt.

"That would be Mr. Weingardt," Garrison said, raising an eyebrow slightly. He could tell John had something up his sleeve.

"So, it would be understood that Mr. Weingardt had extensive knowledge of the target location and the inhabitants of that location."

"I guess," Garrison muttered. John closed the gap between him and Weingardt.

"So, why when I asked if the family would be involved was I fed a bullshit answer? Why was I not given all of the information? Was it because Mr. Weingardt didn't know? Or, did he think I wouldn't mind watching him murder an entire family instead of just one man, fuck else if it's a woman and a five-year-old little girl," John growled.

"I don't see how that matters," Weingardt said apathetically. "Muhammed Bakar Akhmedi has been a significant HVT for months and we took him off the board," Weingardt shrugged.

"I asked you if his fucking family was going to be there! I told you I wasn't going to help you drop a bomb on an innocent woman and little girl!" John yelled, looking to Garrison for some support. "Commander, that's not what I signed up for!"

"You signed on to kill ISB," Garrison commented. His steely gaze was unreadable to John, but he didn't seem to feel like offering any support. "And you just took out their number two. I consider this an absolute success."

"Oh, fuck you," John shot. He knew cursing out a superior officer was a stupid move, but in the heat of the moment, he couldn't be troubled to give a shit.

"Master Chief!" Commander Garrison hollered. "I am your direct superior, maintain discipline."

"How are you taking this prick's side, sir?" John asked, feeling like his own Navy was betraying him. "I was given bad information! I'm not a murderer, I'm not taking innocent lives just so this cocksucker can cross off names on some list!"

"You had all of the pertinent information to complete the mission. I don't give a fuck if his family was or wasn't there. You don't get to come back here and judge me," Weingardt shot back.

John threw a right cross in the blink of an eye, connecting with the side of Weingardt's face. Before anyone could stop him, John threw another punch, shattering Weingardt's eye socket and drawing a substantial amount of blood.

"You two-faced motherfucker!" John screamed, reeling back for a third punch.

Two of the Naval Officers tackled John before he could land another blow, wrenching his arms behind his back and pinning him to the floor. John looked over, satisfied to see Joe Weingardt in a bloody heap—he was blubbering like a toddler. The Navy Officers yanked him to his feet and manhandled him out of the room.

John spent the next day and a half in the brig before the decision came down to strip him of his rank and uniform. He was dishonorably discharged and sent on the next flight home without a chance to plead his case.

Chapter Thirty
Oakland, California

John and Riley sat in silence for a few minutes; John had gotten emotional after concluding his story. All the raw emotions of being forced out of the job he loved came back like a tidal wave—the anger, the guilt, the feeling of betrayal still burned in him.

"So... that's what happened," John muttered and shook his head. He patted his pockets for a cigarette, forgetting that Riley had confiscated his pack. "The Navy gave me the boot knowing I'd never talk. I think that Weingardt guy still wears an eyepatch, but I haven't seen him since that day."

"I'm glad you told me," Riley squeezed his hand. "That's not right what they did to you, John. It isn't."

"None of that matters now, Riles," John said, regaining some of his composure. He wiped his face and eyes with his palms. "Thanks for coming with me, you didn't have to."

"I know, but you're my friend and you need to know that," Riley said, smiling sincerely at him. She got to her feet and held out her hand for John. "Come on, we have a lot of work to do."

John chuckled, and with Riley's assistance, pulled himself to his feet. Still holding onto Riley's hand, John pulled her in and embraced her tightly. She laughed in surprise but hugged him back. Riley couldn't deny that she'd missed him, being in his arms again reminded her of how genuinely happy she'd been with him.

"You go on, Riles," John said, kissing her cheek tenderly. "I have to bury my wife."

"John, I can stay if you want..." Riley offered, trying not to blush from the kiss. She felt conflicting emotions, knowing it was way too soon to expect John to be open to a relationship. But at the same time, she felt like a little girl with a crush.

"Nah, I'll be alright," John reassured her, smiling a little bit more confidently than he had been. "You got a ghost to find anyway."

"I can coordinate with the LA branch of the FBI and run the investigation from out here. When you want... if you want to come back, just let me know," Riley offered.

"I will," John smiled. "Go and get to work, kid."

"Are you sure?" Riley asked. John nodded but stuck his hand out.

"I'm sure. And I'll take my cigarettes back, please and thank you," John smirked wryly.

Reluctantly, Riley placed the pack of Marlboros in John's outstretched hand. He tucked the pack in his back pocket, but not before swiping a smoke and popping it into his mouth. Riley rolled her eyes and turned toward the parking lot.

"See you soon, John," Riley called, waving as she walked away.

Chapter Thirty-One
South Pasadena, California

California was an interesting state to a man like Rahman Saleh. He'd spent most of his life in Iraq, never having left the country until he was well into his 30s. His decision to leave Iraq, the Army, and the rest of his extended family had been an easy one after what happened to his wife and small children. Wandering through America seeking lowlife mercenary work had brought him right to Gray Saxon.

Rahman watched a group of protestors march down the street outside the coffee shop he stood in with genuine interest. He wasn't sure what they were protesting, but he could see the passion and fire behind them. It was almost inspiring if it wasn't so annoying to him. The barista handed him his coffee and he left after dropping a couple of loose bills in the tip jar. Checking his watch, Rahman picked up the pace toward the Orange Grove baseball field. There was a little league tournament going on and plenty of spectators, Rahman blended in with the rest of the crowd.

Sipping his coffee, he leaned against the chain-link fence. Looking to his right, Rahman saw the two Middle Eastern men approaching him, permanent scowls etched on their faces.

"You two need to relax and look a little less homicidal. Otherwise, people are going to get the wrong impression," Rahman sneered, eyeing both men through the lenses of his Oakley Aviators. Neither one said anything, having found no amusement in the quip. Rahman rolled his eyes and took another sip of coffee.

The two men were brothers named Samir and Qaosim, both born in America but had traveled many times to the Middle East. They were fanatical in their support for the ISB, their family hailed from Syria and had instilled their radical views on them from a young age. Rahman had met them through the dark web; they were the perfect fall guys, so perfect that Rahman couldn't pick a better duo if he was casting a movie.

"My brother and I are ready for the next step," Samir spoke. He did most of the talking for the two brothers. "We have been waiting for this moment our entire lives."

"Good," Rahman nodded. "You two are going to help rewrite history as we know it."

"It is the will of Allah that we have been brought together," Samir said crazily, his religious fanaticism showing its true colors. "We are soldiers of Allah and are ready to wash our hands in the blood of the infidels."

"Uh-huh," Rahman agreed, his sarcasm went right over their heads. Rahman had never been super religious and had pretty much stopped believing in any higher power after his family was murdered. "I hope you two are ready for what we have planned."

"We are ready," Samir repeated, the fire burning wildly in his eyes. Rahman was unnerved by the man, but Samir's insanity was exactly what Gray Saxon needed.

"You've said," Rahman muttered, finishing his coffee. "Alright, do you guys remember the 2017 Paris attacks?"

"Of course," Samir nodded.

"Think that, but the US version. That's essentially the plan. You'll meet the rest of the team this week. Keep your mouths shut, listen, and you'll earn a one-way ticket to Heaven," Rahman rattled off.

"What do you mean, US version?" Samir asked, raising an eyebrow at Rahman's comment.

"You'll see, my friend," Rahman clapped Samir on the shoulder. "Come on, I'll show you two where you're going to be living for the next few weeks."

Chapter Thirty-Two
Los Angeles, California

Gray Saxon's small suitcase was opened on the bed, packed neatly to the brim. He double-checked the drawers before returning to the safe and fetching his Para-Ordnance 1911. He tossed the gun into his much smaller backpack and threw it over his shoulder.

The door to the bathroom opened and Taylor appeared, drying her hands on the back of her black yoga pants. She smiled at Gray and wrapped her arms around him, pulling him in for a passionate kiss.

"That was definitely one of the best weekends of my life," she said, touching his face. Saxon smiled.

"Yeah, I think you're right."

"So, where are you off to?" She asked, reaching for her own bag and suitcase; she was due to fly back to Jacksonville with her friends in a few hours.

"I'm gonna be here for a while," Saxon shrugged. "Like I said, I've got business here I still have to attend to."

"You never did tell me what you did for work," Taylor pointed out.

"In all fairness, neither did you," Saxon smirked. "Maybe next time."

"Oh, so there's going to be a next time?" Taylor asked, blushing slightly.

"I think so," he smiled and headed for the door; he held it open for Taylor to squeeze past with her bags. "You need a ride to the airport?"

"It's alright, my friend has the rental car," Taylor said. They walked hand in hand toward the elevator. She looked up at Saxon's stoic face and smiled to herself.

"I would like to see you again, Gray," she said quietly. "I know it's crazy, we barely know each other, but it feels like…"
"Feels like we've known each other for a long time," Saxon finished her sentence for her. She laughed and nodded.

Saxon could not deny the fact that their chemistry was off the charts. She was everything he would've wanted in his previous life. It killed him to know that there was no realistic chance for them to be together. Saxon was on a warpath and he knew the most likely outcome. He knew that he was on borrowed time the second he walked into Sulieman Khatib's hotel room and opened fire on the Lollapalooza crowd. Any extra perks that came with his life, he had to take full advantage of. But Taylor wasn't just a perk. She was the only person, the only thing that had made him pause and think about what he was doing. Was it really worth it?

As the elevator doors opened, Gray Saxon grabbed Taylor and turned her towards him.

"Stay with me," he blurted out. Taylor did a double-take, almost as if she didn't believe what she'd heard him say.
"What did you say?"
"Stay with me," he repeated. "I know it's crazy, I know. And I know it's probably ignorant of me to ask you to stay, you've probably got shit to do back in Jacksonville. But I've got an apartment lined up in Pasadena and I just don't want to say goodbye to you right now. I really don't."

Taylor was silent, her expression unreadable. Saxon had taken a huge risk, something he was no stranger to. This risk, however, made him more anxious than hijacking a Reaper. After a few seconds, Taylor broke into a wide smile. She threw her arms around his neck and hugged him. Taylor took a step back and looked him up and down one last time.

"Ok," she said quietly.

"Really?" Saxon gasped, a little shocked that she accepted his offer.

"It's crazy, but I've always been a live-in-the-moment kind of girl," Taylor shrugged. "I'd love to go to Pasadena with you."

Saxon yanked Taylor towards him, planting kisses all over her lips.

Chapter Thirty-Three
Los Angeles, California

The FBI Field Office was bustling with activity and Riley Hanna was at the head of it. On the president's order, Riley was given permission to run the Gray Saxon investigation from the Field Office. He'd given her authority to use whatever and whoever she needed to prevent anything else from happening.

Her main goal was to find Rahman Saleh, the other man in the picture that she'd found. With Ryan Bueshay dead, Rahman was now her only direct link to Gray Saxon and her only priority for the time being. She was still wary to share how much she knew about Saxon, for fear that the information would leak to the press before they were truly ready to release that kind of information.

James Gutierrez was originally from San Antonio, Texas; born into a particularly wealthy family. His dad owned a successful chain of restaurants and his mother was a podiatrist. Never finding any interest in either of those fields, James joined up with the Marines fresh out of high school.

He'd served two tours—Iraq and Afghanistan—before deciding to go to the FBI. His career in the FBI had been almost as unimpressive as his military career.

He opened the door to Riley's makeshift office and plopped down in the seat, rubbing his temple and groaning loudly. He had been left in the dust while Riley had run all over the country with John Shannon, something he was not happy about one bit. Ever since James had been assigned as Riley's partner, he'd felt completely overshadowed by her. His pride had taken a huge toll since he started working with her. Riley looked up from her laptop and saw his disapproving look.

"What?" she asked, her tone hinted at annoyance. James scoffed but didn't say anything. Riley didn't have the time or the patience for James's attitude.

"I don't understand why you trust some washed-out Navy SEAL more than you trust me. We're supposed to be working this case together," James shrugged.

"You didn't believe in the lead. You were so quick to go right along with what everyone else was thinking. We had enough conflicting evidence, but you didn't back me up in the slightest. So, if you're bent out of shape about being left behind, you've only got yourself to blame. Your attitude has been a problem since you started with the Bureau and I know I'm not the only one to tell you that," Riley finished her verbal ass-chewing and sat back in her chair.

She had never really liked James, she'd tolerated him as her partner, but they were never close like one would assume about partners. His negative and whiny attitude had been a problem for her since their first day together. She pegged him as an ego-maniac.

"We're partners, Riley," James grunted. "But you've never treated me like an equal and now you come back, fly me out here from Chicago, and just start bossing me around like I'm some first-day analyst. I don't appreciate that."

"James, I'm going to be crystal clear so you understand," Riley said, narrowing her eyes. "I really could care less about your feelings right now. We have a serious threat to national security. If you are not going to be helpful, don't let the door hit you on the way out. I don't have time to play therapist with you."

James sat back, feeling dejected, offended, and pissed off. He shook his head in a mixture of disgust and amazement at how abrasive Riley was towards him. His decision was made the second the words left Riley's mouth. He ripped his badge off his belt and threw it at her.

"Fuck you," he growled before storming out of the FBI Field Office.

Stomping down the hall with his head hanging low, James walked full speed into John Shannon's chest. He recoiled back, nearly losing his balance.

"Careful, buddy," John said, catching James so he wouldn't fall. James looked at John with disgust.

"My life was going just fine until she decided we need a burnout chain-smoker to help with this investigation," James spat. John was taken aback by the hostility. "Have fun with your girlfriend, motherfucker."

"Ok," John said quietly through gritted teeth. It was all he could say without cursing James up and down for being such a douche. James huffed and walked away, knocking a computer off a desk on his way past the cubicles.

Chapter Thirty-Four
Los Angeles, California

John knocked three times and waited, not wanting to barge in on Riley if she was on a call or something of that nature. After a few seconds, the door opened.

"Hi," Riley said, smiling at John. "How'd the funeral go?"

"It was a nice service. Plenty of people attended," he said, smiling sadly. He was still dressed in his standard funeral attire—black suit and black Steve Madden's. Riley was surprised that for the first time since reconnecting with John, he didn't smell like cigarettes.

"I'm glad to hear it," Riley said, sitting back behind her desk. Despite the loss, John seemed to be doing much better than when Riley had last seen him. It had only been a few days, but he still seemed almost ok.

"How's everything going here?" John asked, throwing himself down in a chair and propping his feet up on Riley's desk.

"I think James quit," Riley chuckled, shaking her head and sighing. John cracked a smile.

"You still a bully, Riles?" he asked. Riley gawked, taking offense at the remark.

"I am not a bully!" she cried. "I just don't have patience for people who whine and don't have a backbone."

"Harsh words," John chuckled. He changed the subject, not really caring about Riley's partner; he didn't like the man the first time he laid eyes on him. "What're you working on now?"

"Still trying to find this Rahman Saleh character. So far, we've come up empty. And don't get me started on Gray Saxon, he's the definition of a ghost."

"Well, he's going to slip up at some point. We just have to be there when he does," John muttered.

"What do you mean?" Riley asked, looking at him quizzically.

"Well, he's going to slip up. No matter how much he's changed or gone off the rails, that's still the same guy who disobeyed direct orders and launched an unauthorized rescue mission. That's who Saxon is at heart; at least I think he's still got some humanity left to him. My guess is that he's going to have a real come-to-Jesus moment very soon. And when that happens, we need to be ready to take him off the board," John explained.

"You mean kill him?" Riley clarified.

"Honestly," John sighed. "I don't know if I could look him in the eye and pull the trigger. I'd like to think I could, but I don't know. I still remember my old Commander Gray Saxon. He was someone I looked up to. But either way, if we kill him or we capture him, we still need to be ready."

"I'll let you know when we get something on Saleh," Riley said, fidgeting with the papers on her desk.

John nodded and got to his feet; he buttoned his black sport coat and headed for the door. He reached for the door but stopped, his mind abruptly running wild with ideas. Emotionally, he was all over the place; grief will do that to a person. On top of that, he hadn't had one cigarette all day.

"Hey, Riles," John said, turning around. He was suddenly very aware of how sweaty his hands had gotten.

"What's up?" Riley looked up at him curiously.

"Do you want to grab a quick dinner with me tonight? We can talk more about the case and come up with a plan for when we find Rahman," John fumbled over his words slightly. He felt like an idiot, using the case as an excuse to ask her to dinner, but he'd already thrown himself in the deep end.

"John Shannon," Riley crossed her arms and tried not to blush. "I would love to go to dinner with you."

Chapter Thirty-Five
Los Angeles, California

Taylor Lavine was no stranger to male attention, not by any stretch of the imagination. Although she'd always been humble about it, she had been branded the prettiest girl in school since middle school. That title followed her all the way through high school and her two-year stint at community college.

After deciding a Bachelor's Degree was enough school for her, Taylor turned to modeling. It started out pretty innocent but had gotten increasingly explicit over the years. She was never uncomfortable in her line of work; she was proud of her looks and her body, something she worked religiously to keep in tip-top shape.

Despite being desired by hordes of men and women, Taylor wasn't one to sleep around or date multiple people. Usually, that is. But as Taylor sat across from Gray Saxon at Providence, one of Los Angeles's fanciest and most expensive restaurants, she couldn't help but think about home back in Jacksonville.

"You're pretty quiet tonight," Saxon commented, taking a sip of red wine. He'd bought an entire bottle, despite Taylor's protests that it was much too expensive.

"I'm sorry!" she snapped back to reality, suddenly feeling rude for zoning out on her date. Saxon chuckled and reached for a piece of bread.

"What's on your mind?" he asked.

"If I'm being honest, home," Taylor said, sipping her own glass of Pinot Noir. "I don't know, it's a long story."

"I've got time," he offered, leaning in closer towards her.

"Maybe some other time," Taylor chuckled. "I don't know if I know you well enough yet."

"You only agreed to live with me, nothing too major," Saxon quipped. Taylor laughed, understanding that she was contradicting herself.

"There was just a lot that happened before I came out here," Taylor began. "I do modeling all over Florida. It's a pretty big scene down there, obviously not as big as LA, but still good."

"A model, huh?"

"Yeah. That's not a problem with you, right?" Taylor asked. Saxon threw his head back and laughed.

"No, it's not a problem with me," he smiled. He could definitely picture Taylor being a model, she was intoxicatingly attractive and her sex appeal was unrivaled.

"I was hoping it wouldn't be. Anyway, yeah, just a lot of drama before I left. That's part of why my friends and I came out here. I needed it and they knew it. They're good friends."

"They sound like it," Saxon agreed.

Just as Taylor was going to continue talking, Saxon's phone rang loudly in the inside pocket of his sport coat.

"Goddammit," he cursed, ripping his phone out to see who was bothering him—Rahman Saleh's name blinked on the phone screen. Saxon looked up at Taylor apologetically. "I'm so sorry, I have to take this."

"No worries!" she smiled. Saxon hopped up, kissed her on the cheek, and ducked out of the dining room before stepping outside.

"What?" Saxon answered, already heated. Rahman was startled by his immediate aggression.

"Are you ok?"

"I'm fine. Why the fuck are you calling me?" Saxon spat back. Rahman sighed heavily and paused. "Rahman, fucking tell me or get off the phone."

"Something is wrong," he said ominously.

"Explain."

"The same car has been circling the apartment complex all night. Another one is parked on the other side of the street. I got a good look at that car and the men inside. They look like cops," Rahman said.

Saxon's stomach dropped. If Rahman had somehow gotten made, then the entire rest of his plan was in jeopardy. Everything that he'd done would be for nothing. All of those people he killed would have died in vain.

"Rahman, I need you to think long and hard before you answer me. Is there any way you could've gotten made since you got there? Did those two terrorist fucks do something stupid?" Saxon's voice was icy cold, only adding to Rahman's fear of the man.

"No. I swear. I've kept a good eye on these two clowns. They haven't had a chance to slip up and I sure haven't. Should I check with Ilsa and Alaina?"

"I trust Ilsa and Alaina," Saxon growled, the insult intentional. Rahman scoffed, insulted at the insinuation.

"I've never given you a reason not to trust me."

"Until now!" Saxon fired back.

Through the windows of the restaurant, Taylor watched Saxon get more and more animated on the phone. He was pacing back and forth on the sidewalk; she could tell he was getting mad. With her attention on Gray Saxon, she almost didn't notice someone slip into his open seat across from her.

"I'm sorry, that seat's taken," Taylor said, not hiding the annoyance in her tone. She turned to see who had invited themselves over to her table and gasped.

"Hello, Taylor," Bryon Hannaway said without a smile. His eyes were narrowed in anger.

Taylor's hands began sweating instantly and her heart rate skyrocketed. She looked back toward the window, Saxon was still deep in conversation. Turning back to Bryon, she looked him dead in the eyes, trying to push down her feelings of fright and anxiety. Bryon was African American, over six and a half feet tall, and pushing 250 pounds of muscle. He'd played semi-pro football before shredding his knee in a freak injury. After that, his drinking and drug use skyrocketed. The constant substance abuse made him violently angry and short-fused, something Taylor had been on the receiving end of too many times.

"Why are you here?" her voice trembled. Bryon reached across the table, trying to grab her hand. She pulled her arm away quickly.

"Don't be rude," Bryon said. His tone disgusted Taylor.

"Fuck you, Bryon!" Taylor hissed, trying to keep her voice down. "Why are you here? How did you find me?"

"Your friends posted a lot of pictures on Facebook and Instagram," he said. "It was easy to track you down, baby girl."

"Don't call me that," Taylor spat, shivering at the sound of his pet name for her.

"Why do you have to be like that?" Bryon said, sitting back in his chair dejected. Taylor crossed her arms and scoffed in disgust.

"I broke up with you, Bryon. I do not want anything to do with you. And now you're stalking me. That's not ok."

"I'm not stalking you, Tay. I'm bringing you home," Bryon said defensively. Taylor could tell he was getting angry and that was never good.

"Bryon, what more do I have to say to you? I'm not going home with you. I will never ever go back to you, do you understand? You were abusive and toxic and I want no part of it," Taylor hissed.

"Alright, obviously you've been drinking tonight," Bryon remarked. "Come on, it's time to go."

"No," Taylor said defiantly.

"Taylor, come on," Bryon ordered, raising his voice.

"No!" Taylor shot back.

Saxon got off the phone and headed back into the restaurant. He cocked his head in confusion when he saw the African American man sitting in his seat. Taylor looked on the verge of tears, that was enough for Saxon. He quickly crossed the dining room and approached the table.

"You are in my seat," Saxon snarled, glaring daggers at the man sitting in his chair. Bryon looked up at Saxon and scoffed. He outweighed him by at least 50 pounds and was several inches taller. Pushing back from the table dramatically, Bryon stood up, puffing his chest out obnoxiously.

"Oh, am I?" Bryon taunted.

"Yeah," Saxon said quietly, not breaking eye contact with Bryon. He'd known men like Bryon his whole life and he wasn't scared in the slightest.

"Taylor and I were just leaving," Bryon shrugged.

"Oh, really?" Saxon asked, looking at Taylor. She shook her head.

"Yeah. Really. She's coming with me," Bryon reached over to grab her.

Saxon caught Bryon's wrist and twisted it, immediately forcing Bryon to his knees. He turned even harder, threatening to snap the joint. Bryon groaned in agony, sweat started pouring from his temple.

"I'm gonna let go and then you're going to walk your dumbass out of here. And you are never going to bother Taylor again. Otherwise, I'll snap your fucking wrist so badly you won't even be able to jerk off," Saxon growled, leaning down so only Bryon could hear.

The entire waitstaff and the diners were staring at Saxon and Bryon, hesitant to get involved with two equally intimidating men.

"I got it," Bryon wheezed. Saxon let the wrist go and Bryon immediately gripped it, massaging it to alleviate some of the pain.

"Get the fuck out of here," Saxon snarled.

Reluctantly, Bryon got up and walked himself out of the restaurant. Saxon didn't sit back down until he saw Bryon turn the corner and disappear into the city night.

"I'm so sorry, Gray," Taylor said, wiping her eyes with her napkin. "I don't even know what to say,"

"Who was that?" he asked. There was an intensity in his eyes that Taylor hadn't seen before.

"Bryon Hannaway. He's my ex-boyfriend. I've broken up with him a few times but he doesn't leave me alone. I was going to get a restraining order when I got back to Jacksonville."

She continued to tell him about their tumultuous-turned-abusive relationship. Everything he heard made his blood boil.

They got back to Saxon's apartment in South Pasadena and Taylor immediately headed for the shower. Saxon stepped out onto the patio and dialed a number into his phone.

"Hi," Ilsa answered. It sounded as though she had been asleep.

"I need you to do something," Saxon snarled. Ilsa heard his tone and was on edge instantly.

"Yeah, sure. Anything," Ilsa responded. "What is it?"

"Find the hotel where Bryon Hannaway is staying in Los Angeles. Give me any itinerary he has, flights, family in the area... anything."

"Give me a few hours and I'll get back to you," Ilsa said.

"No. Give it to me after tomorrow. I don't need any other distractions before then," he said, rubbing his forehead. Ilsa yawned loudly.

"You sound like you are one little nudge away from breaking," she said honestly.

"I don't need a psych eval. Especially from you," Saxon fired back. There was a significant pause.

"I'm still not over what you had Ryan do. His family didn't deserve that," Ilsa finally spoke again. Saxon sighed, knowing she was probably right.

"Yeah, maybe you're right. But we needed him and we didn't have any way of bringing five extra people with us. We sure as hell couldn't have risked leaving them there. What other options did we have?"

"I don't know," Ilsa muttered. "I truly do not know."

"Alright then. Can we just not talk about it anymore? It's done."

"I guess," Ilsa sighed.

"Get that information. I'll call you after tomorrow."

"Good luck, Gray."

Chapter Thirty-Six
Los Angeles, California

Rahman Saleh slowly pulled the Chevy Tahoe into the cramped parking garage and parked as far away from the massive crowd as he could. He threw the truck into park and turned around; Samir and Qaosim were busy adjusting their military-grade Kevlar vests. Rahman, Samir, and Qaosim were all dressed identically—black suits, black loafers, black gloves, and Kevlar vests over their sport coats.

"You boys ready?" Rahman asked. The two brothers nodded, their eyes full of hatred. Rahman nodded and they jumped out of the truck, forming a semi-circle around the trunk. Rahman looked over his shoulder before opening the hatch.

Inside the trunk were a variety of assault rifles, machine guns, and handguns. Tins of ammo and spare magazines lined the sides. In addition to the guns and ammo, four heavy duffle bags were also among the weapons. Each bag carried a homemade propane bomb. Once again, Rahman looked over his shoulder, making sure no one was getting too curious about them. Everyone in the garage was more focused on getting into Dodger Stadium than the three Middle Eastern men.

Excitement hummed in the air as thousands of fans made their way into Dodger Stadium. The Los Angeles Dodgers were mere minutes away from throwing out the first pitch against their rivals, the San Francisco Giants. The stakes were high for the final National League Championship Series, the winner would advance to the World Series. Every single ticket in the 56,000-seat stadium had been sold out in anticipation.

Gray Saxon walked toward his crew and the Tahoe. He was wearing a navy-blue suit and brown loafers, similar to the others. As he approached the Tahor, Rahman nodded respectfully.

"Gear up," Saxon muttered, pushing past Qaosim and Samir. Samir looked at Saxon with disdain.

"Who is this?" he snapped at Rahman, gesturing angrily. Saxon scoffed.

"I'm the man in charge," Saxon growled, staring him down.

"But you're an American!" Samir countered.

"So are you," Saxon shot back. He reached into his waistband and pulled out his Para-Ordnance 1911 threateningly. "I'm an American and this is my op, so that should tell you all you need to know about me."

"But..." Samir protested. His radical mind couldn't begin to accept that an American would be the mastermind of such a plot.

"Just shut up and do your job," Rahman snapped, Velcro-ing his Kevlar vest.

Although he was still unhappy with the situation, Samir kept quiet. Saxon passed Samir and Qaosim a pair of AK-103 rifles; the rifles were fitted with foregrips and EOTech sights. The brothers were very familiar with the rifle and quickly checked over the weapon. Rahman grabbed his personal weapon from his Iraqi Army days, a Zastava M-70. Lastly, Saxon selected an AKMSU kitted out with a Trijicon ACOG sight and a 40-round high-capacity magazine. He slithered into a Kevlar vest and secured it around his chest.

Heaving the duffle bags onto the parking garage floor, Saxon gestured for Samir and Qaosim to each carry one. Rahman had briefed the brothers thoroughly before leaving for the stadium, so they knew where to carry the bombs to. Grunting in exertion, both brothers picked up two bags apiece.

"Give us your weapons. Drop the bombs in position and then rally up at the checkpoint," Rahman ordered, knowing they would respond to orders better from him as opposed to Saxon. The brothers nodded and handed off their weapons before hurrying off toward a maintenance access door. After squeezing through the door, they disappeared down the restricted hallway.

Saxon grabbed four extra 40-round magazines and stuffed them into the pouches on his vest. He yanked the charging handle on his AKMSU and slammed the trunk shut.

"It's rigged?" Saxon asked as he and Rahman walked toward the elevators. Rahman nodded, pulling a small detonator out of his pocket.

"On your order," Rahman muttered.

Chapter Thirty-Seven
Los Angeles, California

Samir and Qaosim dashed through the maintenance hallway, managing to evade wandering eyes. They turned right at the last intersection and hurried down to the end of the hallway. With Qaosim leading the way, they pushed through a series of double doors and came out just outside the stadium.

"Split off. Drop the bags and meet back here," Qaosim whispered in a hoarse voice. He and Samir split off, heading in opposite directions on the perimeter of Dodger Stadium. Each brother was responsible for dropping one bag in a garbage bin and the second bag under a random parked vehicle. The bombs were only meant to divert attention from inside the stadium, their effectiveness wasn't key to Saxon's plan.

Samir dropped the first duffle bag inside a large trash receptacle, slamming the lid shut to conceal the bomb. He ignored a few of the prying eyes that followed him and hurried down toward the second bomb location, finding a row of parked emergency vehicles, just like Rahman had said there would be.

"In position," Samir whispered into the mic on the collar of his suit. He waited nearly ten seconds for Qaosim to respond.
"Meet back up at the maintenance hallway," Qaosim answered.

Samir buttoned his sport coat and hurried back to the maintenance hallway they came out of. As he rounded the corner, Qaosim was already waiting.
"Hurry, brother," Qaosim urged, holding the door open for Samir.

A minute later, they reappeared in the parking garage. Saxon and Rahman stalked over and passed the weapons back to the brothers. Without a word, Saxon led the group toward the security checkpoint to enter the stadium.
"Do it," Saxon growled to Rahman, who pulled out the small detonator again. He flipped the switch and pressed the ignition.

The Chevy Tahoe erupted in a violent explosion, damaging several other vehicles in the parking complex. The structure shuddered from the blast, throwing a few wandering fans off their feet.

Gray Saxon burst through a set of doors and came face to face with the small screening team and close to 75 fans trying to get through before the first pitch. A handful of armed guards and a trio of metal detectors were all that stood between Saxon and thousands of innocent civilians. The guards looked wide-eyed at the team of heavily armed men before them, visibly shocked.

Saxon raised his AKMSU and pulled the trigger—the rest of his team followed suit. Their bullets cut through the fans and guards like butter. The fans screamed in terror, trampling over each other to get clear of the rampaging shooters. Swaying back and forth, Saxon sprayed bullets indiscriminately into the crowd. He targeted the guards first, killing all of them in a few long seconds before they even had time to react and pull their weapons out to fight back. As Saxon lowered his gun to reload, Samir and Qaosim stepped forward, the AK-103s level with their waists.

"*Allahu Akbar!*" Samir cried out.

The two brothers unloaded, shooting right into the middle of the terrified crowd with reckless abandon. Fans dropped dead left and right, riddled with 7.62 bullets. Their screams were drowned out by the concussive blast of the two AK-103s and Rahman's Zastava M-70. After nearly 30 seconds of non-stop shooting, everyone in the small security checkpoint was either dead or mortally wounded. Rahman, Samir, and Qaosim reloaded, dropping their empty magazines over the bodies of the dead.

"On me," Saxon growled. He nearly slipped on a pool of blood but kept his feet beneath him. Blood coated his brown boots and the cuffs of his pants as he walked over the bodies. He saw a young man trying to crawl away, blood pouring from three separate holes in his lower back. Saxon drew his Para-Ordnance and fired a single round, shooting the man through the back of the head. Samir and Qaosim each fired a few more rounds into the bodies, making sure everyone was dead.

The fans at the various concession stands and gift shops had heard the gunfire, but were not positive what exactly the sounds had been. Security guards and cops were running toward the checkpoint, pushing over fans in the process. Saxon and his team stepped into the middle deck of Dodger Stadium, their rifles lowered.

"Hit it," Saxon grumbled to Samir and Qaosim. They pulled out the remotes for the propane bombs and flipped the switches. A half-second later, the four bombs erupted with a deafening boom. The ground shook from the force of the blasts.

As soon as the bombs detonated, Saxon raised his rifle and squeezed the trigger. He gunned down a row of fans in line for hot dogs, raking both lines with bullets. Blood-curdling screams let loose all across the plaza, fans ran in every direction, desperately trying to avoid getting shot. Samir broke off from the team, chasing down a large group of evacuating fans. Planting his feet, Samir shouldered his rifle and started firing, mowing down row after row of civilians.

"Get back over here!" Saxon screamed to Samir over the gunfire. Qaosim shot his brother a disapproving look as they continued shooting into the concession stands.

A small group of security officers came running into the plaza, their service pistols drawn. The first officer in the group leveled his pistol and fired at Samir. Wheeling around, Saxon unleashed a hellish barrage of gunfire, hitting each of the officers in the legs or stomach. The officers fell over each other, groaning in agony. Samir reloaded his AK-103 and finished off the cops.

Following Saxon's plan, each man split up and ran to a different section of seats. Shooting down the glass doors leading to the seats, Saxon burst through the door. By now, the fans in the stands were climbing over each other, trying to escape the melee. Standing at the top of the concrete stairs, Saxon calmly leveled his rifle and fired, shooting all over the stands. The bullets ripped through the fans and the seats, ricocheting off the ground and sending chunks of concrete all over. He glanced over to the next couple of rows of seats. Samir, Qaosim, and Rahman walked down the steps of their respective sections, shooting wildly into the panicked crowds.

Saxon's AKMSU went dry, he released the rifle, letting it hang from his harness. Drawing his Para-Ordnance, he hustled down the stairs, ignoring the dozens of wounded or dead he left in his wake. He got to the first row and vaulted over the railing, nimbly landing on the field level of the stadium.

The players and managers from both teams sprinted toward the bullpens, trying to get to safety. Holstering his Para-Ordnance, Saxon switched out the magazines on his AKMSU in the blink of an eye. Steadying the AKMSU on the railing, Saxon reengaged, bombing rounds over the field. A couple of managers and players were hit with rounds, they fell onto the grass, screaming in pain.

More security and LAPD officers rushed into the stands, frantically trying to stop the rampaging attack. The stadium had been hurled into complete pandemonium in a matter of seconds—the on-site officers and cops were completely overwhelmed. Not to mention, the bombs outside the stadium had inflicted enough damage and chaos to prevent emergency vehicles from getting to the entrance quickly. Luckily, the LAPD officers on site had gotten several calls out. By now, every uniformed officer in the department would be flying towards Dodger Stadium, along with several helicopters and SWAT units.

A seasoned LAPD officer drew his Glock 17 and pulled the trigger three times, each bullet hit Qaosim in the upper back. The man pitched forward, toppling over a row of seats. The cops swarmed him instantly, rushing down the stairs as fast as they could. Bleeding profusely from his wounds, Qaosim rolled onto his stomach and painfully reached for his AK-103. The same cop fired again, shooting Qaosim in the side of the face. The bullet ripped through Qaosim's head, killing him instantly.

"13-Delta-13, one down!" the cop screamed into his radio.

From the adjacent bay of seats, Samir's eyes flared with rage as he saw the cops murder his older brother. He brought his AK-103 up and yanked on the trigger, yelling obscenities in Arabic as he sprayed lead at the cops. The cops ducked into the stands, the barrage of bullets from Samir was overwhelming. Samir didn't let up, he finished off the magazine in a matter of seconds. Two of the cops had been hit by his bullets. The wounds weren't fatal, but inflicted enough damage to render them useless in a gunfight. Satisfied with his work, Samir reloaded and calmly walked back up the stairs, booting the door open as he strode back into the bay of concessions.

As Samir came into the mezzanine, he was greeted by a hail of bullets that narrowly missed him. Diving back to safety, he peered around the wall. Another large group, close to 20 police officers, was moving toward him; eight of the cops were carrying AR-15 carbines.

"He's in the doorway!" one of the cops screamed, firing another series of shots in Samir's direction.

The cops moved into a swarming formation, preparing to surround Samir. Silently, Samir prayed, knowing his life was likely coming to an end.

Three shots rang out, dropping one of the cops. Gray Saxon somersaulted into the mezzanine, 100 feet past where Samir was hiding.

"Move to me!" Saxon screamed, firing on full-auto and forcing the cops back. Seeing his chance, Samir sprinted back toward Saxon, taking cover behind a hot dog cart. As Saxon knelt to reload, Samir popped up and picked up the pace, firing accurately at the scrambling cops and dropping two more. Saxon yanked the charging handle and continued firing, killing another cop in the process. The cops were completely overwhelmed and outgunned by Saxon and Samir; their numbers had already been cut down drastically. Saxon crossed over and slid toward Samir.

"Keep them occupied, I'm gonna flank them," Saxon snarled, checking his 1911.

"Got it," Samir nodded, he grabbed his rifle firmly.

On Saxon's signal, Samir jumped up, spraying 7.62 rounds all over the mezzanine. With the cops distracted, Saxon ran back into the stands and tore down the rows of seats. He leaped over a railing and kept running, stealing a glance to his right as he ran past the cops' position. Slowing down, Saxon took another right and came back into the mezzanine directly behind the cops. He took a deep breath and raised his rifle.

"Checkmate, boys," Saxon taunted. The six remaining cops turned and looked wide-eyed at him, no doubt in shock as he'd appeared from seemingly nowhere.

Saxon squeezed the trigger, mowing down the cops—bullets riddled their chests and faces. Before the last cop had fallen over, Saxon was already drawing his 1911. Just to be sure, Saxon put a round through each of their heads. The youngest cop in the group was leaning against the wall, blood flowed out of a duo of bullet wounds to his abdomen. He looked up at Saxon with a faint mix of sadness and defeat.

"Please," he choked out. Saxon knelt before the man, knowing he was mere minutes away from bleeding out. The young cop looked at him, surprise in his eyes.

"Not quite what you expected, huh?" Saxon offered. The cop scoffed.

"You're American," he stated, the tone of disgust clear and present in his dying voice.

"Yeah," Saxon nodded, pursing his lips. "You want to ride it out or you want me to end it?"

The young cop began weeping quietly, the realization that his life was at an end hitting him like a locomotive.

"It's alright, kid," Saxon said, patting him on the shoulder. "Just close your eyes."

The cop did as he was told, squeezing his eyes shut. Saxon stood up and aimed the 1911. He pulled the trigger and the cop's weeping ended before the shell casing clattered to the ground.

Saxon fought back the urge to remember all of his fallen teammates from his SEAL days. He had known too many young men that were killed in a war that didn't mean anything to him. Just like the cop, they'd been taken off the board well before the prime of their lives, missing out on so much that life had to offer. But Saxon didn't allow himself to feel guilt. What he was doing was for soldiers—active or retired alike. That was all he needed to focus on.

"Are they dead?" Samir asked, walking up toward Saxon. He nodded slowly.

"Where's Rahman?" Saxon inquired, looking around for his associate. Samir pointed behind Saxon, Rahman was jogging over to them and reloading his rifle as he ran.

"You guys ok?" Rahman asked, bending over slightly to catch his breath. Samir and Saxon both nodded.

"Where's your brother?" Rahman asked Samir.

"Dead," he spat. He was enraged that his brother had been killed, but he knew that Qaosim was now in Heaven, being spoiled with all of Allah's treasures, including the much desired 72 *Houri*.

"Ilsa and Alaina should be in position for extraction," Saxon said. He acted as if he didn't even hear Samir say his brother was dead. In fact, Saxon was pleased that Qaosim had been taken out by the cops. It was less work for him and one more ISB prick off the table.

"Are we done here?" Rahman asked, looking around at the destruction and death they had caused.

"I think we've done enough," Saxon nodded. "Come on, we gotta double-time it to the rendezvous. Cops are swarming this place as we speak."

Chapter Thirty-Eight
Los Angeles, California

Hand in hand, Riley Hanna and John Shannon followed the host toward their table at their favorite restaurant, Majordomo. Located just off Highway 5, Majordomo offered excellent food with a casual, industrial feel. When John was home in Los Angeles, the restaurant had always been a must-do for him and Riley.

They sat down across from each other, as they'd done so many times in the past. Riley couldn't help the nervous knot in her stomach as she sat across from John Shannon. Despite the awful circumstance of their reunion, Riley was extremely happy that he was back in her life. She'd always been too nervous to share her true feelings with him. He had been an impossible person to read when they were together, still too focused on his work overseas to truly give 100% attention to life at home. John's rugged handsomeness and genuine kindness had done Riley in very early on after meeting him.

"This is really nice," John finally said, smiling warmly at Riley. "I missed you, Riles."

"I missed you too, John," Riley smiled back, trying not to blush too noticeably.

"I know I've already apologized, but I hope you know how sorry I am for the way I left things with you," John lowered his voice, the regret was plastered across his face. "Lord knows I regret a lot of things in my life."

"You don't have to apologize," Riley said, touching his hand affectionately. "I mean, yeah, I was pretty upset when you left, but I get it now. I understand."

"I'm glad," John said. He grabbed her hand, feeling extremely comforted by her presence.

"Look, Riles," John began, looking her right in the eye. "Anna and I talked before she passed."

"Yeah?" Riley asked, unsure of where John was going with that.

"Yeah. She made me promise that I wouldn't waste the rest of my life being the same miserable prick I've been for the last few years. But more importantly, she made it clear she doesn't want me to be alone," John explained.

"She sounds like an amazing woman," Riley offered, not wanting to get her hopes up in case John wasn't thinking what she was hoping for.

"She was," John chuckled. "She put up with me."

"You're not that bad, John," Riley laughed. He cracked a smile and shrugged.

"I hope not. Anyway, I just wanted you to know that," John said, giving Riley a knowing look. "I need some time, but if you'd want to, maybe we can go back to Disneyland together."

"You know, John," Riley grinned, trying to downplay her elation. "That sounds absolutely wonderful,"

"You think so?" John asked, grinning. Riley nodded enthusiastically.

"But I have one condition."

"Anything, Riles," John leaned back.

"No more cigarettes," Riley said, narrowing her eyes. John's smile evaporated in an instant, getting a rowdy laugh from Riley.

"Seriously?" he asked, suddenly yearning for his pack of Marlboros in his pocket.

"Yeah. It's disgusting, John," she commented, not budging from her stance on the issue. John sighed loudly, chuckling to himself.

"Alright, Riles," John relented. "No more cigarettes for me."

Feeling a sudden burst of confidence, Riley slowly leaned in to kiss him. They met halfway across the table, falling into a loving kiss. Riley broke away, blushing intensely, which got a laugh from John.

"How about we skip dessert?" John suggested, giving Riley a knowing look.

"Eat fast, Shannon," Riley teased.

After eating their meal without hardly taking the time to chew, John and Riley were back in the apartment the FBI had put Riley up in. Nothing special, but perfectly comfortable for a temporary stay in the city. John wrapped his arms around Riley and picked her up, kissing her neck and lips ravenously. Riley wrapped her legs around his waist, moaning softly as he nibbled on her neck. He carried her to the bedroom, laying down on top of her and kissing her deeply.

"God, I missed you," Riley groaned, leaning up to unzip her dress. She ripped open John's button-down and dragged her nails down his chest.

"Get this dress off," John growled in her ear, sending a shiver down Riley's back. Just as their lips were about to touch again, her phone rang loudly in her purse, ruining the intimate moment. Groaning in annoyance at the horrible timing, Riley rummaged through her purse on the floor and found her phone.

"This is Hanna," she answered.

John raised an eyebrow as Riley's face contorted into a look of absolute horror. Whoever had called her was giving her terrible news. As soon as Riley was off the phone, she jumped up and grabbed her dress.

"What's wrong, Riles?" John asked, concerned.

"There's been another attack," Riley choked out, turning as white as a ghost.

"Wait, what do you mean?"

"I mean there's been another attack. Right now," Riley cried. "Right here in Los Angeles!"

John jumped into action and threw his shirt back on, not wasting time to button it again. They left the apartment immediately and ran for Riley's car—a black Ford Crown Victoria. Riley got back on the phone and fired up her car.

"Where are we going?" John asked, slamming his door shut.

"Dodger Stadium," Riley said in disbelief.

"Holy shit."

Chapter Thirty-Nine
Los Angeles, California

Outside of Dodger Stadium looked like a scene out of a horror movie as Riley Hanna pulled her FBI-issued Crown Victoria into the chaos. Emergency vehicles and personnel were moving in flocks, trying to navigate between the mass exodus of fans and workers. Riley and John could both see a fair number of people with blood on them. Fires from the four propane bombs were still blazing hot, charred body parts were strewn about the bomb sites.

"Oh my god," Riley gasped as she saw the carnage. John was silent, watching through the window in horror. He'd seen plenty of atrocities during his time in the military, but that was war. War was messy, but it was also far away from his home. It was easy to separate. But this was something else entirely, this was war brought right to his doorstep.

Riley threw the Crown Vic in park and leaped out, hand on her service pistol. John was slower to get out but Riley didn't seem to notice. She hurried over to a group of three LAPD Sheriffs.

"Riley Hanna, FBI," she introduced.

"Thank fuck the feds are finally here," the shortest of the Sheriffs said. "I'm Diaz. Come on, follow me."

Diaz led Riley away toward a makeshift commander center on the hoods of three police cruisers. Several Special Weapons and Tactics (SWAT) officers and Emergency Response Team (ERT) personnel were flocked around blueprints and plans, desperately trying to organize themselves before entering the stadium.

"Guys, the FBI is here," Diaz said, gesturing to Riley. She nodded and stepped in the middle of the group.

"Are there still shooters inside?" Riley asked.

"We believe so," the SWAT Captain spoke up. "We made contact with a security team inside, but we lost contact with them. We're trying to coordinate and figure out the best way to get inside without risking any more lives."

"Fuck waiting," John Shannon blurted as he jogged past them. He walked right up to a younger SWAT officer and stuck his hand out. "Gimme your rifle. Sidearm too."

"Excuse me, who the fuck are you?" the captain barked. John ignored him, he stared at the SWAT officer intently.

"He's with me," Riley said, shaking her head in disbelief. "Give him your guns, please."

Reluctantly, the SWAT officer handed over his AR-15 and Glock 17. John racked the slide of the Glock and tucked the pistol in his waistband. Gripping the rifle firmly, John turned to the captain.

"Can you spare me a handful of guys?" he asked.

"To do what exactly?"

"Get in there, you idiot," John said. "We're just wasting time here."

"Captain, trust him, please," Riley pressed. The captain rolled his eyes and got on his radio.

"I need a team going inside now," he ordered.

John nodded his approval and took off toward the entrance of the stadium, a trio of SWAT officers on his tail.

"That's one crazy motherfucker," Diaz commented.

"You're telling me," Riley agreed. She turned back to the group. "Ok, we need to set up a triage unit and start rotating ambulances to all the closest hospitals. The Fire Department needs to get these fires out now. We wait for John to contact us before we go inside, is that understood?"

"Yes, ma'am," the group echoed, each going their own way to get to work.

Chapter Forty

Los Angeles, California

The doors to the elevator creaked open, Saxon was the first one out—his AKMSU at the ready. Rahman followed, scanning the garage tactically with his M-70. Samir, arrogant as ever, was still riding the high of the attack. He strutted out of the elevator with an annoying sense of superiority. The parking garage was vacant, not a single person to be seen or heard. By now, most of the fans and workers had evacuated behind the barricade of emergency personnel.

There was a single ambulance in the far end of the parking garage, used normally to transport injured players to the hospital if needed. The sirens from hundreds of emergency vehicles outside the stadium were blaring continuously. Saxon could even hear choppers as they circled over the stadium.

"Come on," Saxon ordered, lightly jogging toward the ambulance. As the trio of gunmen approached, the side door to the ambulance swung open. Alaina appeared in the port, dressed the role of an EMT.

"Hurry up," Alaina said, waving them inside the ambulance. Saxon nodded for Rahman to get in, he turned and covered their escape.

"This is going to be talked about for years to come," Samir boasted as he walked past Saxon.

"No, it won't," Saxon scoffed. He drew his Para-Ordnance 1911. "This will be."

Saxon squeezed the trigger, blowing a 230-grain bullet through Samir's neck. Samir dropped to his knees, blood spewing from the entry and exit wounds on his neck. His eyes glassed over as he went into shock and struggled to breathe without choking on his own blood. Cold as ice, Saxon stalked over in front of Samir, looking him dead in the eyes. He pressed the 1911 to Samir's temple and yanked the trigger, executing him in brutal fashion.

Saxon unslung his AKMSU and tossed it to Alaina, who caught the rifle and hid it in a compartment of the vehicle. She locked the compartment and climbed back into the cab of the ambulance, alongside Ilsa who was behind the wheel.

"Gray," Rahman said quietly from the ambulance. Saxon turned away from Samir's dead corpse, the sirens were getting louder and louder. "We did it. This is more than enough to take down those ISB motherfuckers."

"I certainly hope so, Rahman," Saxon sighed, taking one final look at the empty parking garage. "Otherwise, all of this was for nothing."

The door to the parking garage swung open, crashing against the concrete wall. Saxon whirled around to see four armed men filing into the garage, three of them had the word 'SWAT' on their body armor.

"Ah, what the fuck?" Saxon groaned, reaching back into the ambulance for his AKMSU. He brought the AKMSU up to his shoulder, flicking the safety switch to full-auto. Staring through the sights, Saxon pressed the trigger.

The first barrage of bullets narrowly missed two of the SWAT officers; they ducked behind a support pillar before the rounds could inflict heavy damage. John and the third SWAT officer took cover behind a Chevy Equinox. Standing up, John smashed the window of the Equinox with the barrel of his AR-15 and steadied the rifle. He pulled the trigger, firing one round at a time, knowing he didn't have any spare magazines on his person.

Rahman soared out of the ambulance, snatching up Samir's discarded AK-103—the more modern rifle was far superior to the older M-70 in a combat scenario. Dropping to a prone position, Rahman fired off a burst of bullets, aiming at the feet of the SWAT team.

"Cover me!" Saxon roared over the gunfire. Rahman leaped up to his feet and unloaded, holding the trigger until the magazine went dry. Under the cover of Rahman's AK-103, Saxon peeled off to the opposite end of the garage, attempting to get a better angle at the SWAT team.

John saw Saxon dashing away and knew exactly what he was trying to do. Throwing his AR-15 into his left hand, John fired off five more rounds, each one almost nailing the moving Saxon.

"Don't let him flank us!" John yelled to his team. He turned to the officer closest to him, his name patch said 'Patterson'. "Lay down cover fire on my mark!"

"You got it," Patterson nodded, slapping a fresh magazine into the breach of his rifle. John waited until the AK-103 stopped firing, Rahman ducked back behind cover to reload.

"Cover!" John shouted, running past the three SWAT officers and through the parking garage.

Patterson kept Rahman forced behind cover, firing round after round. He and the other two officers hopped from car to car, moving closer to the ambulance. Rahman peered around the corner of the car he was using for cover, only to be greeted by a barrage of lead. A bullet smashed into the tail light, shooting glass and plastic fragments everywhere. The jagged shrapnel buried itself in Rahman's face and neck, drawing a substantial amount of blood.

"Fuck!" Rahman cursed, dropping the rifle instantly.

"Rahman!" Alaina cried from the ambulance. She shouldered Rahman's Zastava M-70 and jumped into the fight, firing wildly at the SWAT officers. Keeping the SWAT men pinned down, Alaina moved to Rahman's side.

"Are you ok?" Alaina asked, looking at Rahman's injuries. The lacerations were deep enough for concern, but nothing life-threatening. Rahman nodded through gritted teeth.

"Let's get out of here," Rahman snarled. "Saxon will catch up."

With assistance from Alaina, Rahman got to his feet and into the ambulance. As soon as they were in, Alaina slammed the door shut; bullets smashed into the side of the emergency vehicle, the persistent SWAT officers drew closer and closer.

"Get us out of here, Isla!" Alaina screamed, reloading the Zastava.

Ilsa threw the ambulance in reverse and slammed down the gas pedal. The vehicle shot out of the parking spot like a missile. The three officers dove aside to avoid getting run over.

"Don't let them escape!" Patterson screamed, rolling to his feet and firing another burst at the vehicle. The windows on each of the back doors shattered from the bullets. The first one to his feet, Patterson sprinted after the fleeting ambulance.

"All units, all units, there is a commandeered ambulance exiting the parking garage. Do not, I repeat, do not let it leave! Suspects are on board, armed and dangerous! I say again, armed and dangerous!" Patterson barked into his radio.

His two fellow officers were right behind him, slowing only to shoot at the engine block or driver of the ambulance.

John didn't take his eyes off of Gray Saxon as he ran perpendicular to his former Commanding Officer. Sliding over the hood of a beat-up sedan, John planted his feet and aimed his rifle right at the head of Gray Saxon.

"Drop the fucking gun, Gray," John snarled. Saxon stopped immediately and raised his rifle slightly. His eyes did a double-take.

"John? Fucking John Shannon?" he asked, recognizing one of his old SEALs. John nodded, knowing he didn't need to.

"Drop the gun, Gray," he repeated. Saxon chuckled, ignoring the concussive gunfire going on in the adjacent parking section.

"Come on, John," Saxon scoffed. "We both know that ain't happening. What the fuck are you doing here anyway? Shouldn't you be overseas or something?"

"Not many opportunities to get into a firefight at Dodger Stadium, figured I couldn't say no," John quipped, very aware that Saxon had no idea he'd been given the boot by the Navy.

"Still got your sense of humor, I see," Saxon said. "I am sorry, John. I hope you know this isn't personal."

Before John could react, Saxon whipped out his 1911 and fired two rounds, striking John in the shoulder and arm. The force of the bullets took John off his feet, he landed in a heap, knocking the wind out of himself. Saxon stalked over, keeping the 1911 trained on John.

"If I wanted you dead, you'd be dead," Saxon said quietly. John was gasping for air and writhing in pain, both bullets stuck inside of him.

Gray Saxon tucked the pistol away and ran off, slipping out the exit of the parking garage while the SWAT officers were distracted with the ambulance.

When John Shannon came to, he was being wheeled on a stretcher out of the parking garage. His vision was blurry and there was a consistent ringing in his ears that made his head pound.

"What the fuck happened?" John groaned. He tried to sit up and instantly regretted it, the excruciating pain from the two bullets in his shoulder surged through his body. His eyes watered and he dropped back onto the stretcher.

"Take it easy, sir," the paramedic said. "You've been shot and you've lost some blood, but you're going to be alright, ok?"

"Where's Saxon? Riles... I need to find Riley," John mumbled.

"Just take it easy," the paramedic comforted. "Hey, gimme a hand with this!"

Another paramedic rushed over and helped hoist John into the back of an awaiting ambulance.

Chapter Forty-One
Los Angeles, California

Flanked by a 15-officer SWAT element, Riley Hanna stormed into Dodger Stadium, her AR-15 carbine at the ready. The team fanned out through the security checkpoint, careful not to step on any of the bodies. Riley found it almost impossible to not stop and try to see if anyone was still alive, but the sheer amount of blood on the ground told her any attempt was futile. Besides, someone needed to give the paramedics the green light to enter the stadium and start wheeling out the dead and wounded.

"Moving internal," Riley said into her radio, pushing past a series of double doors and stepping into the actual stadium. The SWAT team followed her lead, breaking off into teams to search the concessions and the plaza.

"Patterson, with me. We're checking the stands," Riley ordered, moving toward one of the shattered glass doors that led to the field.

"Dawkins, Myers, you two with us," Patterson said, selecting the two SWAT officers he knew the best. "The rest of you, clear the mezz and upper decks."

"Copy that," the team echoed one after the other.

Moving skillfully into the stands, Riley moved down the center staircase, making sure every aisle was clear.

Her frustration was reaching a breaking point after they had failed to stop the ambulance from escaping. Patterson's initial call had been garbled by poor reception due to the parking garage. By the time he got the point across, the ambulance was already roaring down the road and away from harm. Not a single other soul had seen Gray Saxon slip out the back amidst the chaos—he'd once again vanished into thin air like a ghost.

"Lower level clear," Patterson's radio crackled. "Moving to upper decks."

"Copy that," Patterson answered, keeping one hand on his AR-15 at all times.

After getting to the last row of seats, Riley was satisfied that the section was clear. She shook her head and gestured for the team to go back up.

"We're clear over here too," Riley said into her own radio.

"You think John is going to be ok?" Patterson asked as they bounded back up the stairs. Riley had been trying not to think about it, knowing it would only upset her further. The wounds didn't sound too bad, but there was no way of knowing the amount of internal damage the bullets had done.

"God, I hope so," Riley muttered.

"Patterson, got a body over here," a SWAT officer called over the radio. "Looks like one of the attackers."

Riley, Patterson, Dawkins, and Myers hurried over to the duo of SWAT officers hovering over Qaosim's body. His attire and weapon by his side gave away that he had been one of the attackers.

"Well..." Patterson sighed. "Looks the part, doesn't he?"

"Yeah," Riley agreed, knowing that was exactly what Gray Saxon had intended. The body of Samir had already been moved, but a second attacker of the same Middle Eastern ethnicity screamed terrorism, regardless of who was truly behind the attack. "Unfortunately for all of us."

Ten minutes later, Riley and her team were exiting the stadium, giving the 'all clear' to a massive team of paramedics and doctors. They rushed inside, pushing stretchers and carrying field aid kits.

Riley walked back over to the makeshift command center, letting her rifle hang from the harness she'd borrowed.

"Get forensics to start collecting evidence immediately," Riley said to Diaz. "Swipe all the security camera footage and get me a goddamn location on that stolen ambulance. Not a word to the media until we get everything straight, understood? We have two bodies in there of the attackers and I don't want CNN or Fox News causing a fucking national panic."

"I understand," Diaz nodded. "I'll make sure my guys are extremely careful."

"FBI will be taking over as soon as they get here," Riley continued. "Please help with whatever you can."

"Where are you going?" Diaz asked as Riley turned away. She didn't feel the need to answer.

Chapter Forty-Two
South Pasadena, California

Rahman Saleh swore loudly in pain as Alaina carefully removed the many shards of glass stuck in his face with a pair of forceps. He leaned away and took a swig from a bottle of Jack Daniels. The lack of anesthesia available to him made the process excruciatingly painful.

"Can you hold his head?" Alaina asked Ilsa. Ilsa had been staring out the window of their third-story apartment since they got back, assuming a full SWAT team would be kicking down their door at any moment.

"Uh, sure," Ilsa mumbled, steadying Rahman's head between her two strong hands. Rahman took another sip and slammed his eyes shut as Alaina went to work again.

After escaping from the stadium, the trio had ditched the ambulance and torched it; their switch car had been unnoticed and allowed them to get back to the apartment without drawing any attention to them. On the other hand, none of them had seen or heard from Gray Saxon, which was enough to give all of them a nervous stomach.

"Alright," Alaina sighed loudly, tossing the bloody forceps into the bowl collecting all of the shrapnel. "All done."

"Jesus," Rahman groaned, taking another heavy sip. "Stitch me up and let's finish this for good."

Alaina went to wash her hands and Ilsa returned to the window. Rahman turned around, studying her.

"Hey," he said. "Relax, no one's coming."

"And how would you know that?" she asked without taking her eyes from the road below.

"Have you heard from Gray?" Rahman asked, ignoring her question. Ilsa shook her head.

"No. I don't know about you, but that worries me immensely."

"Why?" Rahman asked, sitting up in the chair. Ilsa finally peeled herself from the window and grabbed a small manila folder from the kitchen table.

"Two days ago, Gray called me and wanted a full file on this guy. Bryon Hannaway," Ilsa explained, handing the file to Rahman. He opened the file and began reading. "He wanted everything and the hotel he was staying at here in LA."

"So?" Rahman raised his eye. "Maybe he knows him or something, what's the big deal?"

"You didn't hear him on the phone, Rahman," Ilsa insisted. "His voice was... deadly. Whoever this guy is, I'm sure Gray is going to kill him. And that's just another audible he's calling without consulting us."

"If you haven't noticed, Ilsa," Rahman sat back in his chair. "Gray isn't the type to share information. If he's going out to kill someone, who are we to stop him? Doesn't affect us."

"It does when a fucking SWAT team comes through the door and either arrests us or shoots us!" Ilsa shouted. "I don't want to spend the rest of my life in prison!"

"You knew that was a possible outcome," Rahman said simply. "We all did. Ryan was smart enough to kill himself and avoid that."

"I don't want to die either!" Ilsa hissed, storming out of the room.

Rahman was too far gone to understand Ilsa's loss of faith in Gray Saxon. She had believed in his crusade, but it turned into something more violent than she could've ever imagined. The prospect of killing did not bother her, she'd been asked to do much worse during her time with Britain's MI6, their Foreign Intelligence Service. But Gray's inability to share his true intentions and his unpredictability scared Ilsa more than she cared to admit. Something had changed him recently. She wasn't sure what it was, but she was going to find out before he got her killed.

Alaina came back into the room, drying her hands on a wool towel.

"Alright, let's stitch you up, Rahman," Alaina said, sitting down alongside him once again. She grabbed the needle and suture.

"Wish me luck," Rahman winked at Ilsa and took another massive sip of whiskey.

Almost as if on cue, Ilsa's burner phone began buzzing on the table. She snatched it up and answered.

"Hello?"

"It's me," Gray Saxon whispered on the other end. "Are you alone?"

"Hold on," Ilsa said, going into the bedroom and shutting the door behind her. "Ok, I'm alone."

"I need the information I asked you for," Saxon growled.

"Where the hell are you, Gray?" Ilsa shot back. "And who the hell is this Bryon Hannaway? What does he have to do with any of this?"

"Which of those do you want me to answer first?" Saxon asked. He was clearly annoyed at Ilsa's bombardment of questions.

"Where are you?" Ilsa rolled her eyes.

"None of your concern. Next question," Saxon shot back.

"How is it none of my concern?" Ilsa gaped, raising her voice. "Please tell me how that is none of my concern, considering what we just did."

"It's none of your concern, Ilsa," Saxon repeated. "If it was, trust me, I would tell you where I am."

"I don't trust you, Gray," Ilsa admitted. "Not anymore."

"I don't need you to trust me, Ilsa," Saxon said, losing his patience by the second. "All I need is the hotel and room number."

Ilsa groaned loudly, fed up. As much as she didn't want to admit it, she was pretty much stuck with them now. She'd helped with too much and at the end of the day, she was still a believer in what Gray was trying to do. He was an asshole for sure, but he was an asshole with a mission that she fully supported. Most likely, Rahman was right. If Gray wanted someone's hotel and room number, he had a good reason.

"He's at the Westin Bonaventure Hotel and Suites," Ilsa closed her eyes as she spoke, knowing she was sentencing another man to death by giving Gray Saxon the information. "Room 339."

Saxon hung up without another word.

Chapter Forty-Three
Los Angeles, California

After spending nearly four hours at the hotel bar of the Westin Bonaventure, Bryon Hannaway stumbled out of the elevator and toward his hotel room. He'd consumed enough alcohol for at least five people and was starting to feel the adverse effects of his binge drinking. Since giving up on drugs, Bryon's drinking had multiplied to fill the gap.

Leaning on the wall for support, Bryon sifted through the pocket of his hoodie for his room key.

"Where is the fucking thing?" Bryon grumbled. He reached into the pockets on his jeans and finally found the card, then slipped it into the reader. The small indicator light turned green, and the door unlocked.

Bryon slithered inside his small hotel room and kicked off his shoes. The curtains were drawn and the only source of light came from the bath-room. Bryon rapped at the wall, feeling around for the light switch.

The lamp on the desk turned on; Gray Saxon sat at the desk, his Para-Ordnance resting on the glass desk. The gun had a suppressor fixed to the end of the barrel.

"What the fuck are you doing in my room?" Bryon slurred. Despite being heavily intoxicated, his eyes still portrayed an expression of sheer surprise. Of all the people he'd expected to run into, the man who'd been having dinner with Taylor was not one of them.

"Sit down, Bryon," Saxon said, gesturing for the love seat in the corner of the room.

"I'm not in the mood, get the fuck out of here," Bryon swore. Saxon picked up the 1911 and flipped the safety catch off. He aimed the pistol at Bryon's head.

"I said sit down, you asshole," Saxon snarled. Bryon threw up his hands sarcastically and plopped down in the chair. It was not the first time in his life someone had pulled a gun on him. He had grown up dirt poor in Detroit, so getting guns pulled on him had been a regular occurrence as a teenager.

"So, what... you've come here to tell me to stay away from my girlfriend or some noble bullshit like that?" Bryon scoffed, getting comfy in the chair. "Because I'll tell you right now, if you try some of that shit again like you did in the restaurant, I will beat you silly."

"Oh, really?" Saxon said sarcastically, raising both his eyebrows. "You played pro football, right?

"Arena football," Bryon corrected.

"Oh, arena football," Saxon rolled his eyes. "So, I guess that's why you think you're some big badass, right? 'Cause you played *arena* football?"

"Who the fuck do you think you're talking to?" Bryon snapped, wanting nothing more than to pummel the smug man sitting at the desk. The 1911 quickly made him rethink that plan.

"Shut up and listen," Saxon said, resting the weapon on his knee. "Taylor is off-limits. Got it? I don't want to see or hear of you bothering her ever again."

"No, you listen to me," Bryon shot back, pointing a thick finger at Saxon. "You ain't got no right to come here and tell me not to see my girlfriend. Fuck you and your entitlement."

"She's not your girlfriend," Saxon shrugged. "So, stay away."

"Or what?" Bryon challenged. "You gonna use that gun? I bet that thing ain't even loaded, probably just for show. I've met pricks like you my whole life, get a gun and all of a sudden think they're the shit. But I see 'em for what they really are."

"And what's that?" Saxon smiled.

"You're a pussy," Bryon spat. "Just like the rest of those motherfuckers."

"A pussy, huh?" Saxon chuckled. He stood up and walked over to Bryon, kneeling down less than a foot from the man. Saxon's unbreakable gaze barred down on Bryon. He slowly pressed the gun into Bryon's gut. Bryon's eyes widened as he felt the gun touch his stomach, sweat began beading from his forehead.

"Please!" Bryon squawked, all of his macho posturing evaporated in an instant. "I won't even look at Taylor, I swear."

"I don't know if I believe you, Bryon," Saxon said, slowly pulling back the hammer on the 1911.

"I won't, I promise!" Bryon squealed. "Please, don't kill me."

Bryon's eyes were fixated on the weapon. Saxon's face broke into an evil smile, relishing in the fear he was causing Bryon. The second the hammer clicked back all the way, Bryon let his bladder go.

Saxon laughed to himself and stood up. He patted Bryon on the shoulder as the man continued pissing himself.

"Better clean yourself up," Saxon said as he headed for the door.

Sitting in his own urine and feeling utterly humiliated, Bryon wasn't about to let Saxon get the last word.

"See?" he wheezed. "I told you that you were a pussy."

Saxon wheeled around, raised the 1911, and pulled the trigger, firing a hushed round right into the base of Bryon's neck. Bryon's hands instinctively shot up and gripped the wound as blood began spewing out like a geyser. He fell out of the chair and onto his back, gagging on the blood in his throat.

His boots not making a sound, Saxon stepped over and above Bryon Hannaway, the 1911 resting at his side.

Tears were running down Bryon's face as he looked up at Saxon. Rolling his eyes, Saxon raised the gun and popped off two more rounds into Bryon's chest. His body jerked viciously from the bullets.

"Pathetic," Saxon scoffed as he watched Bryon take his last breath.

Tucking the gun into his waistband, Saxon put the 'Do Not Disturb' sign on the handle outside the hotel room and headed for the stairs.

Chapter Forty-Four
Los Angeles, California

John Shannon was thrown into surgery as soon as he arrived at the Southern California Hospital in Hollywood. The bullets had shredded most of his shoulder and upper left arm, causing severe damage to his tendons and rotator cuff.

"How's he doing?" Riley asked as John's surgeon stepped out of the operating room. He peeled off his medical mask and gloves and inhaled deeply.

"He'll be alright, the injuries were not life-threatening," the surgeon explained. "However, that shoulder is not going to be the same. He's going to have issues with mobility for a few months, physical therapy is a must."

"Fuck," Riley swore under her breath. "Is he awake?"

"Unfortunately," the surgeon rolled his eyes. "I recommended that he stayed for a few days and he just about threw me out of the room. My guess is that he's dressed and ready to go by now."

"Wait, are you serious?" Riley gasped. The surgeon shook his head and shrugged.

"The man is stubborn. I'm not going to argue with a grown man about this, I have a ton of patients from the attack to deal with. If he wants to be reckless, by all means," he said, clearly annoyed at John, but also relenting to the fact that there was nothing he could do to change his mind. He reached into his white coat and pulled out a thin bottle of pills. "Make sure he takes one a day, they'll help with the pain."

"Thank you, I'll make sure he takes them," Riley nodded, stuffing the bottle into her pocket.

"Good luck," the surgeon offered before hurrying away to another victim.

Riley pushed open the door to John's hospital room and put her hands on her hips.

"What the hell do you think you're doing, John?" she asked. John was sitting straight up on the hospital bed—he already had his boots and pants on. He was struggling to get his shirt on around the awkward bandaging around his shoulder.

"What?" John asked, almost surprised that she was questioning his decision.

"John, you literally just had two bullets pulled out of you," Riley shook her head. "Maybe you don't want to rush the recovery?"

"Eh, I'm fine," John waved off the concern. "Come on, we need to get back to the stadium."

John finally got his shirt on over the bandage and stood up, wincing at the pain. Riley rolled her eyes and shook her head. She pulled out the bottle of pills and tossed it to John.

"One a day. Please try and take care of yourself," she insisted.

"One a day, got it," John nodded, putting the bottle in the breast pocket of his shirt.

As they were walking out of the hospital, Riley's phone began ringing. She answered as soon as she could and took a few steps away from John out of habit.

"I'll go get the car," John said. Riley tossed him the keys to her vehicle and shook her head as she watched him walk away like he hadn't just been shot twice.

"Agent Hanna," she answered. She didn't recognize the number but the caller had a Los Angeles area code.

"Hey, this is Patterson. From the stadium," the SWAT officer sounded excitable.

"Hey," Riley said. "What's up, is everything ok?"

"I think I got something for you," Patterson responded, keeping the details vague. "How soon can you get to Garfield Park in South Pasadena?"

"About a half-hour," Riley said, checking her watch to figure for traffic at that time of day.

"Alright. Meet me there, be discreet," Patterson hung up without another word just as John was pulling Riley's Crown Victoria up to the entrance of the hospital. Riley hopped in the passenger seat, tucking her phone away.

"Where to?" John asked, slipping on his sunglasses.

"Garfield Park, South Pasadena," Riley ordered, pulling the directions up on her smartphone.

Chapter Forty-Five
South Pasadena, California

Grady Patterson was accompanied by two LAPD officers, Wes Daniels and Jeremy Olsen. The officers had been undercover for nearly a year, working the various drug cartels operating in the Los Angeles area. The three of them had been in the police academy together and had stayed in touch, despite taking different rounds in their policing careers.

When Jeremy Olsen had called Patterson with valuable information about the stadium attack, Patterson immediately reached out to Riley Hanna. He knew she was running point on the case and had the best chance of doing something with the information.

"How long are we supposed to wait?" Wes asked nervously, checking his watch. Being undercover for so long had made Wes extremely paranoid about being in public with other officers.

"Relax, buddy," Jeremy said, always the voice of reason in Wes's corner. "The FBI needs to know what we saw. Just focus on that and we'll be alright."

"I know, I know, but I'm still keeping my head on a swivel," Wes huffed, patting his Sig Sauer P229 handgun tucked in the front waistband of his jeans.

"I would hope so," Jeremy chuckled. Like Wes, he also had a powerful Sig P365 SAS handgun in a shoulder holster.

"Look alive, boys," Patterson said, gesturing to the black Crown Victoria coming to a stop along the curb of Garfield Park. "She's here."

Riley Hanna and John Shannon climbed out of the Crown Victoria. Patterson was utterly shocked to see John Shannon with Riley, considering the injuries he'd sustained. The two groups met halfway across the park before moving to a more secluded area.

"Thanks for coming," Patterson said, shaking Riley's hand. He looked at John and smirked. "Didn't you get shot? Figured you'd sit this one out."

"Tis but a scratch," John smirked, quoting the famous *Monty Python and The Holy Grail*—one of his personal favorite movies. The joke got a laugh from everyone.

"Alright, Patterson," Riley chuckled, getting down to business. "What's up? Your call sounded urgent."

"Yeah," Patterson nodded. He gestured to the two men he was with. "This is Jeremy and Wes, LAPD. They have some information I think you'd be interested in."

"We work undercover in the Narcotics unit," Wes began. "We've been staking out this crew of Mexicans that have been running dope out of an apartment complex not five minutes from here."

"A few days ago, we noticed two women and a man that we hadn't seen before. Keep in mind, we've been watching this building on and off for weeks," Jeremy took over. "Anyway, one day, the guy brings these other two dudes in. Real mean-looking assholes. Tall, black hair, definitely Middle Eastern descent. Initially, it wasn't that weird. The main guy also looked Middle Eastern so we figured maybe they were family or some shit."

"Ok," Riley nodded, anxiously waiting to hear the rest of the story. She was nervously optimistic for the break she was hoping these two undercover officers would provide.

"We saw the two women and the guy coming back a few minutes after the attack. The two women were wearing paramedic uniforms and the dude was bleeding pretty badly, looked like he got hit in the face or something," Jeremy continued.

"That's when we called Patterson. We heard the calls over the radio and knew he responded to the stadium call," Wes added in.

"Holy shit," John gaped, running his hand through his hair. "That's the rest of Saxon's group. I saw him escaping Creech with a woman, that's gotta be one of the women you guys saw."

"Where's the building?" Riley asked, pulling out her cellphone.

"Right down the street," Jeremy said, gesturing behind him. "They were still in the building before we came here to meet you guys. We've got another officer watching it just in case. Couldn't come here without maintaining eyes on."

"Call the FBI now!" John yelled to Riley. She gave John a dirty look, she was already on the phone with the Los Angeles Field Office, trying to coordinate a response team to meet them at the apartment building. John shrugged off the look and turned back to Patterson. "You got a spare piece I can use? Don't think I can maneuver a rifle right now."

"Course I do," Patterson nodded. "You two get back over there and make sure they're still there."

"Got it," Wes nodded. He and Jeremy took off running toward their car, a dirty gray Chevy Camaro. Once they were out of earshot, Jeremy looked at Wes and frowned.

"That's a year's worth of work out the fucking window," he commented. "The second we raid that building, those cartel guys will disappear and we'll be back to square one."

"I was just thinking that too," Wes grunted. All of their long hours and hard work infiltrating the gang would be worthless the second the FBI stepped foot into the building.

"Alright, the FBI is mobilizing a SWAT team. We need to get over there immediately and I don't want them to make it to us before SWAT can get here," Riley said.

"Come on, I'll drive," Patterson gestured for them to follow. They took off running towards Patterson's police-issued Ford Explorer.

Patterson got to the SUV first and threw open the trunk; he grabbed a small lockbox and fed a key into the lock, snapping it open with a quick turn of the key. Inside was a Beretta M9 pistol, a 9mm handgun that had a 17-round magazine. He picked up the weapon and carefully handed it off to John, keeping the barrel pointed at the ground.

John accepted the weapon and performed a brass check, the gun was loaded and ready. He made sure the safety was on before tucking the gun in the front of his jeans.

With Patterson behind the wheel, Riley riding shotgun, and John in the back, they headed for the apartment building after Wes and Jeremy's Camaro.

Chapter Forty-Six

Los Angeles, California

Gray Saxon had given up trying to fall asleep, he didn't want to disturb Taylor with his incessant tossing and turning. Gently slipping out of the king-sized bed, he slipped his feet into a pair of Vans and crept toward the kitchen. The apartment was in an alias's name, Alexander Graham, and Saxon had prepaid the first three months' rent ahead of moving in; this was contingent that the apartment would be furnished, which it was.

Saxon opened the kitchen cabinet and grabbed a half-empty bottle of Captain Morgan Spiced Rum. He twisted the cap off and flipped it on the counter, not bothering to grab a glass. Raising the bottle, Saxon took a long gulp, then cracked open the door to the patio attached to his seventh-story apartment, letting the cool night air rush into the apartment. He squeezed through the door and slowly shut it before plopping down in one of the lawn chairs.

Sleep had been hard for him to come by, pretty much since the night before he led the unauthorized mission to rescue Cassidy Minor. His subsequent capture and torture destroyed any chance he had of ever returning to a normal sleep schedule. It was too vulnerable, too calm for him to ever fully allow himself to sleep peacefully.

With everything that was going on in his life, Saxon understood that taking out Bryon Hannaway had been a stupid and careless decision. He'd never been one to second guess himself, but there was a lot at stake. The future for every single serviceman and woman was on the line and Saxon had risked his mission over a scumbag like Bryon Hannaway. He silently cursed himself for allowing him to be so foolish as he downed another couple of shots worth of rum.

"Can't sleep?" Taylor asked as she creaked the door open. She looked half-asleep and was wearing an oversized t-shirt.

"Sorry, didn't mean to wake you," Saxon said, taking another sip of rum. "Just needed some air."

"You know, we've spent several nights together now," Taylor said quietly, sitting down in Saxon's lap and resting her head on his strong shoulder. "And I don't think you've slept through the night any of those nights."

"I don't sleep much," Saxon admitted, setting the bottle down so he could wrap both his arms around her. He kissed the top of her head. "I'm sorry I woke you up."

"You didn't," Taylor said. "But when I rolled over and you weren't there..."

"Sorry," Saxon offered anyway.

"Do you want to talk about it?" Taylor asked.

"Which part?"

Taylor looked up at him seriously.

"You've been pretty quiet since Bryon interrupted our dinner," she said. She was hesitant to bring up her ex, but knew it was the smart and right thing to do. She liked Gray and did not want to give him the wrong impression.

"That's your business," Saxon muttered. Truth be told, the last thing Saxon wanted to talk about was Bryon Hannaway. For reasons unknown to Saxon, that kill was still bothering him immensely. Talking about the man certainly wouldn't help him feel any better about it.

"You can tell me whatever you want or don't want to, at the end of the day, it's your business," Saxon took another sip.

"I just don't want you thinking things about me before I've had a chance to explain," Taylor offered sincerely.

"Taylor, the guy seemed like an asshole," Saxon shrugged. "Not much else to it, right?"

"No, Gray," Taylor shot back, getting out of his lap and glaring at him. Saxon. "There's a lot more fucking to it!"

"Ok, ok, ok. I'm sorry, I didn't mean anything by that," Saxon threw up his hands. "I just don't like prying."

"It's not prying if I'm offering to talk to you about it," Taylor said with strong defiance.

"You want a sip?" he asked, offering the bottle of rum to Taylor.

She cracked a small smile and took a swig, sitting down in the lawn chair next to him. Turning his chair slightly, Saxon faced Taylor and leaned forward. Just as she was about to start talking, Saxon pulled her in and gave her a quick kiss. She blushed and shoved him away.

"I'm trying to be serious here, Gray."

"Alright," Saxon prepared himself. "What's the deal with Bryon Hannaway?"

"We met years ago, back when we were in college," Taylor began, smiling kind of sadly as the fond memories came flooding back. "He was really sweet; I was a freshman and he was a junior. Real 'big-man-on-campus' type."

"I'm familiar," Saxon muttered.

"I'm sure," Taylor chuckled. "He was an All-American defensive back in college, we both went to the University of Miami. He proposed the day after I graduated, he was already playing arena football. I said yes and we were engaged just like that. We never did get married, though..."

"What happened?" Saxon asked, taking another sip of rum. He could feel the alcohol starting to make him sleepy, which meant it was doing its job.

"He got cut from the team after a pretty bad knee injury," Taylor said. "After that, it was all downhill. He started drinking and popping pills and became a completely different man. I tried to leave him a few times, but it was complicated. I still loved him, but I couldn't take it anymore."

"Taylor," Saxon leaned forward and stared at her. He could tell by the tone of her voice that there was something she wasn't telling him. "You can tell me anything, you know that, right?"

"I do, I do," she nodded, wiping her eyes as tears were starting to form. "Even though we were together, he forced himself on me. More than once. I tried to stop him a couple of times and that's when it got violent."

Saxon sighed heavily and took a long pull from the bottle, emptying it in one gulp. He suddenly felt a lot better about having murdered Bryon Hannaway hours earlier. But as he watched Taylor blink the tears from her eyes, his guilt began gnawing at him. She'd been horribly mistreated by Bryon and was clearly still dealing with the repercussions of being in such an abusive relationship.

And Saxon was living a total lie with her. She'd allowed herself to trust him, to open up to him. All the while having no idea what he truly was.

"I'm so sorry," Saxon whispered. "I don't even know what to say."
"Don't be sorry, Gray," Taylor smiled. "I'm just so glad that I met you. I've never had a guy be nice to me the way you are."

That was enough to make Saxon consider swallowing a bullet from his Para-Ordnance. Silently, he was cursing himself up and down for getting her involved in his mission. No matter how noble Saxon thought his intentions were, he was smart enough to understand that Taylor would most likely not feel the same way.

"Yeah," Saxon choked out, hanging his head in shame. He looked up at her sadly. "You deserve better than him. And better than me, Taylor."
"What do you mean?" she asked, visibly taken aback by his statement.
"Taylor," he began, holding her hands as tightly as he could. "I don't deserve you. I've done and seen too much. And if I told you all of that, you'd see me differently. You'd see how... damaged I am."

Taylor threw her arms around Saxon and held him for a long time, not wanting to let go. When she finally let go, she looked deep into his sad, piercing eyes.

"I told you about Bryon," Taylor said. "Now, it's your turn."

Saxon sighed and patted his lap. Taylor climbed back into him and rested her head on his shoulder once again.

He started from the beginning. He told her about Cassidy Minor and how their friendship turned romantic for one night. He told her about

Cassidy's abduction and the horrific video that was made. He told her about ignoring orders and rounding up a group of shooters to rescue Cassidy. He told her about the mission and how it went horribly wrong, killing every single man who entered the building except for himself. He told her about rescuing Cassidy at his own expense.

And then he told her about his year in the hands of the ISB. How he was tortured and beaten relentlessly; the meanest militants would take turns cutting Saxon open with knives, hooks, and sharp pieces of metal—the dirtier the tool, the more likely they were to use it on him. Every time the infections would get so bad and he'd be close to death, the village doctor would give him antibiotics and heal him just enough to keep him alive. How he was fed food laced with various poisons from the area. How he was locked in rooms and cages alike for weeks at a time until the passage of time lost all relativity. How he was forced to watch the ISB militants murder and rape people to torture him even more.

He finally got to his escape, detailing how he managed to break out of captivity following a Russian airstrike. He still had to fight and kill several fighters, but the majority of the camp had been decimated. Saxon never went back to the US military and he was formally listed as MIA, though everyone assumed he'd probably been killed. He spent the next few months working his way back to the United States, under a variety of aliases.

Taylor was quiet through most of the tale, only interrupting to ask small clarifiers.

"After that," Saxon concluded. "I guess I kind of lost faith in the military."

"My god," Taylor breathed in disbelief at the harrowing account Saxon had just shared. "You mentioned you were tortured before, but I had no idea, Gray. I don't even know what to say."

"There's nothing to say," he shrugged casually. "It happened, nothing you or I can do to change it. But it changed me. I mean, it really changed me. The Gray Saxon before all of that was not the one you know now, I promise you that."

"How could it not change you?" Taylor said. "You went through hell and back. But you're still here, Gray. That's a testament to how incredibly strong you are."

Saxon pulled Taylor in for a deep kiss, slipping his tongue inside her mouth. She smiled brightly as they continued to kiss.

"Come on," Taylor whispered, breaking off the intense kiss. "Let's go back to bed."

Chapter Forty-Seven
South Pasadena, California

Patterson parked alongside the adjacent street to the apartment building. Wes and Jeremy had gone around to have eyes on the back exit. A trio of unmarked FBI SWAT vehicles were parked further down the street. Each of the three Ford Explorers had four officers inside, each man was armed with a police-issued AR-15. A pair of snipers were getting into position on top of the buildings on either side of the target building.

"You see that window right there?" Patterson pointed to the second window on the third floor of the building. "That's their apartment. Wes and Jeremy confirmed."

"Jesus," Riley breathed, pulling a pair of binoculars from the glove compartment. She popped the caps off and held up the scope, focusing on the window.

"See anything?" John asked. He was laying on his back across the bench seat in the back of the Explorer, fighting the urge to have a cigarette. This was the longest he'd gone without one since he picked up the habit in the Navy.

"Movement inside. They're definitely in there," Riley lowered the binoculars.

"Hey, Wes, you got a copy?" Patterson said into his two-way radio.

"Copy," Wes answered a second later. "Jeremy and I are in position."

"Agent Hanna just confirmed visual on targets. Targets are in the nest."

"Understood. Give the word and we're ready," Wes said, a slight anticipation in his tone. "Be advised, most of the cartel activity we've been monitoring is from the sixth floor. As long as we avoid that, we should be good. "Last thing I want is for us to get ambushed by a bunch of cartels."

"Yeah, I agree," Riley chimed in, getting on her radio. "All teams, be advised, avoid the sixth floor. We do not want to cause more trouble for ourselves."

"Stand by," Patterson said. "Malcolm, get ready. We're moving in."

"Copy that, the team is prepped and ready," Malcolm, the FBI SWAT Captain, answered.

"How do you want to play this, Riles?" John asked, pulling out his M9.

"Smash and grab," Riley said. "Kick down the door and take them all. Alive. If they are who we think they are, they'll have a way to find Gray Saxon."

"They're going to be armed," John muttered. "They're not going to want to come quietly with their hands up."

"I know," Riley said. "But we need them alive. Is that understood?"

"Yes, ma'am," Patterson said. John nodded in agreement.

"Alright, let's do it," Riley said, drawing her pistol and opening the door. Before John got out after Riley, he popped two of his prescribed painkillers into his mouth and gulped them down with a sip of water. Hopefully, the intense pain he was in would subside. Otherwise, he'd be a total liability in a gunfight.

"All teams, we're moving in," Patterson said into the radio.

Riley led the way to the apartment, her gun drawn. The 12-man SWAT team met them at the front door. Patterson smartly sent half the team around the back to link up with Wes and Jeremy. The plan was simple—both teams enter the building from opposite sides and converge on the apartment. But in Riley's experience, it was the simple plans that always got screwed. As she led the team toward the front door, she felt a nervous knot forming in her stomach. She was used to the feeling but hadn't dealt with it in a while. Since becoming a Special Agent in Charge, there had been a drastic decrease in the number of raids she actually conducted. Sure, she helped plan or run them, but she hadn't actively participated in one in a long time.

John held the door open, letting Riley, Patterson, and the SWAT team rush into the building ahead of him. He slipped inside after them and brought up the rear. Although he had no idea what to expect, he was positive they were about to get into a gunfight. The attackers he'd fought in the parking garage at Dodger Stadium were heavily armed, which made him incredibly nervous as they climbed the stairs to the third floor. In the apartment building, there were too many opportunities for collateral damage, not to mention Riley and the rest of the team.

Riley swung the heavy steel door open and moved into the quiet hallway. The team filed into the narrow corridor, their boots barely making a sound on the carpeted floor. At the opposite end of the corridor, another access door slowly opened. Wes, Jeremy, and their SWAT team stepped into the hallway.

"Which door is it?" Riley asked Patterson.

"Second door on their side," he said, gesturing to the other team. "Let's move."

They moved down the hall, moving in near silence. John slithered through the SWAT officers to the front of the group, no way he was letting Riley go in first. He nudged Riley and gave her a subtle smile.

"Be careful," he whispered to her. She nudged him back.

"Stack on the door," Patterson whispered to the teams. He turned to John and Riley. "You two hang back, I don't allow tourists to go in first."

"Dick," Riley muttered under her breath. John chuckled as he and Riley stepped back, letting the SWAT men move ahead of them. The two teams moved into position on either side of the door, Patterson and Jeremy were the first ones on their respective sides.

One of the SWAT officers jumped out of line and stepped in front of the white door. He was carrying an enforcer, a specially designed manual battering ram.

"Breach!" John hissed to him.

The officer swung the ram with every ounce of strength available to him and hit the door just above the lock. The door violently swung open, partially hanging off the hinges. He stepped back, tossing the ram aside and raising his AR-15.

"FBI! FBI!" Patterson screamed, announcing their presence to everyone in the apartment.

Patterson leaped over the broken door with his AR-15 leading the way into the small apartment. The second his boots hit the hardwood floor, bullets snapped past his head, narrowly missing him. He hit the deck, avoiding the gunfire. The team outside ducked down as a burst of fire cut through the drywall. He could hear three distinct guns—three shooters.

"Engage, engage!" Patterson screamed at the team, bending around the corner and firing five rounds from his rifle. Moving into the apartment in front of Riley, John squeezed the trigger on his pistol, shooting into the kitchen where he knew at least two of the shooters were. The third was still unknown to him.

"Patterson, I got you covered!" John screamed at Patterson, waving wildly from the SWAT team to enter the apartment. The pain in his shoulder had decreased significantly, the pills worked like a charm.

Ducking down and gritting his teeth, Patterson ran deeper into the apartment, sliding against the back of a couch for cover. Two more SWAT officers followed suit, taking cover down a short hallway that led to one of the spare bedrooms. John once again jumped up to return fire, this time catching a glimpse of a blonde woman and a Middle Eastern man shooting back at them; still no sight of the brunette John had seen at Creech Air Force Base or Dodger Stadium.

"Two shooters in the kitchen," John said as slid in alongside Patterson. "No sign of the third, but I'm positive I heard three guns."

"Yeah, me too," Patterson agreed. He grabbed his radio and ordered the rest of the team to move in.

Riley was next through the door, she fired three rounds from her Glock 17 pistol before ducking down the hall with the SWAT team. The opposing gunfire kicked up as all three guns were firing rapidly, John peered around the couch and finally got eyes on the brunette. She was kneeling in the back end of the living room, firing a military-style AR-15. The other two shooters were using the same weapons, with slightly different styles.

"Any of you fuckers got a flashbang?" John asked Patterson, attempting to reload his pistol one-handed. Patterson groaned in annoyance and took the gun away from John, reloading it for him before handing it back.

"I thought you SEAL guys were supposed to be tough!" Patterson said, giving John a wry grin.

"Fuck you. How about that flashbang?" John repeated. Patterson unhooked a small cylinder from his vest and yanked out the pin.

"Flash out!" he warned.

Patterson tossed the flashbang over his head and into the kitchen. As soon as the cylinder hit the ground, the shooting abruptly stopped. John slammed his eyes shut and pressed his hands over his ears, the flashbang went off with a blinding flash of light and the signature high-pitched ringing.

Two of the SWAT officers from out in the hall rushed in, moving past Patterson and John right into the kitchen.

"Hands up!" John heard one of them yell.

Gunshots rang out, followed by the sound of two bodies dropping to the floor under the weight of their police gear.

"Motherfuckers!" Patterson hissed, rolling to a knee and returning fire. The flashbang seemed to have little effect on the shooters. "We gotta nail these fuckers now! Fuck taking them in alive."

"Cover my ass," John hissed, crouching behind the couch. As soon as Patterson leaped back up and began shooting, John darted out of cover and rushed into the living room.

He kicked off from his right foot and flew over a small sofa. As he went airborne, John raised his M9 and fired two shots with lethal accuracy.

Chapter Forty-Eight

South Pasadena, California

The second Rahman Saleh saw the grey cylinder hit mere feet away from him, he dove aside, covering his eyes and ears. He assumed it was a flashbang, but had less than a few seconds to react—flashbangs had an incredibly short fuse. While the flashbang would still affect him, protecting your vision and hearing was paramount for a quicker recovery. Alaina and Ilsa were less familiar with flashbangs and were incapacitated as soon as the grenade went off.

Rolling onto his back, Rahman saw the two FBI SWAT officers rushing towards him. As they were barking nonsensical orders at him, Rahman flipped his AR-15 around and fired four shots, gunning down the two SWAT officers. They toppled over, still barely alive as they lay in a heap, bleeding all over each other.

Rahman got on one knee and reloaded his AR-15, slapping the fresh magazine into place. Alaina groaned in agony as her eyes were still recovering from the blinding light.

"Get up!" Rahman hissed, knowing they were about to be engaged once more. "Ilsa! Move to me."

Alaina sat up slowly and rubbed her eyes, trying to get over the effects of the flashbang grenade. Rahman's eyes went wide with surprise as he saw the man from the parking garage come flying through the living room. He fired two rounds, aimed right at Alaina. The bullets hit Alaina square in the heart, killing her instantly. She fell onto her side, her lifeblood pouring out of the two separate bullet holes.

Rahman crawled behind the small island in the kitchen, avoiding a barrage of rifle rounds. The rounds blew through the cabinetry in the kitchen, raining down wood splinters and wall fragments all over him.

Dodging the onslaught of bullets, Ilsa crawled over to Alaina, trying to find a pulse. Rahman saw her completely exposed and jumped up, unloading a 20-round burst on the cops in the apartment.

"Get some fucking cover!" Rahman screamed, grabbing Ilsa by the neck and throwing her behind the fridge. Isla fought him, trying to get back to Alaina's side. "Listen to me! She's fucking dead. If you don't want to be in the ground next to her, pick up your fucking gun and move it! We need to get out of here!"

Still in shock, Ilsa grabbed her AR-15 and ran through the kitchen to the laundry room. With Rahman laying down suppressive fire, Ilsa threw open the door at the back of the laundry room. It led to a second exit from the apartment and a back staircase.

"Get down to the car, I'm right behind you," Rahman yelled, ducking into the laundry as another response of gunfire came at him. Ilsa nodded and hurried down the stairs.

Rahman slung his rifle over his shoulder and checked his sidearm, a compact Glock 26. Tucking the pistol in the front of his pants, Rahman headed down the stairs after Ilsa.

The gunfire ceased and John rolled over onto his back. He'd landed on his bad shoulder; even with painkillers and adrenaline surging through his body, the pain was debilitating. He took a couple of deep breaths and cursed before he jumped up and moved into the kitchen. Patterson and Riley were right behind him. Shell casings littered the floor. John took a knee alongside Alaina's body, feeling her neck for a pulse.

"Anything?" Riley asked. John grimaced and shook his head, using his good hand to gently massage his bad shoulder.

The only other woman he'd ever killed had been four years ago on the mission to kill Muhammed Bakar Akhmedi. Although John had not physically dropped the bomb, he'd still called in the strike and felt guilty about it all the same. But this was a little different. This time, it had been in close quarters. John shook the rising thoughts of regret and guilt out of his head. They had a mission to finish.

"Move," John growled, raising his M9.

The SWAT team spread out, clearing the apartment room by room. John kicked the door to the laundry room open and saw the back door leading to the staircase.

"Fuck! Back exit over here!" he screamed as he took off, running as fast as he could through the door and down the stairs.

"John! Wait for us!" Riley called. John ignored her and kept running. He could hear Ilsa and Rahman at the bottom of the staircase.

"Jeremy! There's a back exit!" Patterson yelled into his radio. "Get back outside and cut them off!"

"We're already on it!" Jeremy called back. He sounded like he was sprinting.

"Sniper teams, be on the look for a man and woman exiting the building! We need them alive! I repeat, do not shoot to kill."

"Copy that," the sniper team leader answered.

"Come on," Patterson said to Riley, shaking his head. "We gotta get downstairs now."

"I know, I know," Riley agreed.

John threw himself against the door, forcing it open just in time to see Rahman and Ilsa running down the sidewalk.

"I have eyes on!" John said into his own two-way radio. "In pursuit!"

"We're coming in from the front!" Wes's voice crackled over the radio.

John came to a stop and aimed his M9; he yanked the trigger, firing a single nine-millimeter bullet. Rahman's body jerked awkwardly as the bullet hit him in the side. He lost his footing and stumbled, falling on his face. His rifle fell from his grasp, tumbling under a car parked on the curb.

Ilsa wheeled around and leveled her AR-15, firing half a dozen rounds at John. Diving behind a parked car, John avoided the bullets. He turned and saw Wes, Jeremy, and three SWAT officers running as fast as they could.

"John, we got you covered!" Jeremy yelled, leveling his Sig P365. He pulled the trigger four times, his rounds missed hitting Ilsa by mere centimeters. As Wes and the officers began shooting, distracting Ilsa and forcing her to take cover, John jumped up, moving down the row of parked cars as fast as he could.

"Ilsa!" Rahman snarled, struggling to stand back up. The bullet had severely damaged his hip. There was no way he'd be able to keep running, let alone walk. Ilsa knelt next to him, but not before blasting off a few more rounds at the small team of cops.

"Come on, Rahman," Ilsa urged. "We're almost to the car."

"Go," Rahman said through gritted teeth. The sidewalk around him was coated in a thick layer of red blood.

"I'm not leaving you, I already left Alaina," Ilsa responded.

Rahman drew his Glock 26 and aimed it at Ilsa. Her eyes widened.

"Goddammit, Ilsa," Rahman panted. "Just get the fuck out of here. Forget me. Find Saxon and finish this fucking thing. I don't want to have died for nothing."

"Rahman... I can't leave you," Ilsa said. Rahman rolled his eyes.

"Ilsa, fucking go!" he barked. He shifted his aim slightly, firing a round into the car next to Ilsa, intentionally trying to scare her into going.

She finally got the message and ran toward their car, not once stopping to look back. Rahman lowered the gun and smiled to himself, proud of Ilsa for doing what she needed to do.

John slowly stepped toward Rahman, keeping an eye on the Glock 26. He couldn't afford to have Rahman shoot himself like Ryan had.

"Drop the gun," John snarled. Wes and Jeremy appeared on either side of John, their guns equally trained on Rahman. The trio of SWAT officers took off running after Ilsa.

"Fuck you," Rahman spat.

John made an executive decision and squeezed the trigger, firing a single round through Rahman's upper arm. The Glock 26 fell to the ground instantly as Rahman clutched his shattered arm, screaming in pain.

"Cuff him," John ordered.

He dropped down and snatched the AR-15 from under the car. Hitting the release, John checked the magazine, which was a little more than half full. He slammed the magazine back into the breach and sprinted after the SWAT officers.

Ilsa jumped into their car—a Honda CRV SUV. She turned the car on and threw the vehicle into drive, slamming on the gas pedal. Spinning the wheel, she expertly spun the car around and accelerated away from the apartment.

John ran into the middle of the street, emptying the entire magazine at the back of the fleeting car. His bullets shattered the back windshield but did nothing to stop Ilsa's escape.

"Goddammit," he breathed, bending over at the knees. His lungs were on fire and he was feeling lightheaded. John knew he was horribly out of shape and it was these kinds of moments that reminded him of that.

"John, you got a copy?" Riley's voice crackled.

"Yeah, go ahead," John panted, sucking in air.

"We have one in custody. What's your status?" she asked.

"The woman got away. Get an all-points bulletin out on a silver Honda CRV."

Chapter Forty-Nine
Los Angeles, California

Gray Saxon was a nanosecond away from snapping his phone in two. A relatively peaceful night's sleep had been ruined by no less than ten phone calls. His phone would not stop ringing.

"I can't get one motherfucking goddamn night of peace. Fucking bull-shit," Saxon swore like a trucker as he got out of bed. His tirade got a small chuckle from Taylor, who was still snuggled up warmly in bed.

Saxon picked up his phone and his heart skipped a beat seeing all of the calls had been from Ilsa. Looking back at Taylor, Saxon left the room, not wanting her to hear any part of his conversation with Ilsa. He called her back as soon as he got into the kitchen and she answered immediately.

"Gray!" she cried. "They hit the apartment! Alaina is dead, Rahman's been taken into custody, what do I do? I don't know what to do, I'm just driving, but I don't know where to go!"

"Woah, woah, slow down," Saxon said. "What the fuck are you talking about?"

"The cops hit the apartment! I don't know how they found us, we were careful" Ilsa yelled, completely shaken by the whole experience.

"Fuck!" Saxon cursed. "And Alaina is dead?"

"They shot her twice," Ilsa said. "I tried to help her but Rahman wouldn't let me. We tried to make it to the car, but he took one in the side. It was bad but it looked like he was still alive. The cops were arresting him last I saw."

"Ditch the fucking car as soon as you can. After you and I hang up, you trash this phone. Get rid of anything else that could give your identity to me. Meet me at the safe house in Monterey Park. Do not get followed."

"Alright, alright," Ilsa said, actively trying to calm herself down. "I can be there within the hour. I'm gonna ditch the car and find a different vehicle."

"And you're positive they took Rahman?" Saxon clarified.

"Yeah," Ilsa confirmed. "And that guy from the parking garage was there too. Just so you know."

"Fucking Shannon," Saxon spat. "Alright, we'll figure it out. Talk soon."

Saxon hung up and started getting dressed. He threw on a pair of ripped jeans and a flannel shirt, along with a pair of tan Timberland boots. Lastly, he grabbed his Para-Ordnance and slammed a full 14-round magazine into the breach. He picked up a suppressor and stuffed it into his pocket, then tucked the pistol in the back of his jeans.

"I gotta go out for a little bit," Saxon said to Taylor. She rolled over to face him, a look of concern spread across her beautiful face.

"Is everything ok?" she asked. Saxon nodded.

"Yes, just work stuff," he said, knowing it wasn't a total lie. Taylor huffed.

"You still haven't told me what you do for work," she pointed out.

"That's more of a seventh or eighth date thing, baby," he smiled.

Taylor smiled, but Saxon could tell that comment annoyed her. Unfortunately, he did not have time to appease her or try to come up with a sufficient enough lie as to what he did for work.

"I'll be back later," Saxon said, kissing Taylor on the cheek. She kissed him back.

"See you later."

Saxon left, leaving Taylor with more questions than she cared for. She didn't have the slightest idea why he was so secretive about his job, but then again, he had been in the military. Saxon had not given her any other reason to not trust him, but as she got up and jumped in the shower, her mind couldn't help but wonder.

Chapter Fifty
Monterey Park, California

The safehouse was exactly what a safehouse should be—simple and unassuming. Monterey Park was consistently ranked as one of the best places to live in California due to its steadily increasing economy, excellent schools, and prime location. Because of this, a lot of young families populated the area. In fact, either side of the safehouse was occupied by younger families with kids still in elementary or middle school.

Ilsa was waiting nervously in the kitchen of the small house, knowing Saxon would be there any minute. She could hear the neighbor kids playing baseball outside and, strangely, that made her feel more relaxed. Ilsa had always wanted to have a family, but it just never worked out for her. Unfortunately, she'd given up on that dream many years before. The thought of adoption still nagged at her, but that was far-fetched, considering her current line of work.

There were three quick knocks at the door. Ilsa jumped up and peered through the glass window. Gray Saxon had his back to the door and was watching the street like a hawk, making sure no one suspicious was watching the house. Taking a deep breath, Ilsa unlocked and opened the door.

"Hey," she greeted, stepping aside and letting him into the house. She shut the door and locked it as soon as he was through the portal.

"Are you ok?" Saxon asked, looking over Ilsa for any injuries.

"I'm fine, I'm fine," she insisted.

"Alright, walk me through what happened," Saxon said, sitting down on the couch and propping his feet up on the coffee table. Ilsa sat down in the chair across from him.

"We went back to the apartment like we had planned," Ilsa said, leaning forward and resting her arms on her knees. "Next thing we knew, cops were busting the door down. We were able to hold them off for a while, but after Alaina got killed, Rahman and I decided to fall back. We were running to the car and then he got shot. I wasn't going to leave him, but he pulled a gun on me and forced me to go. I think he thought he was done for and didn't want me to join him."

"Noble motherfucker," Saxon scoffed. "But I thought you said he was taken into custody?"

"He was," Ilsa nodded. "As I was driving away, I saw them slapping cuffs on him. I thought he would've put a bullet in his head before allowing them to take him."

"He should've," Saxon shook his head.

"What are we going to do, Gray?" Ilsa asked, looking up at him. She was genuinely scared and completely unsure of what they were going to do having lost half of their team in the span of a few minutes.

"What do you mean?" Saxon asked, raising an eyebrow. Ilsa cocked her head, surprised by his lackadaisical response.

"I mean what are we going to do? We don't have a team anymore."

"A team?" Saxon chuckled, standing up. "Ilsa, honey, we never had a team. All we had was a group of damaged expendables. Ryan and Alaina did their jobs perfectly. Rahman, however, has just become a massive liability. That'll have to be dealt with."

"Dealt with? Jesus Christ, Gray. Rahman is one of us, he's counting on us to get him out, not kill him," Ilsa exclaimed.

"You clearly have the wrong idea of what it is I do," Saxon retorted. "Rahman should've eaten a bullet. The fact that he didn't proves two things. He doesn't have what it takes to do what is necessary and his heart is clearly not completely in what I'm trying to accomplish."

"I can't even believe what I'm hearing from you," Ilsa spat. "I thought you would show a little bit of compassion."

"Ilsa, there is no room for compassion in our line of work."

Saxon had made the decision to remove her from the equation the second he laid eyes on Ilsa. Her nervous and anxious state was of no use to him anymore. Like Rahman, she had become a liability. And like Rahman, she was a liability with too much information. Turning his back to Ilsa, Gray pulled out the suppressor from his pocket and screwed it onto the barrel of his pistol.

In the blink of an eye, Saxon drew his Para-Ordnance Black Ops 1911 and pulled the trigger, the gun popped quietly as the round exploded from the barrel. The .45 ACP round sliced through Ilsa's throat and blew out through the back of her neck. Her eyes bugged out and her hands shot up to her throat, clutching the grisly wound. Blood seeped through her fingers and leaked from the exit wound, covering the chair in a vivid red. She struggled to breathe, choking on her own blood.

Saxon walked over and fired another hushed round into Ilsa's face, executing her right in the middle of the living room. Ilsa's body fell off the chair, dropping onto the floor with a loud crash. He removed the suppressor before tucking the gun away. Saxon carefully picked up the two shell casings and stuffed them into his pocket.

He closed the blinds and drapes all over the house and made sure everything was locked before sneaking out the back. Saxon could not risk Rahman divulging any information about their plan to the cops or federal agents. If the FBI had taken him into custody, then chances were high that Rahman would be at their Field Office in Los Angeles.

Chapter Fifty-One
The White House, Washington D.C., Maryland

The tension in the Situation Room was palpable as news outlets ran and reran footage covering the Dodger Stadium attack. The president sat at the head of the table once again, his hands folded on the table and a look of permanent worry etched on his face. Around the table sat the many Cabinet members, their assistant, and a few other personnel from various three-letter agencies.

"The last time we sat here, I thought I made it crystal clear that I wanted this situation handled," the president spoke. He took a long pause, allowing his fierce eyes to land on every person sitting around the long table. The weight of the president's gaze was felt by a very select group of Cabinet members especially. The president put on his reading glasses and opened a black folder. He flipped through a couple of pages before stopping at the casualty report from the Dodger Stadium attack.

"129 dead. Another 657 injured and countless others who are going to need professional counseling for the rest of their lives. Does that sound like a situation that is being handled? I'll answer that for all of you. No, it fucking does not," the president threw his glasses on the table and sat back in his chair, crossing his arms. His face was red hot with anger and panic. He had an election coming up in eight short months and his response to this type of threat could make or break the election.

"Those numbers are estimates at the moment," the Director of the CIA, Shawn Masterson, said. "Unfortunately, we expect the death toll to be higher by the end of the day, what with all the critical injuries and everything."

"That's great, Shawn. Thank you for sharing," the president spat. Shawn shrank in his seat under the disgusted glare of the president.

"Sir, if I may," Director of National Intelligence Linda Penton spoke up. "My teams have been monitoring the situation developing in South Pasadena,"

"Go ahead, Director," the president said, giving Penton his undivided attention.

"It is my understanding that the same Navy SEAL and FBI agent who were involved with Creech exchanged fire with the attackers in the parking garage of Dodger Stadium," Penton began. "And I've just received word that they conducted a raid on an apartment building where the attackers were living. One attacker, a Swedish national, is confirmed dead. They have one man in custody and another currently at large. Gray Saxon, unfortunately, was not at the apartment and has disappeared again."

"Well, I honestly don't know what we would be doing if it wasn't for John Shannon and Riley Hanna," the president sighed. "The dead woman... what do we know about her?"

"Not much," Secretary of Defense Bill Alders said, opening the dossier he had on Alaina Nilsson. "Alaina Nilsson, 29 years old. She was a pilot in the Swedish Air Force until about a year ago. Her wingman was shot down over Syria during a recon mission. Islamic Syrian Brotherhood took credit. Apparently, she took it pretty hard. Washed out of the military a few weeks later,"

"Again, with Syria," the president sighed. "It seems to me that Mr. Saxon must've assembled a team of veterans who hate Syria and the ISB almost as much as he does."

"I would agree with you, Mr. President," Alders nodded. The president turned back to Linda Penton.

"What about the man in custody?"

"His name is Rahman Saleh. Another veteran, served in the Iraqi Army. And he also has a grudge with the ISB. He left the Army after the ISB murdered his wife and children. Act of retribution for Saleh working with us."

"Jesus. Why haven't we heard more about this ISB group? They sound horrible."

There was an awkward silence as several Cabinet members and agency heads exchanged knowing looks. The president slammed his hand down on the table.

"Enough! What are you not telling me?" he yelled, startling everyone in the room. The president had never lost his cool like that in front of anyone during his political career.

"Sir, this may have been our own doing," Alders said, not wanting to meet the president's gaze.

"Explain," the president growled.

"Well, sir, when we were combating ISIS, we helped arm and train several rebel factions in Syria. The fact of the matter is that a lot of those rebel factions united under a man named Yusuf Bakar Akhmedi. Together, they formed the Islamic Syrian Brotherhood and became nearly as dangerous as ISIS."

"Fuck me," the president muttered under his breath. "Yeah, Bill. I'd say that sounds like our own fucking doing."

The room fell silent again. The president's brain was racing in a million different directions. Finding Gray Saxon still had to be top on the list. The families of the dead and surviving victims were the next priority. And once everything settled down, the president would personally inquire as to how his administration helped arm and train a terrorist organization.

"Someone get John Shannon or Riley Hanna on the line. Tell them to interrogate Mr. Saleh. Use whatever methods necessary. We need to find Gray Saxon now," the president ordered. "And get the plane ready, I'm going to California. This country has a remarkable way of uniting during these times. It's time to remind everyone of that."

Chapter Fifty-Two
Los Angeles, California

Riley Hanna hung up the receiver for the landline in her office, having just got off the phone with the president's National Security Advisor. She'd been given complete authority to interrogate Rahman Saleh, however she chose, as long as she delivered actionable intelligence by the end of the day. The president would be in Los Angeles in a little over six hours and he wanted good news by the time he touched down.

The FBI Field Office in Westwood Village had a small detention area, which was where they elected to hold Rahman Saleh for the meantime. There was a small interrogation room attached to the detention area; roughly the size of a small living room. There was a single metal table, two chairs, and the large two-way mirror. Swiping her badge, Riley pushed open the door to the viewing room. John Shannon turned and nodded, his arms folded across his chest. He looked exhausted.

"How's it going?" Riley asked. John sighed and shook his head, gesturing to the FBI agent who was in the process of trying to question Rahman Saleh.

"He hasn't said a word," John said, defeated.

"I just got off the phone with the National Security Advisor," Riley said ominously. John looked at her quizzically.

"And?"

"POTUS gave us authority to interrogate him with whatever methods we choose. He's on his way to LA now and wants something solid by the time he gets here."

"Holy shit," John breathed, running his hands through his brown hair. "I completely forgot that the election is coming up, no wonder POTUS is getting on Air Force One. He needs us to find this asshole more now than ever."

"You're telling me," Riley agreed, having gotten an earful from the National Security Advisor. John looked at Riley hesitantly.

"What?" she asked.

"I can get him to talk," John said, biting his lip. "At least, I think I can. But you're not gonna like it."

"John, as far as I'm concerned, we just got clearance to do whatever the hell we want to," Riley said sternly. "I am not going to upset the president any more than he already is."

"Alright, then find Patterson," John said. "And I'm gonna need two five-gallon water jugs and towels. Nice thick towels."

"I'm on it," Riley said.

She left the room quickly, hoping John didn't pick up on her discomfort at the thought of him having to waterboard someone. Riley had certainly questioned a fair number of suspects and convicts, but she'd never had to interrogate someone. This was new territory for her.

John rolled the sleeves on his black and grey flannel shirt up past his elbows, buttoning them around the cuffs so they would stay in place. His FBI security badge was attached to a clip on the belt loop of his jeans. Swiping the badge, John unlocked the door to the detention room and swaggered in, kicking the door shut behind him. It locked instantly, buzzing loudly.

"I'll take it from here, kid," John said in his intimidatingly deep voice. The FBI agent looked at John with mild contempt, indignant at his sudden removal from the interrogation he was supposed to be running.

"I've been tasked with the interrogation," he responded, getting up from the table and putting his hands on his hips. "Please, go back outside."

"Sorry, buddy," John said, staring the FBI agent down. "It's my room now."

The agent scoffed in disgust and stormed out of the room, slamming the door behind him. John chuckled under his breath. Everyone at the Field Office was overly annoyed by John's presence. He pulled the chair out from the table and sat down, groaning loudly. His back was acting up again, causing him major discomfort. A few years of bouncing around in an excavator did not help his already injury-plagued body. The military had done a number on him, the construction work only perpetuated the issues.

"Mr. Saleh," John smiled without any warmth. "How are you feeling?"

"I won't talk to you, either," Rahman spat, wincing in pain. He had several stitches in his face; the gunshot wound in his torso was still raw and simple movements, like talking, just plain hurt. The paramedics had done a solid job of patching him up and doping him up with painkillers, but those had already worn off.

"Well," John shook his head. "That's a real shame because I need information that you have."

"Too bad," Rahman said, smirking at John. John chuckled and stood up. He slowly walked around the table, glaring at Rahman, who didn't look up.

Rahman stared blankly at the table, knowing how Americans liked to intimidate the men they interrogated. When he'd worked with a US Marine detachment in Iraq, he'd participated in many brutal interrogations. John did not scare him at all, there wasn't much he could do to him. Rahman had rightly figured that John wasn't FBI, based on his brief interaction with the agent who had been questioning him. Poorly, that is. John sat down on the table, right next to Rahman. He leaned down until his head was inches from Rahman's.

"You listen to me," John snarled. Rahman could taste the cigarettes still lingering on John's breath. "If there is one thing I hate more than a terrorist asshole, it's a terrorist asshole who won't talk."

"Fuck you," Rahman retorted, spitting in John's face.

John wiped his face on his shirt, chuckling at the sheer guts Rahman clearly had. No wonder Saxon had taken a liking to the guy. But, John was on a tight schedule and couldn't put up with childish bullshit. He reeled back and punched Rahman in the side of the head, his fist connecting where the majority of the stitches were.

Rahman shrieked in pain, fighting against the handcuffs on his wrists and ankles. Several of the stitches burst on impact, blood leaked out as the wounds reopened. John grabbed a fistful of Rahman's hair and slammed his face into the table, popping another two stitches. Rahman wept in pain, thrashing wildly, trying to break his restraints. John backed away and Rahman fell back in his chair, his chest heaving.

"Don't worry, Rahman," John said, patting him on the shoulder. "You'll talk soon enough. I promise."

Chapter Fifty-Three
Los Angeles, California

The door to the detention room buzzed open and Grady Patterson hurried inside, carrying a water drum in each hand. He had several towels thrown over his left shoulder; Patterson dropped the towels on the table before slamming down the water jugs. Still sitting at the table, John looked back and nodded calmly to Patterson.

"Is she there?" John asked, pointing to the two-way mirror. Patterson nodded.

"Go ahead, I'll get him ready," Patterson muttered, rolling up his sleeves. Patterson adjusted Rahman's cuffs, locking his wrists and ankles to the legs of the steel chair he was sitting on.

John exited the detention room and slammed the door shut. Riley was alone in the observation room, biting her lip nervously. John didn't have to have a major in psychology to tell that she was uncomfortable. The first time he'd witnessed an interrogation, he'd been the same way. But over the years, he'd grown a little used to the process.

"Hey," John whispered, grabbing Riley gently by the arm. "Are you ok?"

"Yes, I'm ok," she said, more trying to reassure herself than John. "I've just never had to torture anyone before."

"You're not going to lay a finger on him," John said, hoping that would put Riley at ease. "Don't worry, I've done this plenty of times, he'll break after a few rounds."

"Are you sure?" she asked, her eyes betraying how uneasy she was.

"Positive," John said. He gave her a quick kiss on the cheek and headed back into the room.

As soon as John entered, he swiped a towel from the table and folded the cloth in half once. Patterson stood behind Rahman, awaiting John's order to begin. Rahman looked at John through a steely-eyed gaze, not withering under the fear of what was to come. As John locked eyes with Rahman, he was once again reminded that the man possessed a strength few men had. It was almost admirable to John.

"Last chance, Rahman," John said coolly. "Tell me where I can find Gray Saxon."

"Go to hell," Rahman said, breathing steadily. John shrugged.

"Hold him," he said to Patterson. Grabbing Rahman by the shoulders, Patterson held him in place as John placed the towel over Rahman's face, flattening it out over his mouth and nose. John twisted off the cap to the first water jug and lifted it up, carrying it over to Rahman. The process was extremely difficult with his wounded shoulder, but he ignored the burning pain as best he could. He raised the jug over Rahman's face and began pouring the water over the towel.

It didn't take long for Rahman to start struggling, he fought feverishly to get his wrists and ankles free from the cuffs. He started shaking his head back and forth, desperately fighting to get the towel off of his face but Patterson's iron grip was impenetrable. John continued pouring water over his face, increasing the flow steadily. Patterson looked up at John and cocked his head, signaling for John to stop. He obliged, setting the jug down.

Patterson pulled the soaking wet towel away from Rahman's face and wrung it out. Rahman coughed and gagged, sucking in air and throwing up vast amounts of water. His eyes were bloodshot and his skin was pale. He struggled to get his breathing back down to a normal pace.

"That wasn't very fun, was it?" John asked, leaning down until he was eye level with Rahman. "And that wasn't even half the fucking jug."

"You're insane," Rahman gasped, spitting onto the floor. John chuckled and crossed his arms.

"Well, you got me there," he shrugged. "Now, where is Gray Saxon?"

"I don't know!" Rahman cried. "I don't know where he is, he doesn't stay with us."

"You're referring to Alaina Nilsson and the other woman, the brunette, right?" John asked. Rahman nodded.

"Ilsa," Rahman muttered, hanging his head. "Ilsa Davies."

John nodded and stepped back into the viewing room; Riley sat behind the monitors. She looked anxiously at John, having to watch him torture Rahman was a little hard for her. She cared for John immensely and knew that he had done some pretty shady things, especially for the Navy.

"Ilsa Davies," John said, leaning over the monitors next to Riley. "I need you to find out everything you can about her and see if anything comes back to Saxon. So far, that's all we have. I'll keep leaning on this guy and see what comes of it. He knows something, just need to get him to spill."

"Alright, I'll go see what I can find," Riley mumbled, getting up in a hurry.

"Riley," John said as she reached for the door. "I get it, ok. But you have to understand, a man like that isn't going to talk without pressure. He just won't. I've seen guys like him before, they don't crack easily."

"I understand, it's just weird to watch," Riley admitted.

"Which part?" John asked, stuffing his hands in his pockets.

"I care about you. A lot. And I know what a good person you are and how sweet and gentle you can be. And then I see you become this entirely different person and it's just weird," Riley admitted.

"This is just part of the job," John said, knowing he didn't have the time to assuage Riley's discomfort. "I'm sorry."

"Don't be," Riley said, opening the door to leave. "I'll see what I can find."

John nodded and hurried back into the room. Rahman had his breathing back under control, and with that, some of his confidence. Patterson had the towel flattened out across the table, ready to go for another round.

"How do I find Gray Saxon?" John asked, putting his hand on Rahman's shoulder. "You must have a way to contact him, right?"

Rahman stared up at John angrily, keeping his mouth shut. John shook his head and threw a right cross, punching Rahman in the jaw. Patterson held Rahman firmly in place on the chair while John threw another punch, knocking a few teeth out and splitting Rahman's lip.

"Where the fuck is Gray Saxon?" John snarled. Rahman spat out a wad of blood and a lost tooth, but did not answer. Patterson grabbed the towel and wrapped it around Rahman's head, much tighter than the first time.

"So be it," John muttered, shaking his head. Crouching down, John picked up the water jug.

Chapter Fifty-Four
Los Angeles, California

All was quiet in the interrogation room. Rahman was drifting in and out of consciousness, blood leaking from close to a dozen facial injuries. Grady Patterson leaned against the wall, sipping from a plastic water bottle. He was beyond frustrated and exhausted. John Shannon had pushed the table against the back wall and was sitting on it; a bottle of Southern Comfort in his right hand. He had been interrogating Rahman without stopping for nearly three and a half hours, the stress of the situation was becoming unbearable. Instead of smoking again, John had Patterson get him a bottle of SoCo to calm his nerves. If John ever started smoking again, there was no way he would be able to stop a second time. The whiskey, while not the nicotine that John's body craved so badly, did help to alleviate some of the symptoms of withdrawal he was feeling.

John knew that the president of the United States would be landing shortly and it would not be good for him or Riley if they had nothing valuable to report. Riley had chosen not to watch the rest of the interrogation, having got her fill from the first go around at waterboarding Rahman. Though, she was equally frustrated. Her search for an 'Ilsa Davies' had turned up next to nothing. It appeared that much like Gray Saxon, Ilsa Davies was also a ghost.

"Why won't you fucking talk?" John asked quietly, taking a monstrous sip from the bottle. "Why are you making me fucking kill you? Just tell me what I want to know."

Rahman looked up at John, both of his eyes were swollen so much he could barely see the man sitting only a few feet from him. His entire body hurt so badly, he wanted nothing more than to just die. He'd surrendered to the fact that he was going to die the second he fired into the crowd of concert-goers at Lollapalooza. No one could get away with something like that and still walk the Earth. Rahman Saleh had fought his fight, he'd done his part in avenging his family. Now, all he wanted was to see them again.

"My phone..." Rahman croaked. John set the bottle down and jumped off the table. He took a knee right in front of Rahman.

"What about it?" John asked, gesturing for Patterson to get to work. Patterson slipped out of the room, on a mission to find Rahman's phone.

"Saxon didn't stay with us," Rahman spoke in a ragged voice. "I tracked his phone and found out why. He's been living with a woman, Taylor Lavine. The information is on my phone."

"Holy fuck," John breathed, darting out of the room.

A few seconds later, Patterson came running back into the viewing room with a clear evidence bag. Inside was Rahman Saleh's iPhone. John ripped open the bag and grabbed the phone—he tried to unlock the device but was deterred by the passcode lock. An eight-digit code was needed to open the phone. He ran back into the interrogation room, phone in hand; he didn't bother to close the door.

"Rahman, buddy, I need the code to open it," John pleaded, showing Rahman the device. Rahman took a deep breath and began giving him the code.

"Six-Nine-Four-Three-One-One," he called off the first six digits. John punched the code in quickly, awaiting the last two digits.

The rifle sounded like an explosion, echoing through the entire floor of the FBI Field Office. The bullet, a .338 Lapua Magnum, cut through the two-way mirror like butter, shattering it upon impact. Dropping slightly, the round hit Rahman Saleh in the gut; he doubled over in pain. The second round was a millisecond behind the first one. It entered through the top of Rahman's head, impacting at the precise moment he keeled over. The round tore through his brain and skull before slowing down somewhere in his back; he was dead instantly, his head was split open like a piece of wood that had been struck with a broadax.

John threw himself flat against the ground as a third round soared into the interrogation room, hitting Rahman again in the head. Rahman's head popped like a water balloon, spraying blood and brain matter all over the back wall. Like John, Patterson was on the ground as well. He had his Glock 17 drawn, but was in no position to return fire without exposing himself to the sniper.

He looked up at Rahman, his head in pieces all over the room and wall. John had been so close to getting valuable information, and in an instant, it had been ripped away from him. The feeling was both demoralizing and defeating, to know he was so close. An idea popped into John's head and he suddenly looked around frantically. The phone was sitting undisturbed next to Rahman's foot; John swiped the phone and stuffed it in his back pocket. Two numbers would be much easier to crack than eight. The Crime Techs at the Field Office could hopefully gain access to the phone, especially having more than half of the passcode. John made a mental note to bring the phone to them as soon as he could.

Another round blasted through the interrogation room, whizzing past the top of John's body.

"He's dialed in on us," John spat in disgust. There was no doubt in his mind that the shooter was Gray Saxon. The sniper was positioned across the atrium and at least two floors above them, giving him a prime look right into the interrogation room. If John or Patterson were to expose themselves, they'd certainly be shot before they could make it to the door.

"What do you wanna do?" Patterson asked, moving slowly closer to John. "Someone will have heard those shots, backup will be on us any second."
"All he needs is a few seconds to disappear again, trust me," John said. "There's a gun out in the viewing room, right?"

"Yeah, check the drawer," Patterson nodded. "I'll cover you if you're making a move."

"On three," John said, getting to a low crouch. "One... two... three!"

On John's count, Patterson raised his Glock 17 and peered around the shattered mirror. He blasted off the entire 17-round magazine as fast as he could. Under the cover fire, John darted into the viewing room. Throwing open the top drawer on the desk, John found a spare pistol, a Sig Sauer P226. Alongside the pistol, he found three 15-round magazines; John slipped the two spare magazines into his back pocket before slamming the third into the breach of the pistol. He snapped the slide forward, chambering the first round.

"Grady, move to me!" John yelled, raising his gun and firing at the sniper, forcing him back away from view under the metal railing. Patterson sprinted out of the interrogation room, stopping at the other side of the door across from John. He quickly reloaded his Glock 17, tossing the empty magazine back into the room.

"You ok?" John asked, looking over Patterson for any wounds. Patterson nodded, sweat dripping from his established forehead.

"I'm good," he said, breathing heavily.

"Good. Get ready to move," John said. "We're going after that fucker."

Chapter Fifty-Five
Los Angeles, California

Gray Saxon ducked behind the railing as a barrage of bullets from John and Patterson rained down on him, satisfied with his shots. Seeing Rahman Saleh's head explode brought him a strange feeling of comfort. Yet another loose end Saxon had been able to take care of. He'd become accustomed to being alone, only depending on himself. His team had been necessary to complete his plan, but they had always been expendable. Saxon certainly never trusted them with his life or put himself in a situation to rely on them for anything. They had been a means to an end, nothing more. On his own again, Saxon felt comfortable. And in a strange way, that feeling of comfort pleased him immensely.

He rolled behind a concrete planter, unbeknownst to the two shooters below him. His hands worked the bolt of his preferred sniper rifle, a Remington Modular Sniper Rifle that he'd taken from Sulieman Khatib's Chicago hotel room. Back in his SEAL days, the MSR had been his go-to rifle, preferring it over any other sniper platform the military offered. He'd taken the liberty of fitting this MSR with a suppressor, bipod, and thermal scope, which gave him the upper hand when shooting through rooms.

After leaving the safehouse in Monterey Park, Saxon double-timed it back to Los Angeles. The FBI Field Office was the only logical place for them to take Rahman, considering John was working so closely with the Bureau. From there, it was a rather simple matter to get onto the roof of the Field Office, via the window cleaners' gondola. Murdering the two-man crew of washers was a small price to pay for admission to the Field Office.

There was a lull in the gunfire, Saxon could now hear the distinct sounds of the emergency alarms echoing through the building. The FBI would be locking down and flooding the building with cops to seal off any chance at escape. Four floors above Saxon's current position, there was a hole in a glass window where he had entered the building. The gondola was right outside the window and was Saxon's shot at a clean getaway.

Thumbing the release, Saxon dropped his half-empty magazine and fed three more cartridges into the bullet before slamming it home. Peeking over the railing, Saxon saw John and Patterson rushing down the hallway to the staircase. An FBI tactical team, about five agents, were waiting for them. Saxon swung his rifle up and flipped the bipod out, propping the gun up on the railing. Carefully selecting his target, Saxon squeezed the trigger, firing a round through the kneecap of the shortest agent in the tac-team. He racked the bolt, loading a fresh round into the firing chamber, and adjusted his aim a few centimeters before squeezing the trigger again. A second FBI agent was hit, this time in the arm. The round shredded his wrist, nearly blowing his hand off. The appendage was held grotesquely to the rest of his arm by a few tendons, the bone having been shot away by the bullet. With two of them now unable to fight, the team was forced to find cover. He'd deliberately shot to wound, knowing it would be disheartening for the rest of the team to see their comrades shot to pieces.

Attention would turn to the wounded as well, giving Saxon some much-needed time to plot his route back up to the window cleaners' gondola.

Saxon fired another round, narrowly missing Grady Patterson's shoulder. Getting to his feet, Saxon slung the rifle across his back and took off running. As he ran, Saxon drew his Para-Ordnance and flipped the safety off; he expected to run into trouble. Rounding the corner, Saxon saw the same staircase he'd descended down to get into position to take out Rahman. He smiled inwardly and sprinted toward the steps, running as hard and as fast as he could.

John looked up and saw Saxon darting back further into the building. Although John was not super familiar with the layout of the Field Office, he knew there were staircases on opposite sides of each floor. That had to be where Saxon was headed.

"Grady, get Riley on the radio!" John ordered. "Tell her to lock off the staircases on the northwest side of the building and get another team up here now."

"You got it," Patterson said, yanking his radio off the clip on his belt. "Riley, it's Grady, you got a copy?"

"Go ahead," Riley answered.

"Gray Saxon is inside the building! Lock down the northwest staircase and get a team over to our position, we've got wounded."

"Copy that, a team is on their way to you. I'll take a second team and head for the staircases," Riley responded. "Have John meet up with us if you can."

"Tell her I'm already on it," John muttered, giving Patterson a wry grin. "Do any of you have a radio I can borrow?"

Patterson ripped a radio off the belt of the FBI agent who'd been shot through the knee. He flipped the radio onto the right frequency and tossed it to John, who caught it and clipped it to his back pocket.

Ducking, John sprinted down the corridor; he could see Saxon running two floors above him. Saxon was fast—a lot faster than John had expected. John slowed down and turned the corner. The main staircase was less than a hundred feet away. He reloaded his Sig Sauer on the run and bounded up the stairs, half expecting to run into Gray Saxon on his ascent. John paused, listening for Saxon on the staircase. He heard him running hard up the stairs, he was still at least two floors ahead of John.

"He's moving up towards the 12th floor," John said into his radio. "Lock down the 12th floor!"

"12th floor, got it!" Riley yelled back. John sucked in air and bounded up the stairs two at a time, trying to close the gap between him and Gray Saxon.

Chapter Fifty-Six
Los Angeles, California

Riley Hanna, along with a six-man FBI Tactical Team, stepped out of the elevator onto the 12th floor of the Field Office. She kept her finger slightly off the trigger of her M4A1 carbine, but was ready to engage at the first sight of trouble. Close-quarter scenarios had been one of her spe-

cialties during her time at the FBI Academy. As opposed to hard interrogations, which made her incredibly uneasy, the thrill of close-quarter
encounters was something she'd always loved.

"Spread out," Riley said to her team. She adjusted her vest slightly,
which carried several spare magazines for her rifle. The team crept down
the hall, Riley led the way.

"I've got our rear," a female agent said, swinging around to make sure
Saxon didn't come up behind them.

"Where the hell is he?" another agent muttered under his breath.
There was an unmistakable sense of dread among the seven agents.
They'd all heard about Gray Saxon and none of them wanted to get into a
firefight with him.

"Cut the chatter. Stay focused," Riley said harshly, not wanting to give
away her own nerves about the situation. The team fell silent as they kept
moving, clearing a series of offices. The emergency alarm was still blaring, adding a frightening ambiance to their predicament.

"John, what's your location?" Riley muttered into the radio mounted on
the shoulder strap of her vest.

"I'm on the 12th floor moving towards the labs," John said. He sounded
winded.

"Copy that, we'll be right there," Riley turned to her team. "Labs, double-time it."

Picking up the pace to a steady jog, the team cut through a labyrinth of
cubicles, a shortcut to the crime labs at the northeast corner of the building. Riley threw open a door that stood in their way, letting the team
move into the lab before her. John Shannon was at the opposite end, his
Sig tucked in the front of his waistband.

"You didn't see him?" John asked, taking a few deep breaths; sweat was
dripping from his forehead. Riley shook her head.

"I don't understand, I thought you said he was on 12," Riley commented, lowering her gun. John shrugged.

"He was," John muttered. "He's gotta be here somewhere, come on."

John drew his gun and left the lab through the back exit, coming out in the middle of a long corridor. He instantly felt colder as he stepped into the hallway. Turning to his left, John saw the window at the end of the hall had been shattered.

"Jesus Christ," John groaned, running down the hall.

"John! Wait for us," Riley called before taking off after him, the team on her heels.

John guessed the window had been cut open with a small handheld torch—a common tool that could be bought at most hardware stores. He crept closer to the window and saw the window cleaners' gondola on the ground. Shaking his head in disbelief, John stepped back from the window and punched the wall.

"Goddammit!" he cursed, dropping to his knees. He looked up at Riley, who was now just seeing the broken window.

"Who the fuck is this guy?" Riley asked rhetorically, absolutely dumbfounded that, once again, Gray Saxon had vanished into thin air.

"You better have someone check the roof," John commented. "My guess is we've got some dead window cleaners around here."

On the gondola ride to the ground, Saxon had disassembled the MSR and stuffed the components into a grey duffle bag. The coveralls he'd taken from one of the dead window washers had come in handy; he slipped into the dirty blue work uniform and zipped up the front before stepping off the gondola. Throwing the duffle over his shoulder, he walked confidently away from the building, wanting to get back to his apartment and make love to Taylor as soon as he could.

Chapter Fifty-Seven
Los Angeles, California

The presidential motorcade was both intimidating and impressive; close to 20 vehicles all outfitted with bullet-proof glass and filled with heavily armed Secret Service agents. The FBI Field Office had been made aware that was the president's first stop the second he touched down in Los Angeles. Despite the threat of Gray Saxon, the president was insistent that he speak to Riley Hanna and John Shannon first. His next stops would be to visit the various hospitals where victims of the Dodger Stadium attack were being treated.

A secure perimeter had been set up around the Field Office in preparation for the president's arrival. National Guardsmen and FBI Tactical personnel patrolled around the front of the building. In addition to the massive manpower surrounding the building, several armored Humvees and SWAT vehicles lined the street leading to the Field Office. Each Humvee was mounted with a massive Browning M2HB, a .50 caliber belt-fed machine gun.

Riley Hanna paced nervously in the large conference room on the second floor of the FBI Field Office. She had the entire room ready for the president and his group of advisors that would no doubt be traveling with him. As soon as it had been confirmed that Gray Saxon was in the wind again, John took Rahman's phone to the IT specialists, hoping they could get into the phone before the president got there.

"Come on, John," Riley muttered under her breath. She checked her watch for the millionth time. "Where the fuck are you?"

The elevator doors opened and a squad of Secret Service agents stepped off, flanking the president and his advisors. They walked purposefully toward the conference room. Riley barely had enough time to flatten out her blue FBI shirt before the doors swung open and the president walked inside, smiling kindly at her.

"Agent Hanna, good to see you again," he greeted, sticking out his hand. The president was being kind, but Riley could tell he was deeply bothered by the events that had transpired. "I was disappointed to hear Gray Saxon got away. Again."

"As am I, Mr. President," Riley said, hanging her head slightly. "We're still trying to figure out how he managed to breach a secure facility without raising any alarms."

"I'd be curious to learn that as well," the president commented, taking a seat at the table. He didn't bother to introduce any of his advisors. "It's even more disturbing that Mr. Saleh was killed before we could interrogate him further."

"That seems to be the sole purpose of Saxon's infiltration," Riley said, kind of impressed that the president was so up to speed with everything. "Clearly, Mr. Saleh had valuable information that Saxon did not want anyone to know."

"Clearly," the president said, almost sarcastically. Riley winced at the comment, hearing how displeased the Commander in Chief was through the sharp tone of his voice.

"Well, where is Mr. Shannon?" the president asked, looking around the room for John.

"I'm so sorry, he'll be here soon," Riley said, checking her watch again. "And he's hopefully going to be coming with valuable intel."

"Elaborate please, Agent Hanna," the president said, waving his hand. Riley swallowed and sat down across from him.

"Before Saxon killed him, we were able to get partial access to Rahman Saleh's phone. The phone was highly encrypted, but Saleh gave us more than half of the code before he was shot. John brought the phone to our IT guys to see if they could get through the last two numbers."

"And I'm glad I did," John remarked as he walked into the room; he was carrying a folder and Rahman's phone. He stuck his hand out toward the president. "Sir."

"Mr. Shannon," the president shook John's hand firmly. "Please tell me you have something."

"I sure do," John nodded, sitting down next to Riley. "It appears that Mr. Saleh was getting suspicious of Saxon... a little paranoid I guess. Anyway, he was tracking Saxon's phone and found out that he'd been living with a woman, Taylor Lavine."

John opened the folder and took out a small file on Taylor Lavine, including a few pictures. He handed the papers over to the president, who scanned through the pages just long enough to get a grasp on the type of woman Taylor Lavine was.

"She doesn't raise any red flags," the president thought out loud.

"No, sir, she doesn't," John agreed. "I don't think she's involved with any of this. My guess is that she probably has no idea who Saxon really is or what he's been doing."

"What makes you say that?" the president asked, handing the papers off to one of his assistants.

"Call it a gut feeling, but I do have something a little more interesting than that to share with you," John carried on, pulling out a photo of Bryon Hannaway's bullet-riddled body, and sliding it across the table to the president. The president grimaced at the picture.

"Who is he?" the president asked.

"That is Bryon Hannaway," John said. "And before Mr. Hannaway was a washed-out semi-pro football player, he was a legend at the University of Miami. Which is also where Taylor Lavine went to school. Turns out, they were engaged for a while until Taylor broke it off. Bryon must've taken it pretty hard because she filed a restraining order against him a few months ago."

"And now he turns up dead after she's with Gray Saxon," the president shook his head. "You think Saxon killed this guy?"

"Sure do. Bullets that killed Bryon matched the ones we pulled out of some of the victims from Dodger Stadium. Saxon definitely killed him. Which was a major mistake, if you don't mind me saying."

"How so?" the president raised an eyebrow.

"Saxon gave us a thread to pull," John answered. "The thread connects to Taylor Lavine. All we have to do is pull, sir."

"Then by all means, John," the president said, looking at John and Riley sternly. "You pull that thread."

"I'm working on that as we speak," John confirmed. "Once we have a possible address, we'll be able to move on her."

"I'm trusting you two to get this done. If you need anything, you have to tell me," the president stressed. "I'm afraid if we don't, we'll be forced into another conflict. You should have seen the protests outside the White House this morning. They want war."

"I'm not surprised," Riley admitted. "Those protests have been trending on Twitter as well. Looks like a lot of people want to react."

"Sir, that's what Saxon wants," John said. "Think about it, sir. He hates America almost as much as he hates the ISB. What's a better way for revenge than to pit the two sides against each other?"

"That would explain bombing that village with our drone," the president muttered.

Everything was starting to make sense to him. Saxon was trying to get America involved in another war, while simultaneously fueling the ISB's already prevalent hatred for America. The president was now caught in an impossible position. To retaliate against the ISB would definitely earn him positive press with his voters, but the ISB wasn't truly responsible for these attacks. Yes, they'd killed American soldiers; hell, the ISB had filmed the rape of an American pilot and sent it all over the internet. On the other hand, another long-term conflict in the Middle East was the last thing America needed. The president was not sure how many people would buy the Gray Saxon story if they chose to make it public. It was much easier to believe it was the ISB than a former Navy SEAL.

"We need to go public with this," the president ordered. "We need to out Saxon and wipe him off the board. I don't care if he comes in a body bag or handcuffs. Set up a press conference and tell the whole world who's really behind all of this shit. That's an order."

Chapter Fifty-Eight
Mashabim Air Base, Israel

Michael Jameson and Jason Davenport sat outside their barracks, smoking cigars and talking quietly to themselves. They were wearing camouflage pants and DELTA t-shirts, not bothering to wear their full fatigues. Since their raid and capture of Khaled Al-Khatib with John Shannon, the lives of the two Delta Operators had been pretty quiet, save for a few quick recon missions. News of the Dodger Stadium attack had reached the base a few hours prior. They wondered whether or not the attack was connected to the Chicago shooting.

"How long before we go to war again?" Davenport asked, puffing on his Macanudo.

"If the ISB really shot up a goddamn baseball game, I give it a few weeks," Jameson answered, blowing out a thick circle of cigar smoke. "You talked to your wife yet?"

"Tried to call her, no answer," Davenport grunted.

His wife and three small children lived outside of Los Angeles in Anaheim, within walking distance of Disneyland. Davenport had been at odds with his wife for some time now; he hated thinking about it, but he knew that they were likely headed for divorce. She had practically begged him not to deploy again—their third child was less than a year old, and she needed his help. But Davenport couldn't pull himself away from the military. At 33 years old, he still considered himself to be in the prime of his life. The truth was that he loved every second of being in the military, and as much as he loved his family, he wasn't ready to quit.

Michael Jameson was a completely different story. He was counting down the days until his deployment was over, and once it was up, he would never go back again. He was only three years older than Davenport, but looked at least ten. The war had taken its toll on him and he was just tired. Tired of fighting and tired of wishing he was back home. He'd become disenfranchised with the military many years before, but hadn't fully realized it until recently. He had four daughters who were getting older and he did not want to miss the most important years of their lives. To Jameson, nothing was more important than his daughters.

He smiled at the thought of his girls and looked up into the clear sky, not a cloud to be seen for miles. It always amazed him how the strangest places on the planet had some of the most beautiful views. Jameson leaned back in his lawn chair, the cigar resting in between his lips. He closed his eyes, allowing himself to relax and think of home.

Just as he felt himself drifting off, screaming from the front gate jolted him back to reality. Davenport leaped up, tossing his cigar into the dirt.

"Front gate, front gate!" Davenport yelled, scooping his M4A1 up from the ground. He picked up Jameson's rifle and tossed it to him.

"The fuck is going on?" Jameson asked, knowing Davenport was equally surprised by the sudden commotion.

They sprinted toward the front gate, seeing a throng of Israeli and American soldiers just outside of it. Jameson caught a glimpse of two men walking toward the gate, dressed in traditional Middle Eastern garments. Several American soldiers were screaming for them to stop, warning them they would shoot.

Davenport shouldered his rifle and aimed at the two men, taking up position alongside a female Israeli soldier. He flipped the safety off his rifle. Jameson followed suit, raising his rifle.

"Stop moving!" Jameson screamed. The soldiers recognized him and Davenport as Special Forces and let them take charge. The two men ignored the order.

"Stop moving or we will fucking shoot you!" Davenport shouted. He looked over at Jameson, unsure of what to do.

"Fire at their feet!" Jameson said, only to Davenport. Jameson and Davenport each popped off a round, aiming at the sand at the feet of the two men.

They stopped moving and stood in front of the group of soldiers, completely frozen. One of the Americans shined his weapon light on them. Davenport shuddered slightly, he could see the burning hatred in the eyes of both guys. Clearly, they were not friendly.

Jameson instinctively looked at their hands, trying to determine if either of them was carrying a detonator or trigger device. He saw no such device, but that did nothing to comfort him. There wasn't a doubt in Jameson's mind that these two men were wearing explosive vests. If he shot them, a dead-man switch could activate the bombs. And If he didn't kill them, they'd probably still blow themselves up.

"What do you want to do, Mikey?" Davenport asked, taking a step toward the two men.

"Stay right the fuck there," Jameson said to the two. "Everyone, back inside now. Davenport, eyes on these fuckers."

"Sir?" one of the Americans questioned.

Before Jameson could tell the soldier to hurry up, both men produced detonators from their pockets.

"Sheik Yusuf Bakar Akhmedi sends his regards," the shorter of the two men said in perfect English. He gave the soldiers a crooked smile.

Jameson and Davenport threw themselves aside as the two men detonated their vests, blowing themselves up in a horrific explosion.

Chapter Fifty-Nine
Los Angeles, California

Taylor Lavine had been on the phone all morning with several different photographers. As she'd decided to stay in L.A. for the time being, she needed to line up some modeling work as soon as she could. She's always been an independent woman, and as much as she liked Gray, she wasn't about to let him pay for her to live out here with him. There were many perks to being a model in Los Angeles; there was no shortage of work or photographers and the money offered was exponentially more than back home in Florida. The porn industry was incredibly prevalent in Los Angeles and while Taylor had never gotten too involved in that specific industry, she had done several softcore-solo scenes that paid much, much better than regular photoshoots.

After a promising phone call with an acclaimed photographer, Taylor went into the kitchen and got out the supplies to make a margarita, her personal favorite drink. She flipped on the small TV on the kitchen counter, switching to the local news channel, more for background noise than anything else. As she sliced a few limes and began mixing her drink, she heard the distinct theme of 'Breaking News'. Pouring a couple of shots worth of tequila into her glass, Taylor turned up the volume so she could hear better.

"...And in just a few moments, the Federal Bureau of Investigation will be holding a press conference," the older news anchor was saying. "The reason for which is still unknown, but we can only assume it has to do with the horrific terror attack that happened during a playoff game at Dodger Stadium."

"Such a horrific incident indeed, Tom," the female co-host chimed in. "The official death toll has still not been confirmed, but estimates are in the high 130 to 140 range. Countless more are still in critical condition."

Taylor's cell phone began ringing loudly, snapping her attention away from the newscast. She answered her phone immediately, smiling to herself when she saw who was calling her.

"Hi, Mom!" she answered brightly.

Taylor and her mom, Tanya, hadn't always been close, but as Taylor grew up and matured, they developed a very strong relationship. Taylor shared everything with her mom—the two kept no secrets from each other. Even Taylor's racier jobs had been completely supported by her mother. Tanya had Taylor when she was only 17, a few short months after graduating high school. In order to provide a stable life for her daughter, she worked a minimum of two jobs at any given time. Mostly waitressing and bartending, once she was of age. But those jobs rarely covered the bills, which is what led Tanya to the exotic dancing industry.

"Hi, sweetie!" Tanya replied, thrilled to hear her only child's voice. It had been a while since they'd last talked. Taylor had told her mom she was staying in California for longer than expected, but left out the part about Gray Saxon.

"Are you ok?" Tanya continued. "I've been watching the news, I don't know how close you are to L.A. but I needed to hear your voice. I've been so worried."

"Yeah, I'm ok, Mom," Taylor said, instantly feeling bad for not having called her sooner. "It's scary for sure, but I'm ok. I promise."

"Good," her mom sounded more at ease. "Are you still with your friends?"

"Not exactly," Taylor said, not wanting to completely lie. "I'm with some friends that live out here, they're letting me stay at their place until I figure out what I want to do."

"Well, as long as you're ok. You're an adult, I won't judge," Tanya chuckled, remembering how headstrong she had been as a teenager and young adult, even after having Taylor. Despite being a kid when she had Taylor, Tanya knew she had done a good job raising her. She was smart, confident, and hardworking—all things that she'd gotten from her mother.

"I'm sorry, Mom," Taylor said, suddenly overwhelmed with guilt for not calling her. The attack had been world news, of course her mom was going to worry. "That was super selfish."

"Baby, as long as you're ok, that's all that matters," Tanya responded.

Tanya proceeded to tell her about one of the guys at the gym who had been trying to flirt with her for the past week. She looked great for her age and was no stranger to getting hit on, similar to Taylor. Taylor laughed and reached for her drink, catching a glance at the TV. The press conference was just about to start. A young female FBI agent walked out to the podium, flanked by several other law enforcement officials. The subtext on the TV indicated that the FBI agent was Special Agent in Charge Riley Hanna.

"Thank you all for coming and for bearing with us during these last few weeks," Agent Hanna began. Taylor turned up the volume slightly, still trying to listen to her mom's story.

"It's been a very difficult time for all of us, but I am confident that we are at the end of this reign of terror. Make no mistake, the people responsible for these senseless attacks are cowards. They're not strong, they're not powerful, they're weak. They attacked places that we go to have fun, to enjoy life. No one should ever have to fear for their life at a baseball game or a music festival."

"That being said, I'm here before you to set the record straight. There has been lots of talk and discussion online about who is responsible for these attacks. Many of you are familiar with the Islamic Syrian Brotherhood, commonly referred to as the ISB. Three bodies were found in the hotel room overlooking Lollapalooza; the hotel room that the attackers were shooting from. These three men were confirmed to be allies of the ISB. Additionally, there were two bodies found in the parking garage at Dodger Stadium, and they also had connections to the ISB," Agent Hanna paused, looking at someone to her left, out of the camera frame.

"Hey, Mom, are you watching the news?" Taylor blurted, her attention was now glued to the TV.
"No, I'm at the mall right now. Why? What's going on?" Tanya asked. Taylor didn't answer but turned up the TV a little louder.

"After an extensive investigation, we believe that these attacks were orchestrated to look like the ISB was responsible. But they are not. The motive as to why someone would frame them is still officially unknown, but we do have some idea. And that brings us to the 'who' part of this case. Like I said, this is not the ISB, but the work of a small group of former military operatives. A small group that was being led by one man."

Agent Hanna nodded to one of the officers alongside her. He turned just out of frame and grabbed a large printed photo; he placed the photo on top of a tripod, allowing the media audience and cameras to see.

"Former Navy SEAL, Chief Petty Officer Gray Saxon," Agent Hanna gestured to the picture.

The photo was Saxon's official portrait from when he was in the SEALs. Saxon was dressed in his formal military uniform, which was filled with different badges, pins, and patches, and sporting a sneaky grin. He was younger, more clean-shaven, and wasn't sporting the scars that he now had.

But Taylor recognized him—the man she was currently living and sleeping with.

She dropped her drink, the glass shattering into a million pieces on the hardwood floor. Her hand that covered her mouth was shaking uncontrollably. Her eyes began welling and her breathing became inconsistent. A full anxiety attack was surging through her system as millions of questions and a thousand different emotions erupted like a volcano.

"Taylor? Taylor, what's wrong?" Tanya asked, hearing her daughter's shallow breathing. "Baby, talk to me!"

"Mom, I have to go. I'll call you later," Taylor whispered, abruptly hanging up on her mother.

"As of this moment, Mr. Saxon is still at large," Agent Hanna continued, ignoring a slew of reporters who were barking questions at her. "He is armed and extremely dangerous. To everyone watching and listening, if you see this man, do not approach him. Call the proper authorities, numbers will be posted. But we are asking for help; if anyone has seen Mr. Saxon recently, please tell us. Thank you, that is all for now."

Agent Hanna and her escort of other agents walked off the podium, leaving the eerie photo of Gray Saxon for the cameras to linger on.

"Oh my god," was all that Taylor could croak out.

From the doorway to the kitchen, Taylor heard someone clear their throat. She whirled around and froze when she saw Gray Saxon standing not ten feet away from her.

He was holding a gun in his right hand.

Chapter Sixty
Los Angeles, California

"Tell me it isn't true," Taylor's voice was barely a whisper, she sounded more like a ghost than an actual person. She couldn't take her eyes off of the gun, which was more proof than an admission from Saxon. Saxon's eyes were dark and emotionless; Taylor couldn't tell if that was new or if she had just never truly noticed. Yet, the sight of him standing there holding the gun was all Taylor needed to see to know that everything the FBI agent had said was the truth.

Gray Saxon was quick on his feet. Even in the face of extreme adversity, he'd always been able to think clearly and come up with a solid plan. Case in point, he'd been able to get Cassidy Minor out of a horrible scenario when literally no one else in the United States Armed Forces would even try. But even men like Saxon have their moments of weakness. Saxon looked at Taylor, studying her expression. It wasn't just that she was angry or scared or heartbroken, it was all of those combined and amplified to the tenth degree.

He'd slipped inside the apartment, wanting to surprise Taylor. Overhearing her on the phone, he'd kept as quiet as possible. But then she turned the TV up and Saxon heard the FBI bitch expose him in front of the entire world. Not that he hadn't planned for this, but he certainly hadn't been able to plan for Taylor or his feelings toward her, which he could no longer deny were strong. It was painful to know that in a few seconds, he'd lost any chance he ever had with Taylor. He knew without a shred of doubt that she was not going to see eye to eye with him on his plan or his past acts. The gun had been drawn simply out of instinct. For a brief nanosecond, Saxon considered sticking the barrel in his mouth. But that thought evaporated. He'd gotten too far to not see his plan all the way through to the end, no matter who or what got in his way.

"This isn't how I expected you to find out," Saxon muttered, hiding the gun behind his muscular jean-covered thigh.

"Not how you expected me to find out?" Taylor repeated, baffled at the statement. "How the fuck did you expect me to find out? Did you plan on telling me that you are a goddamn terrorist?"

"I'm not a terrorist," Saxon felt his blood boil as he clenched his free fist.

He hated terrorists more than any other group of people on the planet. Saxon was a patriot, a soldier fighting for every single serviceman and woman all over the world. The accusation struck a nerve with him. But outside of his unit—Ilsa, Alaina, Ryan, and Rahman—not many people would agree. But at the end of the day, Saxon didn't care. All he cared about was making sure the ISB were completely decimated and the only way to do that was to get the entire world to believe that the ISB was a clear and present threat. Also, a few thousand US troop casualties would be a nice touch of retribution for abandoning Gray Saxon in the hands of the ISB four years ago.

"I'm calling the police," Taylor whispered, still holding her cell phone. Saxon hung his head and sighed. She unlocked her phone, but stopped just as she dialed the first number. Taylor couldn't hold it together any longer and broke down, crying harder than she had in a long time.

"Taylor..." Saxon whispered, taking a step toward her. He reached out to take her hand, but she pulled away quickly. She backed away from him, staring him down through her watery eyes.

"Don't you dare fucking touch me," Taylor spat, wiping her eyes with the back of her hand.

"Taylor, I'm sorry," Saxon said, tucking his 1911 in the small of his back. "I never wanted to hurt you. Please, you have to believe me."

"Believe you?" Taylor shouted. "Every fucking thing you told me was a lie!"

"I've never lied to you once, Taylor," Saxon challenged. "In fact, I've been more honest with you than anyone else in my life since I left the military."

Saxon's response surprised Taylor, she stumbled over her words, unsure of how to respond to that. When Saxon had told her about the mission to rescue Cassidy Minor and his subsequent capture, she'd seen it in his eyes that he was telling the truth. She was feeling a million different emotions, realizing that Saxon probably hadn't ever lied to her. The only question he'd ever dodged was about what he did for work, which made sense to Taylor now. She couldn't pretend that she didn't have strong feelings for Gray. The connection, physically and emotionally, had felt rock-solid to her right from the first time they'd met. Sure, it had been a complete whirlwind, but Taylor had always been one to jump first and figure it out later.

"Why?" Taylor asked, setting her phone on the kitchen counter, next to a scabbard of knives.

"Why did I do it?" Saxon clarified. Taylor nodded.

"Don't lie to me, Gray."

"I've got no reason to lie to you now," he muttered. "I don't want anyone else to ever have to go through what I went through. That's why I did it, so those fuckers wouldn't ever hurt anyone again. I don't have the ability to go to war with a terror group, but this fucking country does. They should've bombed the living Christ out of them after that video went viral, but they didn't. All I did was give them a little push in the right direction."

"You call killing hundreds of innocent people a little push?" Taylor asked.

"What would you call it?" Saxon countered. "It's a small price to pay if you ask me."

"And say they do go to war over this," Taylor pointed a finger at him. "What about the soldiers, men and women, who will get killed fighting a war that doesn't need to be fought? What then?"

"Retribution," Saxon's eyes narrowed. "For leaving me in the hands of those goddamn savages. They could've tried to get me out, to do fucking anything, but I sat in a fucking cage for a fucking year! A year, Taylor! You can't possibly pretend to understand what that was like for me!"

Taylor backed away under the volume of Saxon screaming at her; her eyes caught the knives just next to her phone, if it came to that. She knew deep down she should've just called the police, but her feelings for Saxon counterattacked her inhibitions like the side effects of a drug. Saxon was right, she couldn't begin to comprehend what he'd endured in his life, but she'd endured quite a bit too and that didn't turn her into a murderer.

"Gray, I can't even pretend to understand what that was like," she said softly.

"No, you can't," Gray spat. He looked at Taylor intently, struggling with the consequences of his choice to try and have a normal relationship during his mission.

"I really thought I could love you, Taylor. Love you and see this thing through to the end. I never opened up to anyone, not a soul. But you... you got it out of me. You made me feel like a completely different man. For a brief time, I pictured a life where I wasn't constantly surrounded by death and violence and absolute fucking misery. You are an amazing woman, Taylor, and you deserve someone who is going to be good to you. Someone who is excited every second of every day to be with you. I thought I could be that guy... but I can't be. Not now and not ever. I'll never be able to give you what you deserve or need."

"I know," Taylor said sadly. "Why is it that I can't ever pick a good fucking guy? I mean, first Bryon and now a fucking terrorist."

"You don't have to worry about Bryon ever again, Taylor," Saxon admitted. Taylor raised an eyebrow.

"You... you killed Bryon?" she asked. Saxon nodded.

"Shot him twice," he said casually. "He won't bother you ever again."

"Jesus Christ, Gray! Is that your answer to everything? Just shoot whoever pisses you off?" Taylor shouted. Taylor picked up her phone and unlocked it, getting ready to redial 9-1-1. As much as it hurt, she knew there wasn't any other option. If she didn't call and Gray went out to hurt more people, she'd always feel guilty about that.

"Taylor, don't fucking call!" Saxon shouted.

"Fuck you!" she screamed back, pressing the final number and raising the phone to her ear.

Saxon crossed the room in a second, hitting the phone right out of Taylor's hand. The phone dropped to the ground with a loud crash. Raising his boot, Saxon brought his heel down on the device, crushing it. Taylor reeled back and drew the butcher's knife from the wood scabbard. With all her strength, Taylor thrust the blade towards Saxon's gut. Moving on primal instinct, Saxon side-stepped the blade and caught Taylor's wrist with both hands. Jerking her arm up, he forced the blade around and drove it into Taylor's chest, stabbing her between the breasts.

"Oh fuck," Saxon gasped as he saw what he'd done. He'd acted on reflex, not even realizing what he was doing until it was too late. The blade stuck out of her chest in brutal fashion, looking like something out of a Rob Zombie horror movie.

Taylor whimpered like a dog that had its tail stepped on, and tears began free-falling from her glassed-over eyes. Blood sprayed out from the vicious wound, covering Saxon's face, clothes, and hands in vivid red plasma.

"No, no, no! Taylor! God, no!" Saxon cried, holding onto Taylor as she bled over him. He wrapped his arms around her and gently lowered her to the ground, her ragged breaths becoming less and less frequent as she bled out while simultaneously choking on her own blood. She reached up and touched Saxon's cheek with a bloody hand, looking into his eyes one last time before she closed them, never to see the light again.

"Please wake up, Taylor!" Saxon screamed, snatching a towel from the counter and pressing it over the wound, frantically trying to cull the bleeding. "Taylor, please stay with me, baby! Please, don't go! I'm begging you!"

He felt her entire body go limp and knew it was over. A wave of nausea rolled through him and his head started spinning.

Saxon fell back against the island, sobbing hysterically as he stared at his work. He howled in pain, not caring who heard him. He had been right when he told Taylor his life was completely drowned in death. Saxon had killed so much in his life that the act itself was trivial to him. He had visualized a future with Taylor, one where he could've been happy. One where he could allow himself to love and be loved in return, something he had never truly experienced, even with his first wife. But as he focused on Taylor's dead and bloodied body, twitching slightly, he was overcome with despair, guilt, and self-loathing. Reaching behind his back, Saxon drew the Para-Ordnance.

In between animalistic howls, Saxon stuck the barrel of the gun into his mouth and slammed his eyes shut. He yanked the trigger of his 1911.

The gun didn't cycle. The trigger didn't move.

"What the fuck?" Saxon breathed, opening his eyes slowly and removing the gun from his mouth.

The safety was still engaged.

In all his years using and handling guns, Saxon had never forgotten to disengage the safety when he was about to fire. Call it whatever, but Saxon knew there was only one reason why he was still alive. He still had a mission to complete.

Saxon tucked the gun into his waistband and wiped his eyes free of tears.

Chapter Sixty-One
Los Angeles, California

    The three LAPD cruisers came to a screeching stop in front of the apartment building. Riley was the first one out of the lead cruiser, drawing her Glock 17; John exited through the passenger side. The two undercover cops, Wes Daniels and Jeremy Olsen, jumped out of the last two cruisers.

Riley took point, leading the three men through the glass double doors and into the lobby of the upper-class apartment building.

"Can I help you with anything?" the concierge in the center of the lobby asked. He was very obviously gay and slightly uncomfortable with the sight of armed law enforcement in front of him.

"Don't let anyone leave until we come back down," Riley ordered, flashing her FBI badge clipped to her belt. She hit the 'up' arrow on the elevator. "Wes, stay in the lobby. Jeremy and John, you're with me."

"Is it just me or is she insanely hot when she's barking orders at everyone?" Wes said to John under his breath. John couldn't help but crack a smile, he'd been thinking the same thing.

"Secure the lobby, Detective," John smirked, hurrying onto the elevator with Riley and Jeremy.

Once the press conference had concluded, the four of them had mounted up and headed to check out the address that came back from Rahman's phone. According to the intel, Gray Saxon and a woman named Taylor Lavine had been living in the apartment building. Riley found a solid amount of information on Taylor Lavine—a published model and amateur pornstar from Jacksonville.

The elevator doors opened on the tenth floor of the building; Riley once again was in the lead, keeping her Glock 17 at the ready. Moving quietly after her, Jeremy produced his Sig P365 SAS from the holster on his right hip. John brought up the rear, still wielding the Sig Sauer P226 he'd grabbed from the interrogation room at the FBI Field Office.

"Here it is," Riley whispered, pivoting to face the door to the apartment. She looked over at John. "Care to do the honors?"

"Yes, ma'am," John nodded, stepping in between Riley and Jeremy. He turned around and donkey-kicked the door, busting the lock; the door swung open and smashed against the wall.

"Police!" Riley called out, moving into the apartment with Jeremy on her heels. John hurried in after them, ducking into the bathroom to clear the room. Seeing nothing, he rejoined them and continued further into the apartment. Jeremy swung into the bedroom, clearing the living quarters in a few seconds

"Clear," he called out before reappearing. Riley moved into the family room, scanning every inch. John hugged the wall and moved into the kitchen.

Taylor's body was lying in a pool of her own blood, the knife still sticking out of her chest. There was a boot print in the pool of blood, but nothing else that indicated what exactly had happened. John dropped to his knees and felt Taylor's neck for a pulse, her skin was still warm to the touch.

"Jesus," Riley breathed as she took in the gory scene. Jeremy shook his head, disgusted, and got on the phone, calling for an ambulance. "Is she breathing, John?"

"No," John muttered. "She's dead."

John had looked extensively at the photos Riley had gathered of Taylor. Even though she'd lost almost all of her coloring, John could tell that he was looking at the body of Taylor Lavine. Another body connected to Gray Saxon had been dropped.

Standing up, John wiped the blood from his hands on the back of his jeans. He took a step back and saw something in the pool of blood; he reached down and picked up the shattered phone with his thumb and index finger, not wanting to contaminate the evidence any further.

"I got a phone," he said quietly to Riley. He set the busted device on the island. "We must've just missed him, she's still warm."

"How is he always four steps ahead of us?" Riley asked, her frustration evident.

John didn't get a chance to answer, the landline next to the fridge began ringing. Praying it wasn't a family member of Taylor's, John picked up the phone and answered.

"Hello?"

"John," Gray Saxon spoke in a cold whisper. There was a long pause where neither man spoke. John looked over to Riley and cocked his head toward the balcony.

"Is that who I think it is?" Riley asked. John nodded and walked over to the balcony, slipping outside, and closing the door behind him.

"Gray," John finally spoke.

"I didn't mean to kill her," Saxon said, the words almost killing him to actually speak. John picked up on the remorse in Saxon's voice and decided against an aggressive approach. The last thing he needed was to push an already volatile guy over the edge even more. Saxon had proven his capacity for violence was unlike anything John had ever seen before. He had no idea what Saxon was truly capable of if he was pushed into a corner.

"What happened?" John asked, leaning on the railing of the balcony.

"I-I don't even know," Saxon grumbled. "It all happened so fast. And then I was sitting there and I put my gun in my mouth... but I just couldn't do it. I couldn't pull the trigger."

"She meant a lot to you?" John asked. Again, another long pause.

"Yeah," Saxon was finally able to speak. His voice was shaky, it sounded like he was crying. "Yeah, she was a good girl. Hell, she was a great girl. Not the type of girl I ever deserved. Fuck, John, I didn't mean to hurt her."

"I know you didn't, Gray," John said, trying to calm the man down. "But, Gray, you've done some horrible things. You know how this has to end, right?"

"Yes, John. I do," Saxon growled. "There was only one way this could ever end."

"So, come in, Gray," John took his chances and pressed. "You can't run forever. Sooner or later, this is going to catch up to you. So, why not come in on your own terms?"

"John Shannon, if you think I've come this far just to throw my hands up and let you put handcuffs on me, you're sadly mistaken," Saxon shot back, his voice was threatening.

"Well, I can't let you kill any more innocent people. This has gone far enough, Gray," John responded, remaining as calm as he could.

"You know, John," Saxon said ominously. "You really should stop smoking, you look like shit."

John's eyes went wide as he saw Gray Saxon stand up on the roof of the building across the street from the apartment—Saxon was carrying a sniper rifle. He had been lying flat against the roof, with his eyes glued to the scope of his Remington Modular Sniper Rifle, watching John Shannon and the cops inside his old apartment intently. John stared at Saxon, keeping the phone pressed to his ear. Saxon had him dead to rights.

"You want to take the shot, Saxon?" John asked. Saxon chuckled and put his middle finger up at John.

"Not a chance, John. That's too easy," Saxon said. "You want to end this, we'll do it face to face. We're Navy fucking SEALs after all."

"Time and place," John snarled.

"How about where this all started for us, midnight? And bring that sexy little FBI agent if it makes you feel better. But if you bring the goddamn cavalry with you, I'll make sure she's the next person I kill. Only because I know that would probably hurt you more."

"I'd make sure you dial in that scope, Saxon," John challenged. "I'd hate for your aim to be off."

Saxon laughed and hung up, giving John the middle finger as he disappeared back into the building. John lowered the phone and took a deep breath, wishing he had a cigarette to smoke. There was only one place that Saxon could've been referring to—a place that he and John both knew very well.

He walked back inside, just as the first team of paramedics and crime scene technicians were arriving. Riley hurried over to John, abruptly ending her conversation with the lead CSU (Crime Scene Unit) investigator.

"Was that really Saxon?" Riley asked, keeping her voice low so no one else would overhear them. John nodded and ushered Riley out into the hall, out of earshot of the paramedics and investigators.

"Yeah, that was him," John said. "He sounded like a mess, said he didn't mean to kill that girl. I don't know, I guess he really cared about her."

"Did he say anything else?" Riley asked. She didn't care whether or not Saxon had cared for Taylor, she was dead and he was still out there.

"Yeah," John said, debating whether or not to tell Riley everything. He figured he'd probably need the backup, but did not want to put her in harm's way again.

"John," Riley looked up at him strongly. "Spill it, we don't have time for you to be twiddling your thumbs."

"We're gonna end it, tonight," John said. "Where it all started for him and me."

"Where's that?" Riley asked.

"Fortunately, only about a two-hour drive from here."

Chapter Sixty-Two
Al-Tanf, Syria

The V-22 Osprey descended onto the landing pad, Michael Jameson and Jason Davenport leaped off the back platform before the wheels of the transport fully touched down. A full detachment of Delta Force Operators followed them, disembarking from the Osprey and carrying their gear toward the barracks at the military installation in Al-Tanf, Syria.

Both Jameson and Davenport had survived the suicide bombing at Mashabim Air Base, walking away with nothing more than a few cuts and bruises. The bombing had been one in a series of coordinated attacks orchestrated by the ISB; several bases, including Al-Tanf, had been hit simultaneously. Higher-ups in the military guessed it was an act of retribution for the Reaper attack that destroyed most of a village in southern Syria, where the ISB was known to house their families and kids.

Rumors had been running wild through the military community that the president would authorize an additional 40,000 troops to be deployed to Syria, but the actual number was unknown. In addition to that, the name Gray Saxon had become extremely popular. Many of the older military guys knew the name and all about the mission to rescue Cassidy Minor. The FBI's press conference had essentially gone viral, with everyone chiming in their thoughts as to what was really going on. But even with the media talking all about Gray Saxon, the bombings and the threat of a new war were looming large over the military community.

"Where's Commander Garrison?" Davenport asked an imposing guard outside the Tactical Operations Center, more commonly referred to as the TOC.

"I believe inside the Ops Center, sir," the guard said, opening the door for Davenport.

"I'll be right behind you," Jameson called to Davenport. Davenport gave him a thumbs-up and walked inside the TOC.

Jameson, who was carrying his pack and weapons case, hurried over to the barracks. He dropped his stuff on the first open bed. The rest of the Delta team went to work unpacking, but Jameson jogged back over to the TOC. He found Davenport waiting outside the Ops Center; both of them were dressed down from the usual fatigues and combat boots. Davenport and Jameson both wore jeans and light green 'ARMY' t-shirts.

"He's still inside, I didn't want to just barge in there," Davenport shrugged. Jameson, however, didn't feel like being so polite.

"Buddy, we just got dragged into another damn country and delayed leave. Now is not the time to worry about being polite," Jameson said before throwing the door to the TOC open.

Commander Rick Garrison was seated around a long table, conducting a briefing with all of the ranking military officers on base. Every head around the table turned to stare at the two Delta operators.

"Can I help you, gentlemen?" Garrison asked, his displeasure with the interruption evident in his dry tone.

"Sir, we just got hauled here with no warning and our leaves postponed," Jameson said, trying to remain calm and respectful towards a direct superior.

"Give us the room," Garrison said to his table, not letting Jameson continue on. In an instant, the officers were up and out of the room, not even looking at Jameson or Davenport.

"Sit," Garrison ordered, gesturing to the table. Jameson and Davenport sat down next to each other. "What are your names?"

"Major Michael Jameson, sir," Jameson spoke up first.

"Captain Jason Davenport."

"Pleasure," Garrison said, smiling an emotionless smile. "I assume you're not happy about the situation, I understand. I'll throw you both a bone, however. POTUS will approve the deployment of more troops. As of right now, the ISB is our number one priority. They've been hitting military bases, public areas, and government buildings the last few days. Casualties are skyrocketing, the president can't ignore the situation."

"Sir, I thought the FBI said that Gray Saxon is behind all the attacks at home?" Davenport chimed in. "I watched the press conference on the way over here."

"Yes, I watched it as well," Garrison scowled. He'd been Saxon's superior officer back in the day and had known Saxon particularly well, even considering him a friend at one point. The news was both heartbreaking and confusing. "Look, I can't obviously share classified information with you, but have either one of you heard about what happened at Creech?"

Both men shook their heads in the negative. Neither of them had heard anything about any incident at the Air Force Base in Nevada.

"We've been trying to keep it under wraps," Garrison said. "But Gray Saxon infiltrated the base and commandeered an MQ-9 Reaper. He used the drone to blow up a village where the ISB was known to house their extended families, wives, and kids."

"Oh shit," Davenport muttered under his breath.

"The ISB has responded just about as well as one would expect," Garrison commented. "So, as of right now, we're launching a counterattack. Delta and Green Berets are going to vector in strategic airstrikes on ISB strongholds. Hopefully, we can take out most of these assholes and avoid getting into a full-out war."

"I understand, sir," Jameson nodded.

He was beyond pissed about having his final out delayed, but if he could help stop a war from starting, it was his duty. Not just to his country or his fellow soldiers, but to his family back home.

Chapter Sixty-Three
Coronado, California

Located in San Diego, Coronado was essentially an entire city made up of resorts and tourist attractions. Additionally, Coronado was also home to Naval Amphibious Base Coronado (NAB Coronado). The Naval Base was most popular for being the training site for the United States Navy SEALs and various other Underwater Naval teams. Navy SEAL Teams One, Three, Five, and Seven were run out of Coronado.

Gray Saxon hadn't stepped foot within a hundred-mile radius of Coronado since he graduated from Basic Underwater Demolition/Seal training, known as BUD/S throughout the military community. BUD/S was most popular for the infamous 'Hell Week' in which trainees are forced to go through five days of non-stop training, little food, and no sleep. Hell Week is usually the make or break for most SEAL hopefuls. Fortunately for Saxon, he'd made it through Hell Week and gone on to graduate. Becoming a Navy SEAL had always been his dream from an early age.

He walked along the pier, wearing a black hat and sunglasses to mask his identity. The press conference that Riley held had put Gray Saxon right to the top of the 'Most Wanted' list. But as was normally true, most people were too busy looking for Saxon to realize he was hiding in plain sight. Saxon was watching the beach; a new class of SEAL recruits were in the middle of an intense ocean drill. The sight brought back fond memories.

While the training had been absolutely grueling and pushed Saxon to the edge, it turned him into a fine-tuned fighting machine. He'd always be proud of having made it through BUD/S, regardless of his anger towards the military and government.

Once Saxon got to the end of the pier and was away from most of the tourists, he pulled out his cell phone. He looked over his shoulder, double-checking that no one was close enough to hear him. This wasn't the type of conversation he wanted someone to overhear.

Chapter Sixty-Four
Gilbert, Arizona

A lot had changed in Cassidy Minor's life over the last four years, as much as one's life could change in that span of time. After Saxon's daring rescue that got Cassidy out of the hands of the ISB, she was hospitalized for close to three weeks before she was able to go back home to the states. The recovery process, both physically and emotionally, was long and grueling. Once she was back home, Cassidy found an amazing therapist and met with her twice a week in order to process all of the trauma she'd endured.

Aside from therapy, Cassidy came home with two goals—leave the military and divorce her husband, Mark. Especially after her one night with Gray Saxon, Cassidy realized how unfulfilled she'd been in her marriage. Fortunately, her father was an excellent divorce attorney in Phoenix and made sure that Cassidy got a good deal. Mark, who had fallen out of love with her long before her last deployment, was happy to oblige. They had just gotten married too young, there was nowhere to go but down. Cassidy pretty much knew it had been destined to fail, the feelings only confirmed by her constant desire to deploy to Afghanistan over and over again.

She left the military the second she could, never wanting to get back into a helicopter ever again. Her career as a pilot had been something she truly loved, but the whole event changed her perspective and gave her the opportunity to reprioritize. There always was the constant nagging feeling of knowing the military had never been able to find or recover Gray Saxon. Cassidy carried a heavy weight of guilt over that, something that was a regular topic of conversation with her therapist. She felt utterly responsible for Saxon's fate and struggled with knowing that he had probably died because of her.

But like all things, with time, Cassidy began to feel more and more like herself. She took a job working with other soldiers dealing with PTSD at the local VFW, something she found extremely rewarding. And through that job, she was able to meet the man who would become her new husband, Aaron De La Russa. A veteran of Iraq, Aaron had been involved in a horrific IED (Improvised Explosive Device) incident that resulted in him losing his left foot. He'd turned to alcohol and drugs to cope, but that all changed when he met Cassidy. They helped each other find peace and Aaron was now completely sober. They were expecting their second daughter in a few months and Aaron was almost as excited as Cassidy to be going through that journey again.

The news reports of Gray Saxon the last few days had been both troubling and confusing for Cassidy. For starters, she had figured Saxon had died long ago. The thought of him having been alive that whole time was something she couldn't wrap her head around. She'd known Saxon quite well and would've never thought he was capable of the type of violence he was being accused of. The news anchors were having a field day relaying the gory details of the attacks, which only upset her more.

Cassidy sat in the living room of their comfortable ranch-style home, playing with her one-year-old daughter, Bailey, and their German Shepherd puppy, Dino. She set her daughter in her crib when she heard her phone ringing, assuming it was her doctor. Cassidy had been trying to reschedule her appointment all day. Grabbing her phone off the coffee table, she answered without looking at the caller ID.

"Hello?" Cassidy said happily. The caller didn't say a word but Cassidy thought she could hear the caller breathing rather heavily. "Hello?"

"Hey, Cass," the man said quietly. "It's been a long time."

Cassidy gasped and grabbed onto the large bookcase for support, she felt her legs almost give out from underneath her. She had not heard that voice in four years, since her rescue from the clutches of the Islamic Syrian Brotherhood.

"Gray?" Cassidy asked in a small voice. She could feel the tears welling in her eyes and turned away from her daughter, not wanting her to see her mom getting visibly emotional. "Is that really you?"

"Yeah, it is," Saxon said after another long pause. Cassidy struggled not to get emotional as memories flooded through her.

"How... I mean... I thought you were dead, and then the news this past week..." Cassidy fumbled over her words. "Oh my god, Gray! I'm so sorry."

"Jesus, Cass, for what?" Saxon asked, sounding genuinely offended that she'd offered an apology. "I'm sorry, I probably should have reached out sooner."

"Gray... is it true what they're saying about you? Did you really kill all those people?" Cassidy blurted out. She couldn't censor herself, she had to know.

Saxon fell silent again.

"What would you say if I said yes?" Saxon asked. This time, it was Cassidy's turn to pause. That was an impossible question.
"I'd want to know why," Cassidy answered honestly.
"Yeah," Saxon muttered.

Cassidy knew immediately that everything the news anchors had been saying was true. The tone in Saxon's voice gave him away. It was an incredibly conflicting feeling to know that every horrible thing she'd heard about Saxon was true. But she owed her life to Saxon and could not, would not, forget that.

"Gray, what happened?" Cassidy asked. She walked into her kitchen and sat down at the table. "You can tell me anything."
"A lot of shit happened, Cass," Saxon admitted. "I don't really need to get into that, I know you understand that."
"Of course I do," Cassidy responded. "Can I ask why you're calling? I mean, after all this time, why now?"
"I've done a lot of bad things, Cass," Saxon grunted. "But it's always been for a purpose. I'm so close, so close to completing everything I need to. And I've never hesitated. Not once. And last night, I put a gun in my mouth and pulled the trigger."
"Jesus Christ, Gray," Cassidy breathed, running her hand through her hair.
"I've never forgotten to flip the fucking safety off," Saxon scoffed. "And I don't know, Cass, I just needed to talk to someone. I don't have anyone anymore, Cass. I had someone and I..."

Saxon stopped abruptly, almost choking on his words.

"I killed her, Cass," Saxon whispered, his voice trembling as he fought back the urge to start crying again. "I didn't mean to, it was an accident."

Cassidy fell silent, she couldn't believe what she was hearing from her friend. She could hear the pain and the utter devastation in his voice.

"I'm so sorry, Gray," Cassidy said, truly unsure of what to say to him. Words were hard to come by. "I really don't know what to say."

Saxon sniffed and groaned loudly.

"I'm a fucking mess, Cassidy," Saxon spoke in a voice that was barely audible. "I don't know what to do."

"You can't keep hurting innocent people, Gray," Cassidy said. "No matter what you think that's going to accomplish, you can't."

"I don't take what I've done lightly," Saxon growled. "But I'm getting justice for you, me, and every single serviceman in the fucking world."

"I know, I know," Cassidy soothed, trying to ensure that Saxon stayed calm. "What can I do to help?"

"You've already done so much. I know how this ends, Cassidy," Saxon said, sounding oddly at peace all of a sudden. "I just wanted to talk to a friend. A real friend."

"Gray, I owe you my life. And I never got the chance to thank you. Without you, I never would've met my husband or been able to be the mother of a beautiful little girl. And I've got another one on the way,"

"That's awesome," Saxon said. "I'm so happy for you. I'm glad you made it past all that shit we went through. I truly am. I wish I could've, I really do."

"Gray, you did!" Cassidy responded. "You're still alive, you can still come in and stop all of this chaos. And besides, you still owe me that drink," Cassidy remembered the pact they'd made during their time in captivity.

"No, Cass. I'm not," Saxon said coldly. "I've been a ghost since I came back from that place."

"Gray..."

"It's alright, Cass," Saxon reassured her. "I know what I have to do."

"Gray, please," Cassidy tried to stop him.

"I want you to know that you were one of my best friends and one of the best lays I ever had," Saxon chuckled. "You're a good woman and I wish you the best."

Saxon fell silent again, Cassidy was hesitant to break the silence. Tears started falling from her cheeks, her heart breaking for the man she once knew. During their time overseas, Saxon and Cassidy had become as close as two people possibly could be. Cassidy didn't care what Saxon had done, he was still her friend and she would never turn her back on him.

"I'll talk to you later, Cass," Saxon whispered. He hung up.

Cassidy set her phone on the table and broke down, crying harder than she had in a very, very long time.

Chapter Sixty-Five
San Diego, California

The hotel rooms at the Quality Inn San Diego were adjoined by a set of doors. Both living quarters were filled with SWAT officers, equipment, and surveillance gear. In each of the rooms, a sniper lay across the bed, scanning the Coronado beach for Gray Saxon. Each sniper had an 8x10 photo of Saxon propped up next to their Remington 700 rifles.

Grady Patterson sat behind a folding table full of computers, watching CCTV footage from all over the city of San Diego and the Coronado training facility. Riley sat next to him, bouncing her leg nervously as they switched from camera to camera. Behind both of them, John paced back and forth, biting his fingernail.

"Anything yet?" John asked, stopping to lean over Riley's shoulder.

"Nothing," Riley shook her head. "For the tenth time, I'll let you know when we have something."

John continued pacing. Coronado was the only logical place for Saxon to have gone, based on their last conversation. He was just praying he was right. There was no way John was going to meet Saxon without backup. Patterson had mobilized a 12-man SWAT element to accompany him, Riley, and John to Coronado. In addition, Riley and Patterson had both coordinated with the San Diego Police Department and Navy officials from Coronado. The Navy base had been put on high alert as soon as the intelligence came through about Saxon possibly being in the area.

John went into the other room and flopped down on the couch, throwing his legs over the arm of the chair. He was regretting having told Riley he'd stop smoking, especially cold turkey. He knew his stress and anxiety was better managed with the aid of nicotine.

"Hey," Riley said, peeking her head in the adjoining room. "Are you ok?"

"Lovely," John groaned, trying to get comfortable on the couch that was clearly too small for a man his size. Riley laughed at the sight and walked over to John, climbing on top of him on the couch.

"Agent Hanna, there are fellow officers on the premises," John said, giving Riley a wry grin. The comment got a snicker out of the sniper on the bed. His name was Dawkins, one of the SWAT officers who'd gone in after John at Dodger Stadium.

"I don't think Dawkins would rat us out, would you?" Riley asked.

"Lips are sealed," Dawkins chuckled, not taking his eye off the scope. He smiled inwardly to himself, he had a bet going with the other sniper, Koston, on whether or not John and Riley were fucking. With it pretty much confirmed, Dawkins looked forward to getting his $200 from Koston.

"What if we got another room?" Riley suggested. "Just you and me, none of these assholes are allowed."

"I'd say what the fuck has gotten into you, Riley Hanna?" John quipped. Riley rolled her eyes and leaned down, kissing John on the lips.

"I'm fucking horny," she whispered into his ear. John looked over Riley's shoulder toward Dawkins, the sniper paid them no attention whatsoever. For a split second, he considered it, but the room of SWAT officers next door was not ideal.

Without taking his eye from the scope, Dawkins pulled out his cell phone and texted a quick message to Koston.

"I win," was all the message said. He hit 'send' and waited for the inevitable reply.

"We never did get to seal the deal last time," Riley said, recalling their date at Majordomo.

"You're right, but I don't think the middle of a manhunt is a good time," John said, trying his best to let his brain do the thinking and not any other part of his body. Gray Saxon could pop up at any moment and John sure as shit wanted to be ready to go when that moment came.

"Ugh, fine," Riley gave up, knowing John was right. "But after this is over, you and I are getting a hotel room. With very thick walls."

"I'm good with that," John agreed.

"I know a few places in the city that have especially thick walls, sir," Dawkins commented.

"Eyes on the beach, Dawkins," John said dryly, stifling a laugh. Dawkins sniggered.

Rolling her eyes at the comment, Riley got off John and kissed him on the cheek. Before she could walk back into the other room, John grabbed her and pulled her in for another quick kiss.

"As soon as we find this prick, you and I are taking a month off," John whispered in her ear.

"Yes please," Riley breathed, biting John's ear playfully. It took a considerable amount of self-restraint on John's part to remain professional.

She stood up, adjusted her jacket, and smiled brightly at John. John sat back on the couch and took a minute to just admire her. Riley was everything—smart, sophisticated, bad-ass, strong, intuitive, and sexy.

John was so focused on Riley that he almost didn't hear the supersonic round slice through the window with surgeon-like precision. The round traveled through Dawkins's scope before blowing through his right eye and burying itself in his brain. Dawkins pitched forward onto the bed, dead before even knowing he'd been fired upon.

In an instant, John leaped off the couch and yanked Riley to the ground as another round smashed through the window, this time, completely shattering it. Riley drew her Glock 17 in an instant, ready to fight.

"Shots fired, shots fired! Man down!" John screamed into the other room. The SWAT team and Patterson dropped to the ground, almost in perfect unison.

Koston frantically tried to locate the sniper, scanning the rooftops and windows of the buildings in front of the hotel.

"I don't see him!" he panicked. "Any idea where those shots came from?"

"No idea," Patterson answered.

"Stay here," John ordered Riley, sheltering her behind the bed. As smoothly as he could, John reached over onto the bed and grabbed the Remington 700; the scope was done, making the rifle virtually useless.

"Patterson, you got a spare rifle?" John asked, wiping blood from the stock of the rifle.

"Hang on," Patterson grunted, crawling over to the stack of weapons case they had in the corner of the room. He searched through the cases and found an extra Remington 700. As he maneuvered his way back to the adjoining doorway, another round crashed through the room, hitting one of the CCTV monitors.

"Got him!" Koston said, adjusting his aim. He'd seen the muzzle flash from a rifle from one of the rooms at the conference center across the highway from the hotel. "Returning fire."

Before Koston could squeeze the trigger, a .338 Lapua Magnum round blew a golf ball-sized hole through his forehead. His head snapped back and then recoiled onto the bed, blood and brain matter coated the wall behind him.

"Goddammit," Patterson grunted. "John, sniper down in here too."

"Toss the rifle in here, I'll see if I can get a bead on him," John said, moving as close to the adjoining door as he could without exposing himself to the sniper, which he assumed had to be Gray Saxon. Patterson tossed the rifle through the adjoining door; John grabbed the weapon and flipped the safety off.

John thought back to the last time Saxon had him pinned down with sniper fire. Saxon had shot through a wall to kill Rahman and had been deadly accurate. And again, Saxon demonstrated an almost god-like ability to see through obstructions.

"Be advised, he's gotta be using a fucking thermal scope," John warned the team. "We need to get out of here and go after him, this room is a fucking kill zone."

"I know," Patterson scoffed. "Guys, get ready to lay down some cover fire. We're gonna swoop around and go after him. Riley, get SDPD on the horn and tell them the shooter is in the Anchors Conference center!"

"Got it," Riley said, pulling out her phone.

On Patterson's signal, three SWAT officers jumped into action, firing their M4A1s to provide covering fire while another group of four darted for the door. Once those four officers were safe outside, the three shooters darted after them. John kept his aim steady, scanning the conference center back and forth for any sign of movement.

"Patterson, go," John said. "I got you covered."

"Moving," Patterson said, hesitating slightly before he prepared to run.

Saying a silent prayer to himself, Patterson sprinted for the door, slipping around the corner, narrowly missing a round that smashed into the drywall of the hotel room. John yanked the trigger on the Remington 700, the .30-06 (pronounced '30-aught-6') Winchester exploded from the barrel of the rifle and soared exactly where the muzzle flash had just been. The window on the conference center exploded into a million pieces. After a few seconds, Patterson slowly peered around the doorway into the room.

"Did you get him?" he asked John, hoping John had been able to see some kind of indication that the sniper had been killed. John was quiet, he saw no movement through the window at the conference center.

"We need to get over to that fucking building immediately. I may have hit him, but if I didn't, he's going to let us think I did."

"San Diego PD is on the way, a minute tops," Riley informed.

"Good. Let's move out," John said, rolling onto his back and throwing the rifle strap across his chest. "Patterson, cover me."

"You got it," Patterson said, getting to a knee and raising his M4. John turned to Riley and grabbed her hand.

"I'm gonna go, and the second I'm clear, I'm gonna turn around and cover you. You run like fucking hell on wheels, ok?"

"Please be careful," Riley said, sweating from her brow. She was calm for the most part, but the thought of exposing herself to the sniper was terrifying.

"Patterson?" John called out.

"You're good, John! Move!" Patterson shouted back.

"Ah, fuck it," John swore.

John jumped up and bolted, leaping over the bed and running as fast as he could to get outside. Miraculously, there wasn't another round fired at him as he fled.

"Maybe I really did nail that son-of-a-bitch," John muttered to himself. He took up position on the other side of the door, across from Patterson. "Riley!"

"I'm here," Riley called back, her voice a little shaky.

"On my three, you're gonna run for the door, ok?" John shouted.

"Got it!"

"One... two... three! Now, Riley, now!" John screamed. His eyes were glued to the scope of his rifle, watching that shattered window like a hawk.

With her Glock in her right hand, Riley ran for the door, moving nimbly around the scattered equipment cases. John heard the concussive report of the sniper rifle and his eyes went wide as he saw the muzzle flash in the far-left side of his scope, the shooter had maneuvered three windows down to take the shot.

The round hit Riley in the right shoulder, the momentum of the round spun her around 180-degrees. The second round hit her right between the eyes, her head popped like a watermelon. Blood, gore, and skull fragments splattered all over the room. She fell back like she'd been hit by a 300-pound linebacker, collapsing in a heap of her own blood and brain.

Patterson unloaded, spewing rounds from his M4A1 and stepping back into the room, the SWAT officers behind him followed suit. They moved right back into the face of danger and formed a protective line in front of Riley's body while two officers took a knee next to her.

John felt like he'd been hit by a train as a wave of sheer dread fell over him. He stared blankly at Riley's mangled head, which was barely recognizable. Blood poured out of her head wound like a dam that had just been opened.

John leaned back against the wall and threw up before he screamed in agony.

Chapter Sixty-Six
San Diego, California

"Hold him back right fucking now!" Patterson screamed at two of his officers as John rushed back into the hotel room, desperately trying to get to Riley's side; he was screaming incoherently. The two officers each took a side, holding John back from the gory mess of Riley's corpse.

"Get the fuck off of me! You cock-sucking motherfuckers!" John wailed, tears spraying out of his eyes uncontrollably. "Riley! Riley, please! God-fucking-dammit! Riley!"

"Get him out of here!" Patterson barked, swapping out the magazines on his M4.

The two officers manhandled John out of the room, each of them taking an inadvertent fist from John; he was thrashing and fighting back like a toddler, completely beside himself.

"Pick her up and get her out of here, we'll cover!" Patterson said to a group of four SWAT officers. They nodded and very carefully picked up Riley's body, maneuvering her swiftly out of the room.

"Fall back, now!" Patterson ordered the rest of his team. Tactically falling back out of the room, the entire SWAT team made it outside without sustaining another casualty.

John was sobbing like a crazy man, sounding like an animal that had been caught in a trap. His eyes were bloodshot and cheeks were streaked with tears, his voice was starting to strain from screaming at the top of his lungs.

"John!" Patterson shouted, kneeling down in front of the man and grabbing his shoulders. "John, snap out of it!"

"Grady, we can't stay here!" one of the SWAT guys yelled. "John's right, that fucker probably has thermal, we need to move out and take his ass out!"

"I know, goddammit," Patterson hollered back. He reeled back and slapped John across the face, trying to bring him back to sanity. John blinked a few times but stopped fighting against the two SWAT officers. His chest was heaving and his eyes were puffy, but he appeared to be coming back around. John looked up at Patterson, a shattered expression plastered across his tear-streaked face.

"Riley..." he panted.

"Is gone," Patterson said bluntly. "Now, if you want to let the man who killed her get away, by all means, sit here and have a meltdown. But if not, get the fuck up, pull yourself together, and let's fucking kill this prick."

John wiped his face on the front of his shirt and cleared his throat. Patterson picked up the Remington 700 and forced it into John's hands.

"Let's do it," John croaked, his voice nearly gone from the constant screaming. Patterson nodded and got on his radio.

"Any units in the area, this is Grady Patterson with the LAPD SWAT. I have three K.I.A. at the Quality Inn, repeat, three officers down. I need paramedics and ambulances to the Inn immediately. Be advised, shots fired from the Anchors Conference Center. Suspect should be considered armed and highly dangerous. I'm sending a detachment after him, the rest of my team will await paramedics at the Quality Inn," Patterson finally paused for a response.

"This is Captain Shayna Evans, SDPD," an older female voice came back over the radio. "Units are en route to your position and we have choppers circling the target building. Send in your team, we can provide overwatch."

"Copy, Captain Evans," Patterson responded. He turned to his own team. "Cole, Mayhofer, and Sewell, you guys are with John."

"Yes, sir!" the three SWAT officers barked in unison. They quickly checked over their weapons and ammo, borrowing a few spare magazines from the SWAT officers that would be staying with the bodies.

"John, do you need an M4?" Patterson asked, offering John his own weapon. John shook his head and worked the bolt on the Remington, loading a cartridge into the chamber.

"I'm good," John snarled. Patterson patted him on the shoulder.

"Go kill that motherfucker."

Chapter Sixty-Seven
San Diego, California

The second that Gray Saxon saw the woman's head explode through his thermal scope, he ducked back into the conference center and took off running for the stairwell. The conference center had been empty, save for a quartet of maintenance workers that Saxon went through with ease. He hated having to waste bullets on them, but he didn't have time to take them down one by one without alerting the others.

Throwing open the door to the stairwell, Saxon slung his rifle across his back and picked up the Daniel Defense M4 he'd stashed. Saxon racked the charging handle, priming the gun. He darted down the stairs, skipping two or three at a time. Once he hit the main floor, Saxon darted toward the side exit, knowing the front of the building would be crawling with cops at any given moment. He came to a stop just before the exit door and slowly slipped outside, looking around carefully. He heard a duo of police helicopters up above, sirens from who knows how many cruisers blared loudly as the entire conference center was being swarmed with cops.

Saxon double-checked his Para-Ordnance before tucking it in the back of his waistband. Flipping the safety off of the M4, he dashed through the parking lot, stopping behind a parked car for cover. Bullets rang out, kicking up the asphalt at Saxon's feet.

"He's behind the blue car!" Saxon heard someone scream. Another hail of bullets smashed into the car, shattering the windows and windshield.

Saxon moved to the front of the car and took a knee, resting his arm on the hood. He calmly began returning fire at eight officers using their squad cars for cover. Conserving his limited ammo supply, Saxon only fired at what he knew he could hit. Pulling the trigger twice, he saw one of the cops fall over in a heap, the two rounds had hit the cop in the neck and head. Immediately shifting a hair right, Saxon blasted the partner through the chest with a three-round burst. Again, shifting to his right, Saxon let loose another burst, wounding two more of the cops. Five more San Diego PD cruisers drove into the parking lot, maneuvering in front of the wounded cops.

Flipping the selector switch to full-auto, Saxon stood up and pressed the trigger, emptying the rest of his magazine at an awe-inspiring rate. Shell casings spewed out the side of the rifle, littering the ground at his feet with hot brass. The gun went dry and Saxon hit the release, dumping the empty magazine.

A bullet cut through the car and smashed into the lower receiver of Saxon's M4 before he had a chance to grab another magazine. The powerful bullet ripped through the gun before taking off two of Saxon's fingers on his right hand—his pinky and ring finger. Dropping the destroyed weapon, Saxon fell back against the car, gritting his teeth in pain. He held his mangled hand against his chest and drew his Para-Ordnance with his non-dominant hand. His military training had allowed him to still be comfortable shooting with either hand, but obviously he preferred his right. There was no time to address the wound or even try to quell the bleeding from the two stumps on his hand. Saxon shredded the rest of his ammo for his M4, which was only four spare magazines. The ammo was useless to him now that his rifle was done. The extra weight would only slow him down. Getting to his feet, Saxon blasted off half of the magazine in the direction of where the shot had come from.

John Shannon and three SWAT officers were in an all-out sprint toward Saxon; John was carrying the sniper rifle. Saxon chuckled and began running toward the street. When they'd served together, John was one of the best shots Saxon had ever seen. And after all these years, John appeared to have not lost his edge.

The street was busy, cars flying by at 45 miles an hour in both directions, but Saxon wasn't fazed. He dashed through the street, narrowly missing the front end of a Peterbilt semi. The annoyed drivers blared their horns until they saw the guns on Saxon's person and the SWAT team in pursuit.

Vaulting over the trunk of a sedan, Saxon dropped behind the car and stuffed the Para-Ordnance away. With his adrenaline running high, Saxon blocked out the excruciating pain in his hand and drew the Remington MSR; he wrapped his mangled hand around the trigger, knowing he was an exponentially better shooter when using his right hand, especially with a sniper rifle.

One of the helicopters hovered over Saxon, no doubt giving information to the officers on the ground. Everywhere Saxon went, the helicopter followed. The second chopper stayed higher, circling the entire area. Saxon aimed his rifle skyward and peered through the thermal scope, focusing on the main fuel tank, just under the rotors.

He squeezed the trigger.

The round hit the helicopter in the fuel tank. Instantly, the chopper jerked wildly as white smoke began billowing out of the engines. Working the bolt on his MSR, Saxon lined up another shot, this time, at the other side of the fuel tank. He pulled the trigger and the round hit the fuel tank, igniting the large reservoir of fuel.

Saxon took off running again before the chopper hit the ground, knowing the crashed helicopter would give him a few minutes to spare.

Chapter Sixty-Eight
San Diego California

The chopper crashed in the parking lot of the conference center, destroying four parked cars, and erupting in a brilliant explosion that shattered the windows of the surrounding buildings. Debris and flaming-hot chunks of steel shot off in every direction, wounding five passersby and two cops.

Through the flames and smoke from the aviation fuel, John saw Saxon darting toward the blue-grey building across the street from the conference center.

"He's going into that building," John said to his team, pointing to the structure; it was a simple three-story structure with exterior staircases on either side. John saw Saxon running up the stairs on the right end of the building.

"Go get him," one of the SWAT officers, Cole, said. He gestured to the chopper crash and wounded officers. "We have to deal with this shit."

John nodded and ran toward the building, throwing the sniper rifle over his shoulder. Dodging traffic, John made it to the building and booted opened the steel gate to the staircase. He drew his Sig Sauer P226 and moved up to the second floor.

"Chopper Two, any eyes on target in the blue-grey building? I'm on the second floor moving internal," John called out over the radio.

"Negative, no sign of target."

"Fuck," John muttered.

Having to go room to room to find Saxon was not ideal, especially now that John was on his own. But it was all he could do to keep himself from breaking down over the thought of Riley's shredded body, the image of her head split open permanently ingrained in his mind.

John moved to the first door on the second floor and kicked it open—no sign of Gray Saxon. He continued the process down the entire floor, clearing every single room and finding nothing but empty office after empty office. With the second floor clear, John stepped back outside to access the staircase. Moving quietly, he climbed up to the third floor, leading the way with his handgun.

There were significantly fewer doors to check on the third floor than the previous, which was a relief to John. He repeated the process once again, kicking open the first door and rushing inside to search. Again, finding nothing, John stepped back into the hall and moved to the next door. Booting the door open, he rushed inside. The second he entered the office, John was hit from the blindside with as much force as a human could muster up. He was thrown violently off his feet and crashed into the wall, smashing through the drywall. The Remington sniper rifle slid off his back, clattering into the corner of the office.

Gray Saxon stood over John's dazed body. His Remington MSR was slung diagonally across his back and he carried his Para-Ordnance in his left hand. His hand was still bleeding profusely.

"I thought I told you to come alone," Saxon panted. He took a few deep breaths, trying to lower his heart rate. John groaned and tried to stand up, but Saxon kicked him in the chest and he dropped back down. Saxon was in much better physical condition than John was. "I told you I was going to kill her if you brought the fucking feds."

Words seemed to fall out of John's vocabulary as he lay under Saxon; his back, shoulders, and legs felt as if they were on fire. John ignored Saxon's warning and Riley had been killed, exactly what Saxon had promised. The guilt was almost too much for John to handle. He already felt guilty enough over Anna, but now Riley too? John didn't know if he had any more fight in him.

"I'm surprised, John," Saxon sneered. "I figured after all of this, you'd have a little bit left in the tank at least. Very disappointing."

Saxon aimed his 1911 and flipped the safety off, preparing to execute John Shannon.

John closed his eyes, accepting his fate.

He could see Riley. He could see Anna. A feeling of peace overcame him and he couldn't help but smile. Pretty soon, everything would cease to matter. No more fighting.

John Shannon had been considered a hero at one time in his life. And when the job that he loved so much had asked him to trade in his morals, John couldn't do it. It would've been easier to just swallow his beliefs and let the Navy or Joe Weingardt spring him loose on whoever. But that was not who John Shannon was.

And through this whole case, John had never once given up. He and Riley had tracked down every lead together, each time getting closer and closer to the real perpetrator. Riley had given her life to stop Gray Saxon. For John to surrender before the man and not at least fight would be a dishonor to himself, and more importantly, to Riley. She would never have allowed him to give up.

John opened his eyes and lunged toward Gray Saxon.

Chapter Sixty-Nine
San Diego, California

The 1911 went off, but John dodged the bullet. He grabbed Saxon's hand and twisted hard; the gun clattered to the ground. John stepped back and threw a one-two combo, battering Saxon with punches to each side of his face. Saxon stumbled back against the door, his vision slightly blurry from the sudden barrage. John was on him in a second, raining down punches with furious anger. Throwing up his hands to defend himself, Saxon kicked out at John's legs, hitting him just above the knee.

John buckled and Saxon launched himself upward, bringing a balled fist right under John's chin. Falling back onto the wooden coffee table, John shook off the hit, determined not to give Saxon the upper hand. Saxon picked up his 1911 and fired four shots at John, who expertly avoided the bullets; he dove behind the long couch in front of the coffee table. John charged his former commanding officer, diving through the air, and executing a perfect scissors takedown. Saxon lost his pistol as he came crashing to the floor; John kicked the gun across the office before planting his steel-toed boot in Saxon's gut. Wheezing as he rolled over in pain, Saxon tried desperately to stand up. John got back to his feet, aiming his Sig Sauer at Saxon's head.

"Stay down, Saxon," John warned. Saxon sneered and wiped a streak of blood from his lip.

"I can't believe you of all people, John," Saxon breathed. "Can't understand what I'm trying to do. You were there, we watched that video together."

John paused, thinking back to that day. A man from one of the three-lettered agencies had sat John, Saxon, and a handful of other SEALs down in a secure room. He explained that what he was about to show them was not supposed to be seen by anyone in the Special Operations community, but the man felt it imperative that the SEALs know what had happened.

The man opened his laptop and let the men watch the horrific rape video. John was repulsed the entire time. Like Saxon, he had known Warrant Officer Cassidy Minor very well, having worked with her on several missions. The video was the worst thing John had ever been forced to witness. He would've gladly gone with Saxon on his rescue mission, but for whatever reason, Saxon only asked Captain Spathe and his team to accompany him. None of the other SEALs on base had been propositioned by Saxon.

"It was fucking horrific," John muttered. "I was so proud of you when you told the Brass to go fuck themselves and went after her yourself. But this isn't that, Gray. This is awful what you're doing."

"Is it, John?" Saxon asked, sardonically. "Is trying to eradicate a group of absolute savages really so bad?"

"If it means killing hundreds of innocent people, then yeah, Gray. It is," John shot back. He lowered his Sig Sauer slightly.

Saxon slowly slipped his hand to his hip, where his combat knife was sheathed to his belt. Seeing John let his guard down for half a second, Saxon drew the knife and rocketed toward John, moving under the Sig's line of fire. Saxon adjusted his grip on the knife and sliced open John's hand that was holding the gun; the Sig fell. Saxon planted his foot on the gun and slid it under the desk in the back of the office, ensuring that John wouldn't be able to use it against him.

Ignoring the burning pain in his hand, John withdrew his own knife—a Benchmade tactical blade. He ran toward Saxon and swung his blade, ripping through Saxon's shirt. This time, Saxon stumbled back, clutching his side; he was relieved that the blade hadn't dug in, but he was still cut and bleeding. The tip of the knife had sliced his stomach.

"This was the only way to make sure the fucking ISB gets what they deserve," Saxon justified. "I thought it through a million different ways, this was the only way."

"Gray, just shut the fuck up," John spat. He took another swing at Saxon with his knife; Saxon leaned back like he was doing the limbo, dodging the attack. Saxon came back up and threw a vicious right cross, knocking John back to the ground. John's upper lip burst in half, blood trickled down his face.

"And you know what the shitty thing is?" Saxon asked. He was more talking to himself than to John. "If I had met Taylor before all of this, I really don't think we'd be standing here. She was my second chance. My second chance at having a normal fucking life."

"If that's how you treat your second chances," John breathed, tasting his own blood. "It's no wonder your wife divorced you."

Saxon ignored the comment and reached for his Para-Ordnance. Snapping out of his daze, John gripped his knife tightly and ran towards Saxon, wrapping his arms around his body and lifting him off the ground. Jumping into the air, John slammed his foe onto the coffee table, smashing the wood table into pieces. The Para-Ordnance clattered aside and out of Saxon's reach. Saxon quickly rebounded and exchanged brutal punches with John; he landed a devastating punch, glancing his fist off John's cheek. Before John could recover, Saxon grabbed John by the throat, holding his knife inches away from his eye. John was holding Saxon's arm back with all of his strength; the pressure on his throat made it excruciating.

Turning his own knife around so the blade was facing up, John jerked the blade upwards, stabbing Saxon right through the forearm. The knife drove through the bone and pierced through the other side, wedging cleanly in Saxon's arm. Howling in pain, Saxon fell back, loosening his grip on both the knife and John's throat. Saxon shuddered as shock and adrenaline flowed through his body; he gingerly tested the knife stuck in his arm. John knelt down and secured Saxon's knife in his other hand.

"You motherfucker..." Saxon groaned through gritted teeth. John winced as he watched Saxon grab the handle of the blade and start to pull the knife out. Blood squirted from the grisly injury, covering the nearby desk in gore. Saxon's entire body was trembling as he finally expelled the knife from his forearm; the blade was coated in a deep claret. Blood continued to leak onto the floor around him. Ignoring the immense pain in his arm, Saxon swung the bloody knife around, holding it like a hammer. Shakily, Saxon unsheathed a second, larger knife on his leg with his wounded arm; the blade rang as he withdrew it.

"Come on, man," John shook his head. Steadying his breathing, Saxon regained composure and stepped toward John. Diving toward the Para-

Ordnance, John gripped the gun and fired a single shot at Saxon. The round grazed the side of his face and tore off a huge piece of skin from his cheek all the way past his ear. The scorching round burned his skin and the ghastly wound started gushing blood immediately. Saxon dropped to his knees, screaming in pain. His breathing became more and more rapid as he desperately tried to push past the excruciating pain he was in.

His hand was shaking uncontrollably as he brought his ravaged hand up to feel his facial wound. He gagged the second his three remaining fingers touched his face, the pain made him sick to his stomach. The torture he'd endured at the hands of the ISB was beginning to look like a walk in the park compared to the pain John had inflicted upon him.

"Alright, that's enough, John," Saxon's voice quaked. "That's enough of this fucking shit!"

As Saxon sat on his knees, memories flooded through his head. His childhood, his SEAL career, Cassidy, the mission, the escape. He remembered how proud he felt when he saw Cassidy getting onto the Osprey, finally out of harm's way. It was one of the best feelings Saxon had ever experienced, knowing his actions hadn't been for nothing. He thought about Taylor and how happy she had made him. And how that had ended so horribly, as most of Saxon's fond moments in life had. Misery was something that had plagued him for most of his life. But those memories served as the rush of adrenaline that Saxon desperately needed.

Chapter Seventy
San Diego, California

Grabbing his knife firmly in his right hand, Saxon leaped up and charged John, moving swiftly through the air. John countered the attack, their knives clashed, making an awful scraping sound. Swinging his leg, John attempted to kick Saxon's feet out from under him. Sensing the attack, Saxon flipped through the air over John's leg and landed behind him. John spun around as fast as he could to block Saxon's knife, which barely missed penetrating John's leg. Saxon jerked the bloody knife forward, desperate to inflict damage on John. Moving rapidly, John sidestepped the knife and caught the blade in his hand. Despite the pain, John clamped down on the blade and ripped the knife from Saxon's grasp, throwing it against the office wall. His hand was dripping blood now; he knew that was a risky move, but one knife was easier to fight than two.

Saxon stepped back before running full-speed at John, attempting to tackle him. At the perfect moment, John turned his upper body and parried the attack, catching Saxon's arm. Swinging Saxon's arm around and using his lower body to power the move, John threw Saxon into the bathroom of the large office. Saxon smashed his face off the sink, cracking the porcelain into pieces before he hit the ground. His lip had been virtually split in half by the blow.

John reached under the desk and picked up his P226 before stalking over to the bathroom. Saxon rolled onto his back, sucking in air through his mouth; his nose had been busted when he bounced off the sink. He looked up at John with panic in his eyes. He had drastically underestimated John.

"You were a hero, Gray," John growled, stepping over Saxon and aiming the P226 at his head once more. "But now, all you'll be remembered for is being a murderous piece of shit. No one will ever agree with what you've done, I promise you."

Saxon wasn't even listening, he was waiting for the perfect moment. He shot his knee upward, catching John right in the groin, just as planned.

John's world exploded in an eruption of pain he'd never experienced before. He dropped to his knees as he struggled to breathe, tears welled in his eyes from the immense pain. Saxon slowly got back to his feet and turned his back to John, looking around the bathroom for anything he could use as a weapon.

Using every ounce of willpower he could manifest and ignoring the pain in his groin, John leaned back and kicked at the back of Saxon's knees. Saxon fell back, bending awkwardly from the hit. Jumping to his feet, John grabbed Saxon by the back of the neck and threw him forward, smashing his face against the glass mirror. Saxon's face bounced off the mirror, the glass shattered and shards of glass dug into Saxon's skin.

John grabbed Saxon by the back of his shirt and smashed him against the mirror again and again, leaving blood splatters all over the splintered glass and porcelain sink. Saxon's face was absolutely mangled—pieces of glass had sliced his face to oblivion. A large shard had cut into his eye, slicing the lens in half. Saxon fell to his knees, wheezing in oxygen with much effort. John stepped out of the bathroom and reached down, picking up one of the discarded knives; he pressed the edge of the blade against Saxon's throat.

Saxon took hold of John's hand and spat out a disgusting wad of blood and glass. He looked at his butchered face in the broken mirror and started crying silently. The tears stung his shredded face and made him cry even more.

As long as Saxon had spent planning his mission, he'd never really considered what it would feel like to look death in the eyes. His entire body felt destroyed, the pain was so numbingly excruciating. He tried to think of anything aside from the pain, but he couldn't. Even his fond moments with Taylor seemed to disappear from his brain, replaced with nothing but anguish.

For the first time, John felt sympathy for the man who he once considered a friend. John slowly lowered the knife, taking it away from Saxon's bloody throat.

"No," Saxon sputtered, gagging on a mixture of blood and glass. "Kill me... please."

"Gray," John whispered.

"Just... do it... goddammit," Saxon wheezed, pulling John's knife against his throat.

"Do it!" Saxon begged, choking on his own lifeblood. "Please."

He thought of the hundreds of people that Saxon had killed during his crusade. All the innocent baseball fans, concert-goers, and the countless cops. But most importantly, he thought of Riley Hanna. He'd never been able to really tell Riley how much she meant to him. How much he appreciated her and loved her in a way that he couldn't even explain. The times they had together were some of the best John had ever had. And now he would never get the chance to tell her.

John took a deep breath and closed his eyes before slashing the knife across Saxon's throat in one fluid motion. Saxon tumbled over, blood spraying out of his neck. He crumpled under the sink, his head resting against the pipes.

John saw the air expel from Saxon's body; all was silent in the wreckage of the office and bathroom. He leaned back against the wall, sliding down until he hit the tile floor. The entire bathroom was covered in blood and gore; John was soaked in a combination of his own blood and Saxon's.

But it was finally over.

John hung his head and began weeping, overwhelmed with emotions.

Chapter Seventy-One
Topeka, Kansas

The president of the United States was still in The Golden State when he'd received word that Gray Saxon had been killed. He finished greeting and talking with every single survivor of the Dodger Stadium attack before holding a press conference outside of the hospital.

He spoke from the heart, not even taking 30 seconds to prep. In his speech, which was racking up views and likes across all social media platforms, he told the nation that the true mastermind behind the Lollapalooza and Dodger Stadium attack had been killed. He explained that this was an attempt at retribution, but spoke little about Gray Saxon, fearing any amount of sympathy that could form for him. At the end, he promised that the ISB would be dealt with, but that the United States would not be drawn into another war.

After he'd gotten done talking, one of his Secret Service agents congratulated him.

"You're gonna win this next election by a landslide," the agent had said.

And he was right. The election would come and go, and the president would be reelected for a second term.

Gray Saxon's body had been cremated and the remains disposed of in the shore off of Coronado. The same treatment was given to Rahman Saleh and Ryan Bueshay. However, Ilsa Davies and Alaina Nilsson were returned to their hometowns in England and Sweden, respectively. Their families would never really know what caused them to join forces with a man like Gray Saxon. To anyone who read into the entire case, this remained the most confusing part, even to the most seasoned investigators.

It wasn't until the president was airborne toward Washington D.C. that he heard that Agent Riley Hanna had been killed in pursuit of Gray Saxon. The news was devastating, the president had liked Riley a lot and respected her greatly.

He told the funeral all of this as he stood next to the casket at the cemetery in Riley's hometown of Topeka, Kansas. There were close to 200 people in attendance—Riley's family, friends, colleagues, and other FBI personnel. Grady Patterson sat in the back, alongside the rest of the LAPD SWAT team that had protected her body while John went after Gray Saxon.

John Shannon sat in the front row, next to Riley's parents. He was using crutches and his face and arms were covered in stitches and bandages. But he still wore a crisp black suit. He had a vacant look on his face, trying to stay composed sitting next to Riley's parents. They were both crying quietly, holding onto each other for dear life.

"Special Agent Riley Hanna was a true patriot and a true hero," the president concluded his address. He wiped tears from his eyes, unable to stay composed in front of her devastated parents. "I'm proud to have known her."

The president stepped away as an officer began playing 'Taps' on the bagpipes. The beautiful song overwhelmed the audience.

John fought back the urge to cry. It was the third funeral he'd attended in as many days. The first two had been in San Diego for Dawkins and Koston, the two snipers who'd been killed in the hotel room. Both services for the two snipers were emotional, but it was nothing compared to Riley's. Having the president speak to the mourners only added to the heavy mood hanging over everyone.

John was the last man sitting in front of the casket, all of the other attendees were long gone. He watched as the two workers began lowering the box into the hole in the ground. The president came up and sat down next to him, he was accompanied by an older man.

The older man was nearly six and a half feet tall, wore glasses, and had a wild head of salt-colored hair.

"I'm so sorry, John," the president said, patting John on the shoulder.
"My condolences," the older man offered. His voice was less kind than the president's.
"Do I know you?" John muttered, looking over at the older man. He shook his head.
"Probably not," he said. He stuck his hand out toward John. "Jasper Crane, Director of the Central Intelligence Agency."

John scoffed, ignoring Crane's hand. He gave the president a dirty look.

"Not the right place to try and recruit me," John spat.
"That's not what this is, John," the president assured him. "Just listen, please."
"I know where Yusuf Bakar Akhmedi is," Crane said flatly. "I assume you know the name."

John nodded. The leader of the Islamic Syrian Brotherhood had been on John's list ever since he saw the video of him raping Cassidy Minor.

"Well, I came here to offer you a shot at him, if you want of course. Figured it was the least we could do after what you did," Crane said, easing up his tone slightly. "He's feeling confident now and becoming reckless, but our teams have been devastating ISB strongpoints for the past few days."

"I'm never going back to the Navy. Not ever," John said. He turned to the president. "I told you that, sir. And I wasn't saying that lightly."

"All due respect, John. The CIA is not the Navy. I don't believe in red tape," Crane said ominously. "I hope you'll consider it, I'd appreciate the opportunity to work with you."

"No pressure, John. But please think about it, we can always use guys like you," the president said. "Come on, Jasper. Let's give John some space."

The president smiled at John and got up, walking back to his Secret Service escort. Jasper Crane stood up and dropped something into John's hand.

"Consider it," he said quietly. "Guys like you are rare."

As Crane left, John opened his hand to see a small business card. He flipped it over and saw a number scrawled on the back with a small message that read 'Think about it – JC'.

"Shit, Riley," John muttered, staring at the casket being lowered into the grave plot. "I think we got some more work to do."

CPSIA information can be obtained
at www.ICGtesting.com
Printed in the USA
FSHW020344040621
81968FS

9 781087 960319